She wanted to say so many things.

Like:

"I have missed you so much. It was dumb to leave."

"Will it always be this way?"

"I left a piece of my dumb heart in Bell Cove."

"Will my already broken heart be broken more when I leave this time?"

"I want you."

"I love you madly, I love you gladly. I love you dumbly, I love you smartly. I love you, love you, love you."

But the only thing that came out when he continued to stare at her inquiringly, waiting for something . . . maybe a commentary on his performance, was, "Hoo-yah!"

How dumb was that?

THE FOREVER CHRISTMAS TREE

A Bell Sound Novel

SANDRA HILL

AVONBOOKS

An Imprint of HarperCollinsPublishers

THE FOREVER CHRISTMAS TREE. Copyright © 2018 by Sandra Hill. All rights reserved. Printed in the United States of America. No part of this book may be used or reproduced in any manner whatsoever without written permission except in the case of brief quotations embodied in critical articles and reviews. For information, address HarperCollins Publishers, 195 Broadway, New York, NY 10007.

First Avon Books mass market printing: October 2018

Print Edition ISBN: 978-0-06-285407-0
Digital Edition ISBN: 978-0-06-285408-7

Cover design by Nadine Badalaty

Cover illustration by Aleta Rafton

Cover photographs © Janis Smits / 123RF (water's edge); © Judy Kennamer / Dreamstime.com (sky); © Jan Havlicek / Dreamstime .com (sky); © 1carson2 / iStock / GettyImages (Christmas tree); © DenisTangneyJr / iStock / Getty Images (beach foreground); © Doug Lemke / Denise LeBlanc / Guas / kurhan /Luba V Nel / Traveller70 / Jmclellon / Roberto Castillo / Shutterstock (eight images)

Avon, Avon & logo, and Avon Books & logo are registered trademarks of HarperCollins Publishers in the United States of America and other countries.

HarperCollins is a registered trademark of HarperCollins Publishers in the United States of America and other countries.

FIRST EDITION

18 19 20 21 22   QGM   10 9 8 7 6 5 4 3 2 1

This book is dedicated to all those people who wish they could have a second chance to do things right. I'm one of them. If only do-overs were possible!

Like my star-crossed lovers, Ethan and Wendy.

This book is also dedicated to my sister Flora, who lives far away but is following a parallel journey with me these days and months and years, as we have become caregivers for beloved husbands who have sustained traumatic medical issues. Wouldn't it be wonderful if we could go back in time and rewrite our history so we could regain our healthy spouses and make decisions that might have avoided all these calamities?

Alas, that is life!

But books do help. I swear they do. Flora sent me *Streams in the Desert*; I sent her *When Jesus Wept*.

And it's not just inspirational books, per se, that help us through hard times, as you readers have told me over and over. Humor and a good story are sometimes the best medicine.

May this book of mine, and all my others, brighten your days and lighten your load.

THE FOREVER
CHRISTMAS TREE

Chapter 1

She'll be home for Christmas . . .
unfortunately . . .

The Wet and Wild was hopping tonight with an overflow crowd of military men and women from Coronado, both the North Island Naval Station and the special warfare command center. Sure, it was TGIF, time for blowing off steam, and there *was* a live band. But, more than that, with only two weeks remaining till Christmas, the air reeked with joy. The Christmas spirit.

Not so much, though, at the long table at the back of the tavern, where Lt. Wendy Patterson, U.S. Navy WEALS, sat with two of her teammates and a half-dozen Navy SEALs.

Started about ten years ago, WEALS (Women on Earth, Land, and Sea) was the female version of SEALs (Sea, Air, and Land). They often bragged that they were as "hard-assed and ever-battle-ready" as their male counterparts "and looked hot-damn-better doing it." Wendy had been with them for eight years.

The band, with its female singer, was just finishing

up their Mariah Carey version of "All I Want for Christmas Is You" for the second time, to the raucous cheers of the mostly male audience.

What is it about Mariah Carey and sailors? I just don't get the appeal, Wendy thought. *It must be a male testosterone thing.*

At least the men at her table weren't hooting and hollering, as they were perfectly capable of doing, she well knew from past experience. And her female friends weren't rolling their eyes with amusement. You'd think they would be in a happier mood with two-week liberties coming for most of them, starting next week. In her case, it was the first break in six months. For reasons Wendy avoided thinking about, she wasn't looking forward to her time off. Gazing around the table, she saw that her friends didn't seem in any better shape.

It was funny how the SEALs and WEALS tended to stick together when out in public, almost like there was a magnetic pull, or they were a bunch of brain-dead homing pigeons. It wasn't deliberate, and certainly not an act of snobbery, like some people thought. In fact, they looked downright scruffy at times, the powers-that-be having lowered the grooming standards for special forces operatives so they wouldn't stick out in foreign countries. No high and tight haircuts, no daily shaving requirements, no inflexibility on military attire.

No GI Jane dress code for the women, either. Once, when Wendy was about to go out on a live op in Kabul, she'd been advised not to shave her legs or armpits for several weeks. Not that anyone could tell under the burka she'd worn, but just in case she tripped over a rock and flipped her hem up to her butt, she supposed, or was captured.

No, the reason these teams clung together was because of their shared experiences. They'd seen and done things no one else had. And, frankly, they were a little, or a lot, burned out by the constant missions to curb global terrorism. The images would give the average person nightmares.

Like the recent pink mist involving one of their own.

Like the reason for them being together tonight.

The group of them here at the table had just returned from a memorial service for one of their fallen team members, Master Chief Travis Gordon. Flash had taken a hit from a suicide bomber in Baghdad ten days ago, leaving behind a wife and two kids.

"Can you believe the music playing when they rolled Flash's casket into the church?" Wendy remarked, attempting to break the silence. "'Should've Been a Cowboy' is hardly the traditional hymn for a funeral."

Everyone grinned at her words, mostly somber grins if there was such a thing. She hadn't realized she'd spoken so loud, but the band had just taken a break. It was one of those odd moments of quiet within a crowd.

Sitting on her right side was Lt. Commander Jacob Alvarez Mendozo, best known by his SEAL nickname JAM. She must have looked confused at the grins because he explained, "Unusual, maybe, but very appropriate. Flash loved country music. That was his favorite song."

Wendy had known Flash, but not that well. "Guess I'm just surprised that the priest allowed it."

"The Catholic Church is more lenient these days about what they'll allow during their services. What surprised me was that they followed the eulogies with the old Roman Rite Mass, the Tridentine Latin Rite. Must have been at the request of his parents. Believe me, that requires a special dispensation." JAM had been in a seminary at one time; so, he would know about all that religious stuff.

"Remember how he and Cody O'Brien used to go at it over rock versus country, The Boss versus Garth Brooks?" Lt. Merrill Good reminded them. Merrill's nickname was Geek due to his genius I.Q. Supposedly, he'd gotten his doctorate at age eighteen.

I do not want to think about what I was doing at eighteen. Or where. Or with whom. Damn! How can it hurt so much, even after twelve years? She steeled herself against the pain, willing the shield to come up over old memories. With a self-deprecating laugh, she thought, *This is just great. Giving myself another reason to wallow. Get over yourself, Wendy. You survived. The past is no big fat hairy deal. Not anymore.*

"Yeah, but did you see how wrecked Cody was today? Even though they were constantly on each other's asses, they were tight as brothers." This from Ensign Diane Gomulka, a sharpshooter in WEALS and one of Wendy's housemates. Diane was from the Northwest where she claimed to have honed her skills on grizzlies and other wild game. No wonder her nickname was Grizz.

Silence followed Diane's words for a moment as they contemplated the brother-and-sister bond that existed among them, even when they disagreed with each other, even if they didn't like a particular person. When you worked in such close proximity, whether in a foxhole, or the jungle, or a Kabul stakeout, you came to know the other person very well. In fact, you came to recognize each other's smell, the sound of their walk, even the way they breathed.

"Well, I'm going on record here. The song I want played at my funeral is 'Another One Bites the Dust.' The pallbearers should be Dallas Cowboy cheerleaders. You can tap a keg at the reception. On my tombstone you can chisel, 'He laid one thousand chicks.'" Only Command Master Chief Petty Officer Frank Uxley would come up with this notion. F.U. was the most obnoxious, politically incorrect, horny SEAL in the world, and that was saying a lot, but he was an explosives expert with unmatched skills. You'd want him at your back in a close quarters situation or any live op.

But make a move on me one more time, F.U., and I am going to karate chop your favorite body part. Not that she was special in that regard. F.U. hit on anything with breasts.

"What makes you think we would plan a funeral for you, asshole?" remarked Commander Luke

Avenil, the highest-ranking and the oldest of their group at close to forty. In fact, he had a few gray hairs feathering the sides of his dark brown, almost black hair, which was long, but not as long as JAM's in its usual ponytail. Handsome, in an edgy sort of way, Slick had been in the original Force Squad, part of the infamous Eighth Platoon in SEAL Team Thirteen. "Don't you have any family?"

"Just my mother."

"You have a mother?" Slick asked incredulously.

F.U. threw a pretzel at him from across the table. Slick caught it in one hand and proceeded to chomp on it, noisily.

"Listen up, all of you. I've saved your sorry asses more than once by disabling a bomb in your friggin' laps. You owe me, and I want the whole military funeral shebang. Ten-gun salute, parade with a horse-drawn hearse, and all that. No, wait. Forget the ten-gun salute. A cannon would be better."

Unbelievable! And he's probably serious.

Everyone shook their heads at F.U.'s cluelessness.

In an obvious attempt to lighten the conversation, Geek said, "Hey, I got some news yesterday. I was talking to Peach, and—"

"Who's Peach?" Wendy interrupted.

"Caleb Peachy. He used to be a Navy SEAL. An Amish SEAL." At her arched brows, Geek shrugged in a "go figure" way, then continued, "For a while, after he left the teams, Peach worked for a treasure-hunting company, Jinx, Inc. The Jinkowsky family business. Its headquarters is in New Jersey."

"I remember them," Slick said. "They recovered

some kind of pink diamonds from a shipwreck. And then they worked the Louisiana bayous searching for Jean Lafitte's buried stash."

"Right." Geek nodded. "Anyhow, they're involved in shipwreck salvaging, mostly, but lots of other stuff. Cave pearls and pirate booty, like you said, Slick. Also, Nazi stolen artworks. Buried gold or precious gems. Tomb artifacts. Caves with drawings or hidden items, like those famous Scrolls. That kind of stuff. Anyhow, the company is for sale."

He had the interest of everyone at the table.

"Why did Peach call you about this?" Slick asked.

Geek blushed a little. A SEAL who blushed? Had to be a first. He was as wild as all the SEALs, but gave the appearance of an innocent because of his boyish features. It was one of his charms. "He figured I have the cash to buy them out, I guess . . . if I was so inclined."

Everyone knew that Geek was wealthy, probably a millionaire, from all his inventions. Most famous, at least among this crowd, was his "penile glove," which sold by the thousands on the Internet. Enough said!

"And are you so inclined?" Slick took a long draw on his beer. Everyone at the table was drinking beer. No food had been ordered yet. Probably wouldn't be in their present moods.

"No. Well, probably not. Oh, hell, maybe," Geek admitted.

"Wow! Just like Indiana Jones! I'm in," Hamr Magnusson exclaimed. He was the youngest of their group, although he had spent a few years in the NFL (*Can anyone say "The Hammer"?*), which probably meant that he, too, had the cash to invest in such a venture. He gave up football during the uproar over concussions and had been about to go into the family vineyard business, but then he'd been lured by his older brother Torolf into joining him in the SEAL teams. Torolf had bet his brother that he couldn't make it through Hell Week. Hamr had done so, bruised and sore, but no concussion, and too stubborn and prideful to quit.

"Look at it this way," Geek went on. "I read a blog one time where some Marine said there were only three reasons why any fool would want to become a SEAL. To prove something to someone, to prove something to themselves, or because they're monkey-ass crazy. Well, I say there are three reasons why a person would become a treasure hunter. Fame, fortune, and monkey-ass adventure. Same thing, in a way." Geek grinned and raised his bottle, drinking deeply, then set the empty bottle on the table with a clunk, as if making some point.

"Works for me," Slick said, "but my ex-wife has me in court again. I'm about tapped out." For years, Slick's ex-wife had been suing him for more and more alimony. Rumor was that she wanted the Malibu house that Slick had inherited from some relative.

"Did anyone ever watch that *Oak Island* program on the History Channel?" Delphine Arneaux asked. Delphine was a mocha-skinned former body-builder from New Orleans, now a master chief in

WEALS, and another of Wendy's housemates. Her nickname was Arnie, not because of her surname but a play on Arnold Schwarzenegger, the quintessential bodybuilder. "That's Oak Island in Nova Scotia, not North Carolina, by the way. No one is exactly sure what's buried on Oak Island, but it's almost certain that it's something important. Could be buried treasure, Marie Antoinette's jewels, some Templars' secret relic, Shakespeare's manuscripts, even the Ark of the Covenant. It's creepy, but exciting."

They all chuckled at that wide range of potential treasures, mostly unbelievable. And the idea of some venture being both creepy and fun.

"Seriously, you guys," interjected K-4—that would be Kevin Fortunato, who'd joined the SEALs after his wife died of cancer, "we're all burned out at the moment. Eventually, we have to give up this life, maybe sooner than later. Unless we have other talents or degrees . . ." He glanced pointedly at Geek. ". . . which I don't, we usually ease into one of the paid military security companies, like Northbridge or Academi. But think about it. This treasure-hunting gig would be a great alternative, a better transition to civilian life. Still the element of danger. Excitement. And financial reward."

"And women," F.U. added. "Betcha the babes would be hot for treasure hunters, just like they are for SEALs. We'd be regular Harrison Fords, younger and tougher versions."

K-4 rolled his eyes.

And Wendy said, "You are delusional."

"What? You don't think I'm a chick magnet, Flipper?"

Flipper was Wendy's WEALS nickname because she swam and dove like a fish. Years of competitive swim teams and dive meets. She still did a mean swan dive. Actually, she'd had another nickname originally, "Windy," and not as a play on her name. No, during her first week of WEALS training, she'd accidentally broken wind when doing duck squats, and the SEALs instructors, never ones to be sensitive or politically correct, had slapped that tag on her. Luckily, she'd outgrown that incident and the nickname.

"Like I said, delusional," she remarked to F.U.

F.U. looked as much like Harrison Ford as she resembled Kim Kardashian. Wendy took a sip of her beer, not really her drink of choice, but asking for a watermelon margarita at the Wet and Wild would be like asking for filet mignon at McDonald's.

"So, what's everyone doing for liberty over the holidays?" Delphine asked. "I'm going to spend at least a week with my family. Lots of Creole food. Music. Dancing. A week is more than enough, though. I can only take so much of kids yelling, babies crying, and my aunt Estelle getting drunk on what she calls 'sweet tea' but is actually straight bourbon."

No one spoke while the waitress took away their empties and gave them new bottles, but then Hamr said, "I have to go home to Blue Dragon Vineyard or my father'll whack me on the head and give me the concussion I didn't get in football, and that's no joke. He'd do it with the long sword he keeps in the hall umbrella stand."

Wendy had met some of the Magnussons, who prided themselves on their Norse heritage. The men all looked like fierce Vikings, perfectly capable of going a-Viking for fun and plunder. Even Hamr, with his long blond hair pulled off the sharp features of his face into a long braid, would look comfortable on the prow of a longship.

"Talk about kids and babies and yelling and laughing," Hamr continued while Wendy's mind had been wandering. "All one hundred of us Magnussons will be there, between my father, my stepmother, eleven sibs, their significant others, and a gazillion rugrats, no exaggeration."

"I'll be alone in Malibu and loving it. No tree. No jolly Christmas songs. No fruitcake or cookies," Slick said. "Me and my friend Jack . . . Daniels."

"Sounds lonely to me," Wendy commented.

"Sometimes lonely is good," Slick said enigmatically, holding her gaze for a long moment.

What does that mean? Is Slick hitting on me? Nah. He's had plenty of chances to make a move over the years if he was interested in me that way. He must sense a fellow loner, which is what I've been, sort of, ever since . . . no, I am not going there. Not now. She shook her head to clear it and said, "I'm going home for Christmas . . . for the first time in twelve years."

Everyone looked at her and waited for her to say more.

"I own a house on the Outer Banks, which my

aunt Mildred has been taking care of since my father died. I'm hearing rumors that Aunt Millie has gone a bit bonkers, turning the place into some kind of B & B for swinging seniors. Well, 'lively' seniors, but you get the picture." She revealed all this in a rush, already regretting having brought up the subject at all.

"Whoa, whoa, whoa," K-4 said. "My wife and I honeymooned on the Outer Banks. Houses there run in the millions. I mean, oceanfront real estate. Flip? Wow!"

"My house isn't oceanfront, and Bell Cove isn't like other touristy towns along the Outer Banks."

"What do you mean by banks?" Delphine asked, her brow furrowed with puzzlement. She and Diane would be grilling her for sure when they got back to the cottage.

With a heated face and wishing she could change the subject, Wendy inhaled deeply. Best to get it all out and over with. Well, not all. Some of it. "The Outer Banks is a string of barrier islands in North Carolina that separates the mainland from the Atlantic Ocean. It's only about 200 miles long and three miles at most in width, but more often only a mile across. A ferry is needed to cross in several places, including to my town, near the southern edge of the OBX—that's an acronym for the Outer Banks. While a lot of the Outer Banks is commercialized with open sea beaches and state parks and, yes, even shipwreck diving sites . . ." She addressed that last to Geek. ". . . Bell Cove has been waging the good fight to keep its character for a long, long time. They want visitors to spend their dollars there, but only if they're passing through to Beaufort or the Crystal Coast. We're like Mayberry at the Beach."

"My parents used to vacation on Nags Head and Hatteras," Geek said. "They liked to sail."

"Tell us more about your house and your hometown," Diane persisted.

"Like I said before, Bell Cove isn't like those others. Built around an inlet off Bell Sound, it's never catered to the tourist crowd, not because it isn't attractive, but the beaches are too wild, and its deepwater harbor hasn't been maintained enough over the years to bring in the boaters."

"So, if there's no tourist industry, how do the people there make a living? Do they travel to the other towns?" JAM asked.

She shook her head, and realized suddenly that the reason everyone was so interested in her hometown is that it had given them a subject to discuss, rather than the looming one . . . the death of their friend. For that reason, Wendy elaborated, "Some do, but mainly the town was founded around Bell Forge, a small factory. The Conti brothers, Italian immigrants, settled there back in the early 1900s. They were craftsmen who made incredible bells, the kind that hang in cathedrals and city towers, but they also made bells as musical instruments. A dying industry, like all things today that can be made cheaper in mass production."

"Bells." Diane sighed again. Diane had a tendency to romanticize everything.

"Anyhow, it's a lovely place, built around a town square, with a Catholic church at one end and a Presbyterian one at the other, their bells often appearing to be in competition. The streetlights are in the form of bells and are adorned with red bows at Christmastime. It's the kind of place where Christmas carolers walk down its streets in period costumes. Everybody knows everybody."

"Does it snow there?" Diane asked, probably hoping for a warm climate with sunny beaches, a sharp contrast to her home state where snow lay on the ground throughout the winter, often neck-deep.

"Rarely, usually only an inch or two a couple times a year, but there are exceptions. When I was about six years old, we got twenty inches." Wendy's throat closed up for a moment as she recalled her mother, who had been alive then, out by the dunes, making a snowman with her. Her mother had been wearing a red coat, and her auburn hair had been powdered with snowflakes, and she'd been laughing. But then, there were other memories. When Wendy was sixteen, her hair a darker shade of auburn than her father's Scottish ginger, she'd been walking on the snowy beach, hand in hand with Ethan. She'd been the one laughing then, with joy, and wearing her mother's red coat, which she'd refused to give away. Wendy's heart hurt at that mental image.

"Flip, you okay?" Diane asked under her breath as one of the guys called for another round.

"What? Oh, yeah," she said. "Just caught back in time for a moment. Anyhow, there's nothing prettier than snow on sand dunes, I can tell you that."

"Tell us about your house," Delphine encouraged.

"Oh, really, you guys don't want to know all this stuff."

"Yes, we do," almost everyone at the table said, except F.U., who was eying a woman at a nearby table who was wearing a T-shirt that said, "Ask About My Tattoos."

"It's a big house, with eight bedrooms, most of which we never used. My parents wanted a big family, but it never happened after my mother got sick. Dad was a doctor, the old-fashioned kind, who had his office and surgery on one side of the ground floor. There are nice views of the ocean and bay from the second- and third-floor windows. Anyhow, that's it. Big house, small town, a trip I'm not looking forward to. End of story." She exhaled with relief and seeing some of the guys' eyes glazing over at what must be as boring to them as a Home and Garden TV show, she asked, "So, anyone interested in ordering dinner, or should we go somewhere else?"

But not all of them were as bored as she'd thought or willing to let her go so easily.

"Sorry to be so nosy, Flip, but why haven't you been back in twelve years?" Diane inquired.

Wendy's face heated once again. "It's not that I haven't been back at all. I've made several short visits. Once when Aunt Millie was in the hospital. For my dad's funeral. Anytime I was needed. Usually just overnight. The last time I went back was five years ago. My family visited me out here, though."

She could tell that they had lots more questions.

"Sounds like a charming place," Diane said then. "Can I come home with you for Christmas?"

Huh? What? "Are you serious, Grizz?"

"Yeah. Everyone's going to my brother's place in Spokane for the holidays, and my mother will be harping on me about why I don't have a real job, and when am I going to get married and have kids, like my sister. And Dad pumps me for *secret* information about the SEALs. And my sister Marion wants me to introduce her to a SEAL."

"What's she look like?" F.U. wanted to know.

Diane ignored him and concluded, "The idea of a quiet Christmas in a small town with freakin' bells, well, that's heaven to me. Can I come?"

"Sure."

"Me, too," Geek said. "As long as there's wi-fi, have computer, will travel." He waggled his eyebrows at her.

"I'm game." This from K-4.

"I could cut my time in Nawleans short, please God, and head out there for a week," Delphine said.

With each person self-inviting themselves, Wendy's jaw dropped even lower. *Oh . . . my . . . God!*

"Great, and Flip mentioned some shipwreck diving places on the Outer Banks. I could check them out, firsthand," Geek said, then pointed to his iPhone on the table in front of him. "I just checked. Did you all know that section of water off the Outer Banks is known as the 'Graveyard of the Atlantic' because there are still so many shipwrecks still out there, undiscovered?"

"Oh, hell! Count me in, too," JAM said, then addressed Geek. "Maybe we can go to Jersey first and look over that Jinx operation."

"Sounds like a plan," Geek agreed.

"You're not going without me," Hamr proclaimed.

"What about your family?" JAM asked.

Hamr shrugged. "I'll think of something."

Wendy was stunned, but then she realized that this might be a good thing. She'd managed to avoid seeing Ethan all these years. If her friends were with her, it would provide a natural barrier.

"You guys do realize it will be boring there," Wendy cautioned. Really, there weren't more than two bars open during the off season, if that.

"I'm getting too old to be a Liberty Hound anymore," Geek said.

"Same here," JAM agreed. "Party animal days are long gone for me, not that I don't enjoy a party now and then." He waggled his eyebrows at Wendy.

"Will you have enough room for all of us?" Diane asked, a bit sheepishly, realizing she started all this.

"Should be fine. You might have to share space with some senior citizen swingers until I get things straightened out, but it's a big house."

"How senior?" F.U. inquired.

They all laughed then.

Geek glanced around the table. "So, road trip to the Outer Banks for Christmas?"

"Hoo-yah!" a bunch of them at the table said, raising their bottles of beer high, like toasts.

Later that night, Wendy called Bell Cove. "Aunt Mil, it's Wendy."

"Well, hello, sweetheart. You're still coming next week, aren't you?"

"Yes, but I want to bring some friends with me. It might be four or five. Is there enough room?"

"Absolutely. Harry is going to his son's home for the holidays, and Gloria is moving into one of those assisted-living places. Elmer and Claudette might still be here, and Raul sleeps with me," her aunt said, as if thinking aloud. Then, she concluded, "Easy peasy, darling. Bring as many friends as you want. The more the merrier."

"Raw-ool?" Wendy choked out, repeating the name the way her aunt had pronounced it.

"Yes, Raul. R. A. U. L. Our dance instructor. You'll love him, honey."

"And he sleeps with you?"

"Where else would he sleep?"

There were a million questions she wanted to ask about this Raul but the one that popped out was, "How old is Raul?"

"Oh, he's a younger man. Once a woman reaches a certain age, she wants a man who can still tango, if you get my meaning."

Aunt Millie was seventy-two. Wendy didn't want to picture her aunt doing the "tango" at all, and definitely not with some young stud looking to steal an old lady's savings.

"How young?"

"Sixty last month."

"What's that noise I hear in the background?" Wendy asked, noticing the music suddenly blaring and people laughing. "Are you having a party?"

"No, it's just the usual. Foxtrot Friday."

Before she hung up, Aunt Millie asked in a sly voice, "Should I get a Christmas tree, or do you want to pick it out yourself when you get here?"

Over the years, Wendy had demanded that no one ever mention the name of Ethan Rutledge to her. Not her father before he died, or Aunt Millie, or her longtime friend Laura Atler, who was editor of the small weekly newspaper, *The Bell*. She didn't want to know where he was or what he was doing. But there were three things she did know. He was married. He had a child, who must be going on twelve years old, in fact probably more than one child by now. And his family owned tree farms . . . Christmas trees, to be precise, at this time of the year.

That had to be what Aunt Mildred was alluding to, although Ethan probably didn't even live on the Outer Banks anymore. His dream had been to become a veterinarian and move off the barrier island.

But then, my dream was to become a doctor, a general practitioner like my dad. And look where I ended up.

Their compromise plan was that they would live off-island after marrying the summer following their sophomore year at UNC–Chapel Hill, where they'd been accepted for admission in the pre-med and pre-vet programs. It would probably take Wendy ten years to get through undergraduate and medical school. For Ethan, it would be a few years less. After that, they would move back to Bell Cove where she would join her father's GP practice and Ethan would set up a veterinary clinic.

What did they say about the best-laid plans of mice and men going awry? Boy, did they go awry for them!

"Do they still sell those Rutledge Trees?" she asked, immediately regretting her first question related to Ethan in all those years.

Aunt Mildred laughed. "Oh, sweetheart, you are so out of the loop. The Rutledge Tree has become famous, at least here in North Carolina. People travel hundreds of miles to get one. They place orders a year in advance."

"Huh?" Ethan's father, and his father before him, had been trying to grow Christmas trees on the Outer Banks for decades, to no avail. The soil and climate weren't ideal for evergreens. What resulted were stunted, sparse specimens . . . glorified Charlie Brown trees. And people bought them, first as a joke, then a conversation piece, even in upscale island homes. Ethan had been embarrassed by them, even when they had only a small, local following.

But that was the past, and Wendy had dwelled on it enough. If just the mention of a Christmas tree prompted these kinds of memories, she could only imagine what she was in for going home. Could she cancel at this late date? No. There were things there that needed to be settled.

With a shake of her head to clear it, she asked her aunt, "Do we have to have a Christmas tree?"

"Bite your tongue, girl."

"Maybe it's time to get an artificial tree."

"Wendy Ann Patterson! You've been living in California too long if you think a Bell Cove home would stoop to a fake tree, although I did see one in the window of the hardware store last week."

"Okay, but you buy the tree, Aunt Mil, and have it delivered, for heaven's sake. Don't think about hauling it home yourself. Wait a sec. The guys can pick up a tree when they get there. They'd probably get a kick out of doing that. Then we can all trim it. Do we still have Mom's old decorations in the attic?"

"Of course. Do you think I would get rid of those?"

"I guess not." Wendy felt a tightness in her chest just thinking about the raggedy angel tree topper that they'd pulled out every year, even after her mother died.

"I'm so excited," her aunt said. "This is going to be the best Christmas ever."

Wendy doubted that. Very much.

Especially when she heard a voice in the background yell, "Hey, Mil, where's the vodka?"

Chapter 2

Ding, dong, ding, dong, dang! . . .

I hate Christmas." Ethan Rutledge hadn't meant to say that aloud, but as he sat at the conference table in the Bell Cove municipal building on a Friday night, drumming his fingertips on the scarred surface, he had to have some way of expressing his exasperation. The emergency meeting of the town council was taking forever to commence.

Everyone at the table turned to look at him as if he'd committed some sacrilege. He supposed it was, for a Christmas tree farmer.

Like I care!

Just then, the bells of Our Lady by the Sea Catholic Church out on the square tolled the hour. One, two, three, four, five, six, seven, eight. That was immediately followed by the bells of St. Andrew's Presbyterian Church. One, two, three, four, five, six, seven, eight. Not to be outdone, the clock in the tower above this building, which had been late for years, rang its own bells. One. Two. Three. Four. Five. Six. Seven. Eight. It was like a freaking bell competition. Day in, and day out.

"And I hate the bells, too," Ethan declared, which was definitely a sacrilege in a town that was built on bells.

His remark prompted some gasps and looks of horror from everyone, except Laura Atler, editor of the weekly newspaper, *The Bell*, who sat next to him. She chuckled and whispered, gleefully, "Way to go, Scrooge!" Laura, who had been best friends with she-whose-name-he-hadn't-spoken-for-many-years, got pleasure in needling him every chance she got.

Frank Baxter, owner of Hard Knocks, the hardware store, glared at him and said, "Don't take your bad mood out on the rest of us." Then, he inquired, not in a nice way, "Business bad, boy? I certainly hope the market isn't dropping for those wonderful Charlie Brown trees."

Ethan was a successful businessman selling Christmas trees—well, all kinds of trees—around the country, but what Baxter referred to was the infamous Rutledge Tree inadvertently developed by his grandfather and further mucked up by his father, a self-taught botanist, which was sold only on the Outer Banks . . . IN HUGE NUMBERS! There was a time when Ethan had been embarrassed by the stunted, scrawny evergreens, but he'd learned to have a sense of humor, and now promoted the hell out of the funny Christmas trees. And people came from many miles away to buy the stupid things. Go figure!

"Business is just fine," *asshole*, Ethan said. "How are those aluminum foil trees moving?"

"They're not aluminum foil," Baxter sputtered. "They're genuine Williamsburg reproduction silver leaf fir trees."

Williamsburg, my ass! "Hmpfh!" Ethan snorted.

He and Baxter had been in a running battle ever since Ethan's grandmother, Eliza Rutledge, opened a Holiday Shoppe (*With two* p*'s and an* e *on the end! Don't ask. Half the people in town called it the shoppie.*) on the lot of their landscape business two years ago and made the mistake of offering some items that could also be purchased at the hardware store, such as removable wall hooks, of all things. Which had prompted Baxter to start carrying Christmas tree lights, which resulted in the shoppie, rather shop, selling electric drills to aerate the trunks of trees. Those drills had been like a gauntlet thrown down. This year, the window of Hard Knocks was stuffed with Christmas paraphernalia, everything from tree toppers to garlands, with the *coup de grace* being those artificial trees. Now, *that* was a sacrilege. North Carolina was one of the largest producers of Christmas trees in the United States, second only to Oregon. Dissing real trees was a Tar Heels sacrilege.

While the other council members conversed softly with each other, trying to ignore the hostility, Ethan sank down lower in his chair and pretended to be reading text messages on his phone. How he'd gotten roped into serving on this body was beyond him. A moment of madness when Leonard Ferguson had died suddenly of a heart attack and

they'd needed a temporary replacement. Temporary? Hah! That had been two years ago.

Leonard Ferguson's shoe store, named simply
Shoes, had been a fixture on the town square for
as long as Ethan could remember. He, his dad,
his grandfather, all of the family, had gotten their
shoes and boots there over the years. It was now
renamed Happy Feet Emporium, whatever the
hell an emporium was, by his widow Doreen Ferguson, who also happened to be the mayor. He
hadn't been in the store lately, but he'd heard some
of the fancy gear there sold for a couple hundred
bucks a pair.

Ethan looked at his watch again and sighed.
Before you knew it, the bells would be chiming
again. Mid-December was the busiest time of
the year for a Christmas tree farmer. His local lot
and its shop were open until nine p.m. tonight,
manned only by his grandmother, aided by two
high school kids and Ethan's daughter, Cassie,
who was eleven going on eighteen. God only
knew what kind of mess he'd find when he got
back. Plus, he had three flatbed trucks of Fraser
Firs, the Cadillac of Christmas trees, up at his
mainland farm set to go to wholesalers early tomorrow morning. He had a seaplane that he kept
over at the airport in Echo Harbor for commuting
across the sound, which saved him hours getting
back and forth to his headquarters, but still time
was a-wasting here.

Just then, the mayor straggled in, thank God!

Her lateness was what had been holding up the meeting. "Sorry, sorry," she apologized. "I got a last-minute phone call that I had to take."

More like a shoe customer, I bet. Wanting to buy a pair of three-hundred-dollar high heels with a name like Man-hole-ah or Jimmy Choose.

"That's all right, Reenie," the suck-up Baxter cooed. Everyone knew the old fart had the hots for the mayor. If Ethan had wanted to be mean, he would comment on Baxter's comb-over, a recent practice designed to entice the merry widow, he guessed. Actually, it wasn't so much a comb-over as a comb-forward. With bangs! He knew what bangs were because he had a eleven-year-old daughter who cared about such things. In a good wind, Baxter would look like a lightbulb with a fur collar.

"Don't worry. It's no big deal," the others said.

Ethan said nothing.

The mayor plopped a pile of papers onto the table, which he hoped wasn't an agenda. If they had an agenda, it would mean hours. Exhaling whooshily as if she carried the weight of the world, or at least Bell Cove, on her shoulders, Doreen sank down into a chair and smiled at each of them. That's when he noticed her appearance.

Doreen, who was a few years younger than his grandmother's seventy-two, was sporting the most godawful hairdo today, probably thanks to her daughter, Francine, who owned the only beauty parlor in town, Styles & Smiles. It was what his mother used to call a bouffant. In other words, a big gray bush. It was the kind of thing you couldn't stop looking at. But it was nothing compared to the deep, orangish color of her skin. He'd heard that Francine had started offering spray tans in her shop, but holy cow! If this was the result, there were going to be a whole lot of dingbat women around Bell Cove looking like yams.

Besides that, Doreen was wearing a Christmas sweater, fluorescent lime green, with two Rudolphs. She probably didn't realize that the red noses were directly over her breasts which were lifted higher than nature ever intended, probably a purchase from that new boutique on the square, Monique's Boutique.

Baxter's beady eyes about popped out.

Despite himself, a smile tugged at Ethan's lips.

"Oh, my God!" Laura whispered beside him.

"Could we get this show on the road, Doreen?" Ethan asked. "What's so urgent that we needed a special council meeting?"

"Yeah," said Tony Bonfatto, owner of the Cracked Crab. "What's the emergency? I have a holiday buffet for the Ocracoke Divers Club at nine-thirty."

"A little crabby tonight, are you, Tony?" Ethan asked his friend with mock sweetness.

Ethan was pretty sure the words Tony mouthed at him were, "Bite me!"

Doreen scowled at all three of them and began to pass out some folders. Ethan opened his and groaned. Yep, an agenda. He would bet his left nut that up next would be new committees. He hated committees almost as much as he hated agendas.

Quickly, he scanned the sheet.

—Factory closing.
—Christmas streetlight malfunctions.
—Town square tree.
—Fund-raiser.

"Jeremy will give us the report on Bell Forge," Doreen said.

Jeremy Mateer, owner of The Cove, a sort of old-time general store that sold everything from groceries to neoprene diving suits, came from a long line of Mateers who started with a "mercantile" back during the Depression. Jeremy, who was wearing a red vest over a green turtleneck and a Santa hat—yes, he was that kind of a dork—pulled out his own folder.

Death by folder! Ethan groaned inwardly.

"Gabriel Conti, owner of Bell Forge since old man Conti died last year, is coming to town next week. Mr. Conti is an architect from up in Durham, and he has no interest in the factory," Jeremy announced and waited a moment for that news to sink in. "Bell Forge has been declining for years, as we all well know. The workforce is down to twenty now. In its heyday, they employed seventy-five to a hundred. We've all been waiting for the axe to drop for some time now."

Ethan remembered Gabe. They were about the same age, and although Gabe had been sent to ritzy boarding schools by his jet-set parents, he had come to Bell Cove on occasion to visit with his grandparents, both of whom were now off to the great bell cathedral in the sky.

"We got a heads-up about Mr. Conti's visit because a commercial developer, that shark Benson from Nags Head, was stalking the grounds last week with some surveyors," Doreen told them. "You know what that means. A high-rise hotel. Beaches loaded with tourists. Motorboats and water skiers." She shivered as she added, "McDonald's."

"There'll be a McDonald's over my dead body," Abe Bernstein of The Deli proclaimed. Abe prided himself on everything in his shop being fresh, never frozen. The Food Network's *Diners, Drive-ins and Dives* had once done a segment on his Reuben sandwiches, declaring them "Reuben's Greatest Masterpieces."

Baxter, on the other hand, chimed in with his often-voiced opinion on the town and tourism, "I don't understand why everyone fights the inevitable. Look at all the customers we would get if they tore that building down and added some popular attractions. Our businesses would double or triple profits."

The hiss of outrage heard around the table shut him down immediately. By the look of scorn on Doreen's face, it was clear that Baxter wasn't putting his overpriced loafers, which he'd probably bought at the em-por-i-um, under her bed anytime soon.

Blushing, and it was not a pretty picture, ol' Bax

slunk down in his chair and muttered, "I'm just sayin'."

Ethan wasn't surprised about the factory closing. It had been mismanaged for a long time, ever since old man Conti had been in and out of nursing homes, and there being no resident owner on site since his death last year. His son and daughter-in-law much preferred living in Italy and mixing with the international crowd. Thus, the place had been left to the grandson, Gabe.

Practically the only thing Bell Forge made these days were bells for church choirs and high-priced wind chimes. But Ethan had hoped the company would be sold to some other company interested in keeping up the tradition. A pipe dream, he supposed. Look at that famous Whitechapel company in London, which had made both the Liberty Bell and Big Ben. It closed last year after five hundred years in business. Bell Forge had been operating for a mere one hundred. "Is it a done deal?" Ethan asked.

"No. Not at all," Jeremy said. "That's where we—the council—come in. I contacted Mr. Conti at his architectural firm, and he agreed to meet with us after he looks over the plant and its books, but before he meets with the Benson folks."

So, there was a chance.

"We need a committee to meet with Mr. Conti," Doreen said. "Who wants to head that committee? Jeremy can't do it because he's having root canal surgery that day."

I knew it, I knew it. A committee. "Don't look at me," Ethan said. "This is the busiest time of year for me."

Doreen narrowed her eyes and gave him "The Look," the one that said, "Stop being a prick, Ethan. I knew you when you ran around the tree farm in nothing but a droopy diaper."

He narrowed his eyes right back at her, not about to be intimidated by an orange yam with a bush on its head.

Which, of course, gave Doreen the opening to ask, "By the way, did you call Natalie?"

"Natalie . . . who?"

Doreen made a tsk-ing noise at him. "Natalie Forsyth, the nurse over at Southern General Hospital. My second cousin's daughter who was recently divorced. Remember?"

"I haven't had time."

"Make time. That daughter of yours needs a mommy. Beth Anne has been gone for three years now. You're starting to act like an old man."

"Oh, good Lord! This is a council meeting. Not Bell Cove Matchmakers," he protested.

"Forget about it, Doreen," Abe said. "I fixed him up with my niece, a very nice schoolteacher who was visiting here last month, and he canceled at the last minute."

"I had the flu."

"A likely story," Tony, whom he had considered a friend, up till now, inserted with a grin. "Women are all over him, like Sunday sauce on homemade pasta, when he stops by the bar, and he ignores them all."

"Maybe he's turned . . ." Baxter started to say.

"That will be enough," Doreen said before her

suitor said what they all knew he was about to say and Ethan jumped over the table to knock the smirk off Baxter's face. "My point, Ethan, was that we're all busy. Besides, you have as much, if not more, to lose than any of us with all that acreage devoted to your island tree farm. You know darn well the vultures will be salivating over the prospects of forcing you out. A perfect place for a strip mall, I'm guessing." She paused when Baxter raised his hand and said, "No, Frank, you are not serving on the damn committee. That would defeat the whole purpose."

"There are a lot of folks in this town who'd agree with me," Baxter argued, but then, realizing the hole he was digging, romance-wise, added, "Not that I don't value your opinion, Reenie. You're the most—"

"Stuff it, Frank," Doreen said.

"I'll serve on the damn committee, but I'm not heading it," Ethan agreed grudgingly.

"How about you, Tony? You would get along with Mr. Conti really well," Doreen suggested.

"Why? Because we're both Italian?"

"Oh, please. Talk about thin skin!" Doreen said. Tony had developed a sore spot regarding ethnicity ever since that reality show, *The Mob,* became popular. "I meant, because you're both graduates of Duke University."

"Oh. All right. Dammit."

"I'll serve on the committee, too," Laura said, which surprised Ethan, but then she probably figured she'd get a news story out of it. "Listen, folks, we're forgetting something here. Bell Forge is the cornerstone of this town. It was founded by the Conti brothers when they immigrated here in 1902. I know because I looked it up this morning. They were fine craftsmen who were known throughout the world for their bells. In its heyday Bell Forge produced bells for some of the most renowned cathedrals and clock towers. Orchestras would settle only for Conti bells for their choirs.

"Are we really going to let that heritage go? I think we need to think about ways to keep the bell factory, not retrofit it for some other purpose, and definitely not tear it down to turn this town into yet another Myrtle Beach."

Ethan felt a twinge of guilt then at having questioned Laura's motives for volunteering to be on the committee.

"Good thinking," Doreen praised Laura. "Okay, so, Tony, Ethan, and Laura will serve on that committee and will call on any of the rest of us, if need be. Is that settled?"

They all nodded. Ethan grumbled.

"Moving on," Doreen said. "The Christmas street lighting in this town is now a clear and present danger. Matthew couldn't be here tonight, but he asked me to convey how dangerous the situation is. We're a lawsuit waiting to happen."

The Matthew that Doreen referred to was Matt Holter, Ethan's best friend and the town's attorney/ treasurer. It was Matt who'd volunteered him to serve on the town council, initially. Ethan was always reminding his pal that he owed him. Now, more than ever.

"I don't even have a light in front of my store anymore," Baxter complained.

"And the one on my corner keeps flickering on and off," Jeremy said.

"The things are almost a hundred years old. What do you expect?" Doreen said. "The state inspector gave a report yesterday. The entire street lighting system needs to be overhauled, but the immediate concern is the Christmas lighting, which must be fixed, or shut down."

"What? At this time of year? Does that mean no Christmas tree lighting on the square, either?" Laura asked, appalled. "What about the Christmas Eve Carol Walk? What about the church concerts? And the Festival of the Bells?"

"Exactly," Doreen said dolefully.

"How much?" Ethan asked.

"Twenty-five thousand dollars. Initially."

Silence followed, because they all knew there wasn't an extra twenty-five thousand in their treasury, not since the sewer project that was completed last summer.

"I've already ordered the work to begin Monday morning. We're short at least fourteen thousand. We can borrow that amount, but we'll have to find a way to repay quickly, or else—"

Ethan could give them that amount, easily, or lend it to them. But he knew they wouldn't accept. Small-town pride and all that.

"You can't raise taxes. We're already sky high. No way!" said Sally Dawson, speaking up for the first time. Sally ran the bakery/ice cream parlor and struggled as a single parent to raise three sons since her husband died in Afghanistan.

"I'd have to double the price of my trees," Ethan mused aloud, though he wasn't really complaining about taxes.

Baxter didn't take it that way, though. "Your trees cost too much already."

"You should talk! You'd think your shovels were gold-plated," Ethan countered.

"Customers are already complaining about the price of my Crab Imperial," Tony inserted to the grumble fest.

The complaints came fast and furious then.

"What will Mr. Conti think about keeping the factory going if the town looks so downtrodden we can't even afford proper street lamps?"

"This stinks."

"What next? Street excavation for new water lines?"

"And if it snows?"

"It hardly ever snows."

"It does sometimes. Remember that blizzard back when we were kids?"

"If we're going to spend money on streetlights, I want something done about the sand dunes piling up on my side of town. You can't hardly see the ocean for the dunes anymore."

"Forget lights and sand dunes, I want the sidewalks repaired."

Doreen pounded the table with her gavel, which was actually a small lady's hammer, probably a gift from Baxter. "Enough! And before I forget, Ethan, isn't it about time you let us have that blue spruce for the town square gazebo this year? It's already too big for an indoor tree."

"You've kept it trimmed to a perfect shape," Sally complimented him.

"It *is* beautiful, at least twenty feet now, I'm guessing," Abe remarked.

It was actually eighteen and one quarter, a star in the midst of a litter of runts on the local Rutledge Tree Farm. The blue spruce had been a pet project of Ethan's which he'd nursed meticulously for many years, succeeding where his father and grandfather had failed: to grow a perfect Outer Banks Christmas tree, especially a type so out of place for barrier island development, even more so than other species. It had only cost about five thousand dollars so far in fertilizer, wind and sun screens, and time, making it commercially unacceptable. But that was beside the point.

"Think about how impressed Mr. Conti would be," Laura said, knowing exactly why he would never cut down that particular tree.

Really, they'd gone too far this time. He had refused to cut that tree down every single year when they'd started asking, once it became apparent that this was the one Christmas tree that had managed to flourish here on the island. He didn't mind donating a tree, even one of the pricey ones from over on the mountain, but not that one. All he said was "No!" but he said it with such finality that no one argued, just indulged in a lot of under-the-breath griping.

The Catholic church bells began to toll, nine

times. Followed by the Presbyterian church. Followed by the town hall clock. Ethan put his face in his hands and counted to ten, then twenty.

"I have never seen such a bunch of grinches in all my life!" Doreen said then. "I swear, Dr. Seuss must have modeled his book on you yahoos. What we need is some ideas here, not complaints."

"Ooh, ooh, ooh! I have an idea for a fund-raiser," Laura said.

Ethan raised his head to stare at her. He didn't like the tone of her voice, way too gleeful. And she was looking at him.

"A Grinch contest. Around the town, we could place posters with nominees for the grinchiest person in town. People would vote five dollars a shot for their choice, or they could add a nominee. The money could be collected in Mason jars. You would donate those, right, Bax?"

Baxter was too stunned to answer.

"Isn't that kind of mean?" Sally asked.

"Nah! It could be fun. All in the spirit of Christmas giving," Laura contended. "We'll probably be able to pay for the Christmas streetlight project in no time, and have money left over. I'll put a running total in the window of *The Bell* every night. Maybe we could even have a crowning of Mr. Grinch at the concert on Christmas Eve. Or Ms. Grinch. Oh, there are so many possibilities. Bell Cove Grinch of the Year. I love it!"

I'd like to crown someone. "Have you lost your mind? I'm not putting one of those posters and a begging jar in the Christmas shop," Ethan asserted.

"Wanna bet your grandmother will?" Doreen challenged, narrowing her eyes at him, *again*. "It's just the kind of thing she would like for her shoppie."

Ethan cringed at the word.

"I know who I'm gonna nominate first." Baxter slapped a ten-dollar bill on the table and stared at Ethan.

Ethan one-upped him with a twenty and gave Baxter an equal glower back.

"See, it's already working. Two people have been grinched, and we don't even have the posters made up yet. I'm going to nominate my circulation manager, Zeke Abrams. He's the grouchiest man alive," Laura said.

And on it went.

It was the craziest, most asinine thing Ethan had ever heard of. They would be the laughingstock of the state, maybe the country. He wouldn't be surprised to see one of the network TV crews land on their doorstep for a morning segment, titled something like, "The Crazy-Ass Things People Do for Christmas." It would be right up there with those nutcases who decorate their houses and yards with a fifty-million-watt light show every year.

If that wasn't bad enough, as Ethan was leaving the town hall, at nine-freakin'-thirty, Laura sidled up to him and said, "Guess who's coming for Christmas, Mister Scrooge? And I don't mean Santa Claus." Then she added, "Ho, ho, ho!"

Later that night, after sending his grandmother and Cassie home and checking over the day's receipts and inventory, Ethan walked to the far end of his local tree farm, to the perfectly shaped blue spruce tree, the one the council kept badgering him to donate, the one that had defied all odds in growing on an island where even the hardiest evergreen trees struggled to survive.

It was a reminder of things long dead. He should just chop the damn tree down and burn it for fireplace kindling. A final end to . . . everything.

He should.

But he didn't.

He couldn't.

He . . . just . . . couldn't.

Chapter 3

Old acquaintances are not forgotten . . .

To Mildred's shock, Eliza Rutledge showed up on her doorstep, for the first time in twelve years, just before the Saturday Samba session. The dance club event was being held this afternoon, instead of its usual early evening hours, because it was going to be a farewell party, as well, for two of Mildred's "renters," who were leaving that night:

Gloria Solomon, who had been the town librarian for forty years, was moving into one of those assisted-living places, at her children's insistence, none of whom lived nearby. Not that Mildred really opposed the move. Gloria was fine, most of the time, but she had become a bit senile on occasion, taking to nighttime strolls downtown in her underwear. Aside from the modesty issue, the cold temperatures posed a danger to her frail body with its susceptibility to pneumonia. Plus, she sometimes needed the assistance of a walker for support.

Harry Carder, a retired financial advisor, was going to Seattle to spend the holidays with his son's family. Harry, before being confined to a wheelchair, had loved to dance, not so much samba, but swing, which had been a favorite for him and his late wife, Julia, a dentist. Harry would be coming back to Bell Cove, but whether to this house, or elsewhere, depended on the outcome of the visit by Mildred's niece.

Wendy was arriving on Wednesday and staying for two whole weeks, which was both wonderful and ominous at the same time, considering her rare appearances over the years. Mildred suspected that Wendy would not like the idea of her having turned her family home into a B & B, or boarding-house, of sorts, let alone a dance club. She might even be thinking about selling the property, a pros-pect too scary for Mildred to contemplate.

All these thoughts flashed quickly through Mil-dred's mind as she gaped at the woman who had been her best friend since kindergarten, until that nasty business more than ten years ago when in-sulting words had been spoken from both sides, words that could not be taken back. This was the person who'd known her best, had shared her deepest secrets, had laughed and cried with her over big and small events in her life, and vice versa.

Mildred had been there when Eliza Metz fell in love with Samuel Rutledge. In fact, she'd been her maid of honor when they'd married and godmother to their one and only child, George. And she'd been the pillar to which a devastated Eliza had clung when Samuel had died suddenly at age fifty in a freak accident up on the mainland tree farm, then still later when her daughter-in-law ran off with her therapist, leaving George and his young son bewildered and unable to cope on their own.

Eliza had been there for Mildred, as well. When her fiancé, Barry Rogers, had been killed in the waning years of the Vietnam War. When she'd miscarried his baby a few months later. When she'd moved into this house to help her sister-in-law Anne Patterson during the latter stages of her cancer and then stayed to raise her daughter.

Ironically, both Mildred and Eliza had been called on to help raise young members of their families. For Mildred, it was her niece, Wendy. For Eliza, it was her grandson Ethan and then her great-granddaughter Cassie, who was born with a hip disease to a mother, Beth Anne, who was already in the beginning stages of MS, which turned out to be terminal a decade or so later. Because of their falling-out, Mildred had not been there for Eliza during those latter crises with Beth Anne and Cassie.

Of course they'd seen each other over the past twelve years, but only in passing. Pride and stubbornness were part of Mildred's Scottish heritage; she had no idea what Eliza's excuse was, if there was one, aside from anger. And hurt.

"Lize?" she said, her heart beating so fast she could scarcely breathe. "Is something wrong?" Maybe there had been some disaster at her farm. To her grandson. Or her great-granddaughter.

Eliza's eyes, the pale blue that Mildred had always envied, misted over with tears. "Something's been wrong for a long time, don't you think, Mildy?"

That old pet name triggered something in Mildred, and she began to weep, too.

"I brought a gift," Eliza said, pointing to the box on the doorstep at her feet containing a beautiful Della Robbia door wreath with evergreens and fruit and dried flowers.

This style of artistic creation had been a favorite of Mildred's since she was a young girl. She remembered the time the two of them . . . well, never mind. "There's also a matching garland in my truck."

Mildred just then noticed the black Rutledge Farm pickup truck parked on the street. If she'd seen it earlier, would she have opened the door? "But why?" she asked.

"It's a peace offering, Mildy."

Mildred had meant, why was she here, not why the gift, but she supposed they were the same thing. "Oh, Lize!" Mildred felt guilty then, that Eliza had been the one to make the first move. "I am so sorry, my friend." Why was it so easy to say those words now when they'd been stuck in her throat for so long? It was like a Heimlich maneuver had been done on her body and all the pent-up emotion came spilling out.

"Me, too. Me, too."

They were in each other's arms then, hugging and sobbing, both of them murmuring disjointed words about missing each other and wasted years and such. But then, Eliza stiffened as she seemed to stare at something over Mildred's shoulder through the still-open doorway.

There was a click, click, click sound, which Mildred recognized as tap shoes on hardwood floors.

"*¿Que pasa?*" Raul inquired of Mildred with concern as he came up beside her. "Have you had the bad news?"

"No, no, just good news," Mildred assured him. "Raul, I don't believe you've met my friend, Eliza Rutledge. She's brought us a gift." She pointed to the wreath in its hexagonal box, tied with a big red bow. "And, Eliza, this is my friend Raul Arias, who is visiting with me. He's from Spain."

Raul reached out and shook Eliza's hand, saying, "*¡Bienvenida, bienvenida!* You have come for our samba party, yes?"

At first, Eliza didn't answer, so disconcerted was she by the sight of Mildred's companion, who was dressed for today's gathering in a white ruffled shirt tucked into slim black pants with a wide cummerbund. Raul did have a nice figure, for a man his age. If not for the thick, wavy, white hair, which he cared for meticulously with expensive hair products he purchased online, he could have passed for forty, instead of sixty.

It wasn't Raul's physical appearance that had flustered Eliza, though, Mildred sensed. It was his mere presence at Mildred's side, as if he belonged. Eliza had to have heard rumors, but Raul's arm over Mildred's shoulder was a clear signal of their relationship.

"Uh, no," Eliza replied finally to Raul's question.

"I didn't know about a party." To Mildred, she added, "I can come back another time when you're not busy."

"No, no," Mildred said, taking Eliza's hand and drawing her inside. "This isn't the usual Saturday Samba dance session, but a little social get-together to say good-bye to two of my houseguests. And it doesn't start for another hour."

"Go, go." Raul shooed them. "I get the Christmas wreath for you, darling. I will put it in the garage for now."

"Darling?" Eliza mouthed silently at Mildred.

Mildred just smiled and led Eliza into the entry-way, closing the door against the chill. She took Eliza's coat and hung it in the hall closet. It was hard to miss the sound of Julio Iglesias coming from the front parlor; so, they paused there, where Harry, in his wheelchair, was talking to Gloria. The other guests wouldn't arrive for another half hour yet. The two of them waved at Eliza, whose jaw kept dropping lower and lower.

"What happened to the furniture?" Eliza asked, voicing what was probably the least important of the questions she must have.

"We moved it into the second parlor so we'd have room to dance," Mildred said. "Let's go in the kitchen. I was in the middle of making Grandma Patterson's Christmas punch."

"The one your brother used to make? With Scotch whiskey?" Eliza arched her brows. "Isn't that a bit risky to serve to your guests who might be driving?"

What she didn't say, but was implied, was "older people" who might be driving.

"Doc would be appalled to see how little booze I put in his recipe." Doc was the nickname that her brother, Alan Patterson, Wendy's father, had gone by ever since he'd graduated from medical school. "Will you sample it for me?"

"Sure, but just a little. I have to get back to the shop. We're busy on Saturday afternoons."

Eliza sat down at the big oak table in the center of the kitchen, which hadn't changed much since she'd been here last, except for a few updated appliances. The same white, glass-paned cabinets, and even the wallpaper, pretty lighthouses against an ocean background, remained unchanged. It was a large room, but cozy, with its windows facing the bay in the distance over the sand dunes and the occasional passing ship. Center stage on the table was Grandma Patterson's cut-glass punch bowl to which Mildred had already added a few jiggers of Glenlivet to ginger tea mixed with cranberry and orange juices, some ginger ale for fizz, and sliced oranges floating on top. She poured a half cup for each of them and topped them with cranberries frozen inside star-shaped ice cubes.

"How festive!" Eliza said, "and delicious," after taking a sip.

Mildred sat down in the chair next to Eliza, not across the table, and squeezed her hand. "Do we need to talk about . . . you know?" A rehashing of that horrendous time when Wendy's boyfriend, Ethan, had gotten another girl pregnant would accomplish nothing and could renew the hurt, but maybe they needed to explain their actions. To get rid of the elephant in the room.

"Oh, God! I hope not!"

Mildred sighed with relief.

"You look good, Mildy. The years have been good to you."

Mildred glanced down at the green taffeta dress that she pulled out of her closet every holiday. It *was* flattering to her still-trim, short figure, but more than that, it had a full, calf-length skirt that was perfect for samba dancing. In her hair, the same blunt-cut, jaw-level bob she'd worn since her twenties, minus the bangs, and the same reddish-blonde shade, thanks to Francine Henderson at Styles & Smiles, she'd pinned a sprig of holly. "You look good, too, Lize."

And she did, although Eliza waved a hand dismissively at Mildred's compliment. Without any effort, Eliza still managed to look sleek and chic in a pair of jeans tucked into low-heeled leather boots, with a white T-shirt under an open plaid woolen shirt. Women of her height and thin frame managed to pull off any outfit they wore, at any age, without any effort, darn it! Her long salt-and-pepper hair, pulled off her surprisingly wrinkle-free face into a coil held on to the top of her head with a claw comb, was no-muss stylish.

"Are you still painting, Lize?" Mildred asked.

"Not so much. Too busy with the shop and taking care of Cassie."

Eliza Rutledge had been painting since she was

a teenager, as a hobby. After marrying, her works featured beautiful winter beach and bay scenes . . . always with a lone Christmas tree. What else? Mildred had one she'd put in the attic twelve years ago. Snow on the dunes, a lighthouse in the far background, and a small, incongruously placed Christmas tree. Although she was an amateur, Eliza's artistic endeavors were lovely and graced the walls of many homes in Bell Cove.

"This Raul . . . is he . . . um, special?" Eliza asked tentatively.

"Yes, but not in the way you probably mean." The buzzer went off on the stove and Mildred got up to remove a tray of shortbread from the oven. The buttery sweet smell filled the room. She put a few onto a plate and brought it back to the table to cool. Only then did she sit back down and continue, "I've been so lonely, Lize. Especially after Alan passed."

Eliza knew how distraught and lonely Mildred had been after Barry's death almost fifty years ago in that damn war and how Bell Cove, her hometown, had been a refuge for her, especially later as she'd moved in to help Alan raise his daughter Wendy. But Wendy left twelve years ago and Alan had been gone five years now.

"I probably shouldn't have retired five years ago." Mildred had been a Bell Cove Elementary School music teacher for more than forty years. "The school board would have let me continue, as long as I was able, but I had all these grand plans about traveling and gardening . . ." She let her words trail off.

"And . . . ?"

"I discovered that it's no fun traveling alone, and I have a black thumb."

They both laughed.

But then Eliza said, "I get lonely, too. Oh, I know that I have Ethan and Cassie to keep me company, and the shop occupies my time, but . . ."

Mildred squeezed her hand. "But, sweetie, you had more than twenty years with the love of your life. That's priceless. Sam was priceless."

"Yes, he was." Eliza sighed and stared off into space for a moment.

Eliza and Samuel's love story was legendary around Bell Cove. When the mountain boy, Samuel Rutledge, met Eliza Metz, an Outer Banks girl from a family of bell artisans, he fell head over heels in love. He was a Christmas tree farmer, of all things, at a time back in the sixties when there weren't that many big commercial growers. Most people went out and cut their own trees.

Because Eliza didn't want to leave the barrier island and because he loved her so much, Samuel moved here, bought five acres, and tried to grow Christmas trees on the punishing land between the ocean and the sound. It was lucky he still kept that tree farm on the mountain because it was their bread and butter while the island efforts proved a dismal failure. And God bless Samuel, he never faltered under the teasing and laughter of the islanders as he produced one stunted, sorry Christmas tree after another. Then, lo and behold, people started buying the ugly trees out of pity, then as a joke.

All for the love of a woman. Sometimes she wondered if she and Barry would have had the same kind of love if they'd had the chance to marry. Probably not. The Eliza/Samuel kind of love was rare. Although it did seem to run in their family. The men loved hard. Look at how George had taken his wife's leaving, never looking at another woman for fifteen-odd years until his death at only forty, some said of a broken heart. And Ethan . . . oh, my God! His love of Wendy and his grief over what he'd considered her desertion, although he was to blame for that . . . well, enough about that!

"And where does Raul fit into your loneliness?" Eliza asked, jarring Mildred out of her wandering thoughts.

"Not just Raul, but my housemates. You have to be wondering about them." At Eliza's nod, Mildred said, "It started with Joy Lowry. Remember her?"

"She used to own the bookstore, didn't she?"

"Yes. I met her in the general store one day, and she commented that she was thinking about selling her house, that it was too much for her to keep up since her husband, who had that insurance agency, ran off with his secretary, but she didn't want to move away from Bell Cove. I offered to let her stay with me, temporarily."

"Didn't she remarry . . . the new minister over at Nags Head?"

"Uh-huh. Over the past two years, I've had a dozen different people stay here. Never more than three or four at a time. And none have been here for more than six months."

By now, the shortbread had cooled, and Eliza took a bite of one triangle, closed her eyes, and pretended to swoon. "You might not have a green thumb, but you haven't lost your touch with baking."

"Thank you, thank you. I'll give you a tin to take home with you. This is the third batch I've made today."

"Again . . . Raul?"

"Right. I met Raul last year at the Swinging Seniors Club over at Ocracoke. No, not that kind of swinging. It was for jitterbug aficionados. He was visiting his daughter who's a marine archaeologist or something, who lives there." She shrugged. "We connected."

"What does he do for a living? Is he retired?"

"He took early retirement as a professor at the University of Barcelona after his wife died. He's writing some kind of history book."

"Okaay. And is this the real deal, long term, committed kind of relationship?"

Mildred laughed. "This is the nice-for-now, let's-see-where-it-goes kind of relationship. He has every intention of returning to Spain. I can't see myself anywhere but Bell Cove." She laughed again. "Your turn, Lize. What prompted your visit today?"

Eliza took another drink of punch before replying. "Two things, actually. Have you heard about that silly grinch contest they're having in town?"

"Yes. Five thousand dollars raised already. Amazing!"

"What's amazing is the number of people who've been nominated. Ethan and Frank Baxter are running neck and neck for first place at the moment, but I suspect they're voting for each other. I came into the shop this morning, and my name was at the bottom of the list. Mine! Can you imagine? Who would ever think of me as a grinch?"

Mildred had to smile at her friend's consternation. "Maybe you were a little grumpy with a customer."

"Who wouldn't be? Some of them are downright impossible. One man came in yesterday and asked for Christmas lights in blue and white. When I told him he could buy a blue strand and a white strand and intertwine them, he told me, no, he wanted me to go through and change out every other bulb, for the same price. Not that I would do it for any price."

"Bet I know who it was. Old man Whitmore. He's still a dyed-in-the-wool Penn State football fan. Practically everything in his house is blue and white."

"You're right! Anyhow, you're the only one I could think of who would understand my upset over being called a grinch. I'll tell you one thing—if I see anyone voting for me in our shop, I might very well hit him, or her, over the head with a wreath."

Instead of pointing out that such action might be construed as grinchy, Mildred said, "Thank you again for the wreath."

"I remember how much you liked Della Robbia decorations. Now you won't have to go all the way to Nags Head to buy one."

Mildred blushed at being found out.

"Anyhow, sometimes a person gets a lightbulb moment. They see themselves the way other people do. And it was a rude awakening to me that someone would think of me as a grumpy old lady. And I asked myself, 'Is this what all your bitterness has made you, Eliza Rutledge?' I didn't like the answer."

Mildred understood. Until she'd invited people into her home—Wendy's home, she corrected— she'd become bitter, too. "You mentioned two reasons for stopping by today."

"I heard that Wendy is coming home."

Mildred stiffened. This was a touchy subject, especially so early in their reconciliation. "Yes, but only for two weeks," she emphasized.

"I was shocked when I first heard that Wendy joined those female Navy SEALs. She always wanted to be a doctor, like her daddy. Is she happy?"

Mildred shrugged. "She seems content, but then, the fact that she rarely comes home should tell you something. How about Ethan? He was going to be a veterinarian, as I recall. Is he happy?"

"Pff! That boy hasn't been truly happy for twelve damn years. Oh, he cared about Beth Anne, and he adores his daughter, but . . ." She sighed. "You know how it was with him and Wendy." Eliza drank the rest of her punch and held out her cup for a refill before looking Mildred in the eye and remarking, "Don't you think it's about time we set things right?"

Chapter 4

Some things never change . . .

Wendy drove her rental car onto the Bell Cove Ferry, the last leg of a five-hour journey since she'd left the airport at Norfolk. Getting to the southern end of the Outer Banks was never easy, but, to many, the inaccessibility was an attraction, not a disadvantage. In any case, in another hour, she'd be in her hometown of Bell Cove. Most of her driving time had been spent on Highway 12, the Beach Road, and that included several other ferry rides, two humpbacked bridges, and slow-downs through a dozen or more small towns.

Normally, during the high tourist season, it would take much longer, but there was little traffic at this time of year and day. Many, but not all, of the hotels and shops were closed. She could have cut her time by hitting the bypass for at least part of the trip, but who could resist this more scenic route?

Diane, apparently, Wendy thought, with a smile, as she glanced over at her friend, who was asleep beside her in the passenger seat, having partied all night prior to their red-eye flight from San Diego.

At first, Diane had oohed and aahed over the oddly named towns along the OBX, like Kitty Hawk or Kill Devil Hills or Nags Head or Ocracoke, not to mention the scenic lighthouses and signs announcing OBXmas holiday events, such as the Winter Lights at the Elizabethan Gardens, or the town where they sang carols after lighting the municipal Crab Pot Tree. Apparently, some of the towns were attempting to amp up winter tourism.

Wendy, on the other hand, couldn't sleep if her life depended on it. She was so hyped up she could barely breathe. The closer she got to her destination, the more nervous she became. Her hands on the steering wheel felt clammy. Her heart raced. She could swear she heard bells ringing in her ears, which was impossible, being so far away from the famous bells of her hometown, not to mention the roar of the ferry boat's motor and the wind which was always strong here on the inlet off of Bell Sound.

It was Ethan, of course, who was causing her distress.

Am I crazy?

That stuff that Geek said last week about SEALs is probably true of WEALS, too. The only reason you'd want to be one is to prove something to yourself, to prove something to someone else, or because you're just plain crazy. I fit all three.

Path-et-ic!

Ethan probably won't even be there.

But what if he is?

About time I put old ghosts to rest.

Easier said than done!

I should have asked Aunt Mildred if Ethan ever came back.

After all these years of banning any mention of his name, she would think I still care.

And I don't.

Really!

That would *be crazy!*

Aaarrgh!

Wendy parked in the slot indicated, and turned off her engine. She undid her seat belt and turned to Diane. "Hey, Grizz, wanna go outside and get some air?"

Diane shifted in her seat and turned her head without moving the rest of her body. Scarcely opening her lids a crack, she asked, "Are we there?"

"Not yet. We're on the Bell Cove Ferry."

"Another ferry!" Diane exclaimed, which caused Wendy to laugh. The first ferry ride had prompted squeals of delight from Diane. The second, not so much. And now, Diane said with a wide yawn, "I'll pass," and turned away, scrooching lower in the seat with her head resting on the window. "Wake me up when we get there."

Wendy got out of the car, and tightened her sixteen-year-old Lands' End down jacket around her body. The pale blue, puffy coat, a gift from her father on her fourteenth birthday, never wore out. She thought about opening the trunk to get a hat out of her duffel bag, but decided not to bother. She noticed that most folks stayed in their vehicles, not wanting to brave the brisk winds. Plus, they were mostly commuters, accustomed to the scenery, and not lured into the coffee shop by the cheap coffee and stale donuts.

There was a time when Wendy traveled this ferry daily, back and forth to high school, usually with Ethan sitting beside her. Bell Cove had its own elementary/middle school up to eighth grade, but after that students had to go to the consolidated high school that served a number of the towns on the Outer Banks.

More memories!

The temperature wasn't really that bad today, probably in the fifties, but the wind was fierce, making the chill factor about forty, or lower. The waves lapping against the boat were choppy, but that didn't bother Wendy. She'd grown up on the waters of the Outer Banks, where she'd become a world-class sailor and diver, not to mention a marathon swimmer, all of which were assets that led to her joining the WEALS.

After taking note of a fishing boat in the distance and a flock of sea birds wheeling overhead, she inhaled deeply of the salt air. In Coronado, where she lived, they had the Pacific Ocean, but somehow the air and the water seemed different here, sweeter, when it came off the Atlantic Ocean and Bell Sound.

She moved around the wheelhouse toward the front of the boat where the only passengers visible were a man and a young girl in a wheelchair. She paused, not wanting to intrude on their privacy.

The girl, probably preteen, wore a pink fake fur coat with a matching earmuff headband. On her feet, propped on the wheelchair footrests, were pink sparkle Uggs. Very tween chic! She appeared to be coaxing her father into something. Tossing her long blonde hair over her shoulder in the coquettish manner young girls practiced with their fathers, she made coaxing motions with her fingertips, wheedling, "Please, Dad, please. Just one. Please." Her father smiled and shook his head. Once, when he turned to stare out over the waters, the girl wheeled her chair to his other side and proclaimed, "You're a grinch!" She didn't say it in an insulting way, though, and her father just laughed. Finally, he pulled a bill from his pocket and handed it to her. Quickly, before he changed his mind, the girl whipped her wheelchair around expertly and headed toward the coffee shop, yelling over her shoulder, "Thank you, Dad. You're the best scrooge in the world."

The man stared fondly after his departing daughter, but then he looked over to the side and did a double take as he noticed Wendy standing there. Frozen in place.

It was Ethan.

Oh, no! No, no, no!

He looked so good. The same, but older, obviously. His dark hair was short. Not military short, but shorter than was the fashion today. Blue eyes were framed with the same incredibly long and sexy lashes that had enthralled her an eon ago. His athlete's body was tall and still lean, clearly outlined by the wind against his jeans and a lightweight, gray North Face jacket.

Be still my heart! No, no, no! No hearts. Just hormones.

Being in the military, surrounded by attractive special ops men all the time, she should be immune to the appeal of a good-looking man. She was. Usually. But not now. *Down, hormones, down!*

Her first reaction was to turn tail and run. But she couldn't do that. What kind of "hard-assed, ever-battle-ready" female SEAL was she if she jumped ship and bailed at the first obstacle? *Buck up, sailor. You know the drill. Show no fear.* "Ethan," she said, stepping forward.

For a brief blip of a second, he gazed at her with hunger, the expression on his face one she recognized from their old days together. It bespoke not just love, but a forever love, the kind of love that only comes once in a lifetime.

Or until a better opportunity comes up.

His expression immediately changed to one of hostility, or was it hurt? "Wendy! What's a hotshot Rambo like you doing in little old Bell Cove? Come to favor the small town masses with your presence?"

She almost flinched, barely catching herself. "Whoa! Rude much?" she snapped back. Then in an ultrasweet voice, she went on, "Hello to you, too, Ethan. What're you doing back in Bell Cove?"

To his credit, he looked a little shame-faced at his impoliteness and revealed, "I live here."

"Huh? I thought you'd be a practicing vet, like you always planned, living off the island."

He gave her a strange look. "Yeah, well, plans change."

Don't I know it! But you love animals, Ethan. Your

dream from the time you rescued that puppy in third grade was to have your own animal hospital.

"Dreams!" he scoffed.

Wendy hadn't realized that she'd spoken her thoughts aloud. Her face heated with embarrassment.

"What about *your* dream to become a doctor and take over your father's practice?"

"Touché!" She nodded. "So what *do* you do, if you're not a vet?"

"Tree farming. I took over Dad's business when he died ten years ago, but I don't suppose you knew that, either."

"But . . ." She frowned, trying to take in what he'd said. "Didn't you go to vet school?"

"No, Wendy, I did not go to vet school. In fact, I didn't go to college at all."

"You were accepted at UNC. Tuition was paid. You were supposed to report for football practice in August."

"You were accepted, too," he pointed out.

"I thought . . ." It was clear what she'd thought.

Oh, my God! All these years I've been picturing Ethan as a veterinarian, living off the island, with his . . . oh, my God! Tears of sympathy smarted her eyes, not that he would appreciate the sentiment from her, apparently. But, really, Ethan had never shown any interest in tree farming, not the big, fairly prosperous tree farm on the mainland mountain, and absolutely not the small business on the island which grew the infamous Rutledge Tree, which had embarrassed Ethan to no end. She blinked rapidly, pretending that the wind whipping her face was the cause of her tears. There was so much she didn't understand. She deliberately veered in another direction. "No, I didn't know about your father," she admitted. "He must have been only forty or so, if he died ten years ago. So young! What happened?"

"Heart attack."

The men in the Rutledge family seemed to die young, Wendy mused with what was probably hysterical irrelevance. Ethan's grandfather had died when she and Ethan had been about eight years old, and he'd been only about fifty, which had seemed old at the time. His death had been due to some kind of lumber accident.

She remembered Samuel Rutledge, a handsome "older" man, and how close he and Ethan's grandmother had been. Their love had been apparent to everyone. One time she'd seen Eliza Rutledge pinch Samuel Rutledge's butt in passing when they thought no one was looking. Back then, Wendy had thought that was the yuckiest thing for two old fogies to do, but now, in retrospect, she considered it cool. "Was that your daughter I saw you with earlier?"

At first, it seemed as if he wouldn't answer. "Yes. Cassie, short for Cassandra."

"Did she have an accident?"

"You really have no clue what's been happening in Bell Cove, have you? Didn't your father, when he was alive, or your aunt Mildred, tell you anything?"

"I warned them not to mention your . . . I mean,

anything personal about Bell Cove, or I would cut off contact with them," she admitted.

"Pff! As if you didn't cut off contact anyhow! How many times have you come back over the past twelve years? Family ties mean nothing to you."

Where was all this bitterness coming from? She'd never known Ethan to be snarky. It was as if he blamed her for something, when in fact . . . *no, I am not going there!* She raised her chin defiantly. "I don't have to defend myself to you."

"You're right. You don't," he said. Then, staring off into the distance, he answered her earlier question. "No, Cassie didn't have an accident. Congenital bone disease, affecting her one hip."

She inhaled sharply. "I am so sorry." She almost reached out to pat his forearm in sympathy, but caught herself just in time when he backed up a step, as if her touch would be repulsive.

But then he said the oddest thing. "You cut your hair."

What? My hair? What does that have to do with anything? Suddenly, she recalled how much he had liked her hair long, how he used to twine his fingers in the long tresses when . . . She shook her head to clear it and said, "It was the first thing I did when I left Bell Cove. Chopped it off myself in a gas station bathroom." What she didn't say was that she'd been bawling at the time, and had completed her task with cuticle scissors from a pocket manicure set. Even so, she'd revealed more than she should have.

He nodded his understanding and told her, "I

burned your letters, the ones you sent from camp each year."

Was that supposed to match her hair cutting? What could she respond to that? Wendy had been a swimming instructor at a youth fitness camp in Nags Head since ninth grade. That was a lot of letters.

He glanced at something over her shoulder. She turned to see his daughter approaching with a gift bag from the ferry shop on her lap.

She had one more question. "How's Beth Anne?" Actually, two questions. "Do you have other children?"

He had been passing her to meet his daughter, but he stopped. "You really are clueless, aren't you?" He stared at her for a long moment, then said, "Dead. Beth Anne is dead."

She gasped.

"And, no, there are no other children."

Then he walked away.

It was news to him . . .

As Ethan drove off the ferry a half hour later, he was alternately fuming and feeling like an ass.

Okay, I overreacted. Big-time. Now she'll think I still care.

Which I do not.

But she makes me so damn mad. I have enough stress in my life. Why did she have to come back now?

She didn't even know about Beth Anne. Or whether I ever actually had a baby, or multiple babies. Hell, she thought I was a practicing vet somewhere off the Outer Banks. What does that say about how little she cared for me?

I should have just walked away when I first saw her.

She cut off her hair, all that beautiful hair. Not that she doesn't look good now. Just different.

He pictured her as he'd seen her on the ferry. Black jeans tucked into knee-high boots. That old Lands' End jacket. Short, mahogany curls cupping her face. Big brown eyes wide with shock. If she wore makeup, he couldn't tell, though her cheeks had been flushed from the wind, *or the sight of me.*

She'd chopped off her hair the day she left, that's what she said. His heart ached at the thought. But damn, he recalled that day, vividly, and her hair wasn't the only thing she'd sliced and diced. His heart had been chopped out, trampled on, and left for roadkill . . . figuratively speaking.

She was so distraught when I confessed, so disappointed in me. I was disappointed in me. But I never expected that she would skip town. Maybe we could have worked things out. Or else, I should have been the one to leave.

Her father had been alive then. Why hadn't Doc Alan stopped his only child from making the mistake of her life?

But was it a mistake for Wendy? She finished college, and, although she never went to med school, she's made a name for herself in that female Navy SEAL program. Which I cannot imagine. Yeah, she was an athlete, a state

champ in swimming, and she probably aced the special
ops physical training, which is supposed to be grueling,
but my Wendy toting a gun, killing people? Impossible!

No, no, no! I have to stop thinking of her as "my
Wendy." She was never mine, apparently, if she could
walk out on me the way she did, without ever looking
back. And she sure as hell isn't mine now.

"Dad, you're talking to yourself," Cassie said.

"Was I?" He shook his head to clear it. "Maybe
I was going over the Christmas list in my head.
I need to mail it off to Santa tonight, and I have
to be sure I covered everything a certain princess
wants." He winked at her as she sat primly in the
passenger seat of his Lexus sedan. He usually preferred to drive his pickup truck, but the height was
a little difficult for Cassie to maneuver with her hip
problem. So, his Lexus or his grandmother's Volvo
were the preferred modes of transportation when
Cassie was on board.

She giggled. At eleven and a half, she probably
didn't still believe in the jolly old fellow, but she
wasn't taking any chances by scoffing or saying it
out loud. And she did look like a princess, all in
pink, including her boots which had inserts for
ankle support when her legs were weak. Like today, after her lengthy exercise session at the rehab
center. "Did you see the latest votes, Dad?" she
asked then, glancing down at the iPhone in her lap,
an extravagant gift after her last operation.

He groaned. That stupid grinch contest! There
were posters and cash jars at more than a dozen sites
around town, including his own Christmas shop,

dammit! Every evening Laura tabulated the results for the day and posted the results in the newspaper office window, as well as on *The Bell*'s website, which was what Cassie must be looking at now.

"You and Mister Baxter are tied for first place, but Delbert Brown from the fish store is gaining. And three new people are nominated. Nineteen altogether now. And, oh my gosh! Guess how much money is raised so far?"

"I haven't a clue," he grumbled.

"Eleven thousand dollars!"

"What? That's impossible. In less than one week? Some people must be stuffing the ballot jars."

Cassie gave him a sideways glance of suspicion. Then grinned evilly, or as evil as an eleven-and-a-half-year-old could. "Can I nominate Miss Elders, my math teacher? She gave us three quizzes last week. Just before Christmas break!"

"I don't think that qualifies as grinchiness."

"I do!"

"And, no, I don't want you wasting your money on that cr . . . contest."

"But it's for a good cause. The new streetlights are so pretty."

"They're not new, honey. Those bell lanterns have been around since I was a boy your age, since my father was a boy, in fact."

"Well, they look new, all polished up."

And working, Ethan had to concede.

"Nana says the extra money raised by the contest will be given to the food bank. That's a good cause, isn't it?"

"Yes, it is."

"Then I can nominate Miss Elders?"

He laughed at the slyness of his daughter. "No way!"

Her phone beeped, indicating an incoming text message. "It's from Nana. She says to stop for bread and milk, please."

He nodded and pulled off the road into Gus's Gas & Goods. Parking next to one of the pumps, he told Cassie, "Sit tight, sweetie. I'll be right back."

"Okay. Nana says to buy some Jujyfruits, too."

"Nice try, kiddo."

She just grinned at him and went back to doing whatever kids did with their phones these days. He trusted her to stay within the limits he'd set for her.

A blond giant of a man in coveralls stepped out of the building and said, "What can I do for you, buddy?" Ethan had known Karl Gustafson all his life, both of them born on the Outer Banks. Gus had gone off to play pro football a few years ago (no, not for the Vikings, though he fit the image with his sharp Nordic features, but for the Cowboys, instead). He'd soon come back, having torn up his knee one too many times. He seemed contented here, despite the trophy wife he'd picked up in Dallas having ditched him once the spotlight dimmed.

"Fill 'er up. I don't need much. I'll go inside for bread and milk."

Gus's was one of those old-time places that abhorred self-service. Windshield washing and an offer of an oil check were still *de rigueur.* Inside, you could buy everything from bait to butter.

While Ethan waited at the register for Gus to come back inside, Ina Rogers, the longtime secretary at Our Lady by the Sea, wheeled her walker over to him. No escaping what he knew was coming.

"You found a wife yet?"

Ina was as old as she looked, and no amount of makeup, which she'd been piling on since nineteen eighty-two, at least, would hide the wrinkles . . . or the orangish tint to her skin. Another Francine victim! She wore a green wool sweater with a huge snowman on the front. It was hard to miss the blinking carrot nose. In any case, ever since Beth Anne had died, Ina, along with every other busybody in town (and there were a lot!), had deemed it their mission in life to find him a new wife.

As if! "Not yet," he replied as politely as possible.

"Your little girl needs a mama."

Says who? he almost said aloud and glanced out the plate glass window to see what was holding up Gus.

Oh, hell! Gus had the hood up on his car and was checking not just the oil, but the windshield washer fluid, too.

"Us ladies in the Altar and Rosary Society said a prayer for you when we were doing an Advent novena last week. How's that darling girl doing, by the way?"

"Cassie's doing much better, actually. Thanks to a lot of painful work in rehab today and some new miracle drugs. I'm sure your prayers help."

"Miracles are good," Ina said, making a quick sign of the cross over the snowman's head, "but it was you we were praying over. Forget that Match-Dot-Com nonsense. Matches made in heaven are the best kind."

Oh, good Lord! And I'm not even Catholic! "That's nice." Time to change the subject. "Shouldn't you be over at Mildred's today for Tuesday Tangos, or is it Two-step Tuesday?"

He meant his question to be sarcastic, but Ina took him seriously. "No. Mildred canceled all the dance parties for this week. Her niece is coming home tomorrow, and she needs to get the house in shape."

In other words, hide all the evidence of her senior citizen shenanigans.

But wait, Aunt Mildred had a surprise coming if she's expecting Wendy tomorrow. He wondered if Wendy had planned a surprise arrival, or was it just accidental that she'd arrived early. Whatever! None of his business.

"Weren't you and Wendy a thing at one time?" Ina inquired, her face brightening at the prospect of yet another "match" possibility.

"A thing? Yeah, that about sums it up." *Gus, where are you? I need to escape.*

Ina apparently didn't understand sarcasm because she cooed, "Oooh, do I sense a Christmas romance in the air?"

Forget sarcasm, he went directly to rude. "The only thing I smell is gasoline and Mrs. Gustafson's Christmas Kraut Cake and some really overpoweringly sweet flowers."

"Oh, that's my Shalimar," Ina said, beaming and waving a hand airily as if he'd given her a compliment.

What the hell is holding Gus up?

"You better get your foot in the door with Wendy real quick, if you're interested. Those SEALs she's bringing here might be heavy competition."

"What SEALs?" he asked, before he had a chance to bite his fool tongue.

"I heard at the market this morning that Wendy invited a bunch of those SEALs here as holiday houseguests. And you know what they say about Navy SEALs?"

Not in a million years would he ask what she meant by that statement.

"Uh-oh! I knew I should have had my roots done this morning." Ina was attempting to fluff her short, unnaturally black hair while craning her neck to alternately see into the mirror behind the deli and out the front window.

Now what? Ethan followed Ina's glance. Looking beyond the pump stations, he noticed what was holding Gus up. Something had caught Gus's attention, along with that of Dylan Hall, an attendant who worked for Gus and had been serving another car, and the fascinated gawking of customers who were lined up for gas, all with a sudden need to be on the premises at the same time. It reminded Ethan of the time there were hurricane warnings for the Outer Banks, and everyone decided to fill up. A royal mess! He recognized his friend Tony's CRACKED CRAB panel truck, Belle Dawson's pink

Mary Kay Cadillac, and Ed McMullin's turkey farm pickup loaded with frozen poultry.

Pulled onto the side berm of the road was the star attraction: a convoy of SUVs and commercial vans with small satellite dishes, all with the logo, "NBX-TV News" and "Morning Show."

He was not one bit surprised to see the anchors Annie Fox and Sam Castile walk into the store then, followed by the herd of Bell Cove gawkers. Over their shoulders he could see his daughter waving at him frantically, wanting to get out of the Lexus and see what was going on.

Not a chance!

"Oooh, oooh, look over there," Annie yelled to Sam. "It's one of those grinch contest thingees. We should get a picture of this for the story."

"Yeah, and that crazy-ass billboard we saw heading into town," Sam agreed, looking around the store, intrigued by the variety of offerings, no doubt. In fact, his mouth dropped open as he noticed the items in the cold case. What? He'd never seen blood pudding (a kind of sausage which Ethan actually liked in small doses for breakfast with eggs) offered alongside homemade Norsk herring-potato salad (Gus's mom's specialty, which Ethan did not like, passionately)? *Can anyone say fish breath?* Flanking the cold case were a display of crudely carved duck decoys (Dylan's work) and a carousel of North Carolina maps.

Ethan homed in on one thing. "Are you talking about the 'Welcome to Bell Cove' billboard?" Nothing unusual in that.

"The one that says: GET GRINCHED! WEL-COME TO BELL COVE!" Sam explained. "It has a picture of a Grinch-like character on it, ringing a bell. Except this grinch wasn't green. He was sun-tanned, wearing shades, a bathing suit, and flip-flops, dragging a scrawny Charlie Brown–type tree."

Ethan gave Gus a questioning stare.

Gus just shrugged, but he was grinning like a Viking baboon as he left to wait on a customer who'd just pulled up, one who actually wanted gas.

"Do you folks know any of the grinches on this list?" Annie inquired, tapping away on some kind of electronic notepad, probably inputting the twenty-one names listed on the poster behind the Mason cash jar.

Everyone in the store turned to look at Ethan.

Just then, Ethan's cell phone vibrated in his back pocket. He gave it a quick glance. A call from his grandmother. He clicked it on. "Doreen is here with a chain saw. Wants to cut down your blue spruce for the town square Nativity scene to impress some TV crew. Should I call the police?"

Since when did they have a town square Nativity scene? The only law enforcement in Bell Cove this time of year was Sheriff Bill Henderson, Doreen's son-in-law, Francine's husband. He would probably help Doreen cut down the damn tree, just because Ethan had failed to vote for his pay hike this year.

"Over my dead body," Ethan exclaimed. "Dammit! It's my tree. I don't care if it's freakin' Christmas, or if the Pope is arriving with the paparazzi in the NBX news truck. Jesus doesn't need a blue spruce tree near his manger."

"Stop blaspheming," his grandmother said. "You've no call to disrespect the Catholics."

"Huh? I wasn't disrespecting any . . . never mind. They probably didn't have blue spruces in Bethlehem anyhow. I'll be there in twenty minutes. Can you hold Doreen off until then?"

"I'll get my rifle."

Ethan would be nervous about that remark if his grandmother actually owned a weapon, or knew how to use one. Shoving the phone back into his pocket, he yelled, "Gus, where are you? Here's twenty bucks for my gas. I'm outta here!"

After he left, three people put five-dollar votes for Ethan Rutledge in the Mason jar on the counter.

Chapter 5

Home was never so sweet . . . sounding . . .

Wendy drove through the small town square, which *was* charming, she had to admit, just like Diane had observed way back at the Wet and Wild, the night all her friends self-invited themselves here for the holidays. The central gazebo and all the storefronts were bedecked with holiday trimmings, most of them featuring the bells for which the town was famous.

The hodgepodge of architecture styles was reminiscent of Cape May, but not so fancy, with its steeples and gingerbread trim. This was, after all, a working man's town from the beginning, fishermen and bell makers. Yes, there were artisans at the bell factory, but mostly they were blue-collar, skilled forge men. Funny, she'd never really thought about it before, but Bell Cove was not at all a beachy town in appearance, but rather an unexpected, attractive contrast to the ocean and large bay that framed its sides.

Everything looked pretty much the same to Wendy, except for a few new businesses and a high polish on the brass bell streetlights. There had been that odd message on the billboard before she'd entered the outskirts of the town, though. What did it mean? "GET GRINCHED! WELCOME TO BELL COVE!"

Just then, the bells tolled to mark the hour, first Our Lady by the Sea Catholic Church, BONG, BONG, BONG, BONG, followed by St. Andrew's Presbyterian Church across the square, BONG, BONG, BONG, BONG, then the town hall. Growing up in a place founded on bells, Wendy appreciated all the variations, according to size, shape, materials, and craftsmanship. These particular church bells were noted for their clear resonant tones. Not at all jarring like some big bells were. And not as tinny as some of the digitized church bells were today.

The noise caused Diane to awaken with a start. She stretched widely as she glanced around. "Wow! I've landed in the middle of Old Timey Town. This looks like the town square in that Chevy Chase movie *Funny Farm*."

"I think that was somewhere in New England, and there was a lot of snow, as I recall."

"A small-town Thomas Kinkade calendar picture then," Diane amended, fascinated by each of the buildings they passed. "Look, a store called Hard Knocks. And over there, Everything Bells. And Blanket-y Blank: Historic South Carolina Quilts. I love it! I'll have to check out Monique's Boutique. I need something for my cousin's wedding."

"You'll be able to walk from my house."

"Oh, good!"

After exiting the town proper, Wendy entered one of the residential areas, heading toward the older section facing the bay, or sound. The homes here were mostly Victorian, made from cedar shakes weathered to a rich gray color, or Italianate, which was popular at the turn of the last century. Some of the shingles were cut in shapes or arranged artistically to create patterns. Turrets and rooftop widow's walks were not uncommon to a neighborhood that had once housed a few wealthy people, the original owners, Italian immigrants turned tycoons, and higher-ups at the factory. Bell Cove had never catered to the "summer people," like those attached to the millionaire mansions along some of the Outer Banks.

In comparison to this neighborhood, Wendy's home was modest, although it was large—three stories—and the shakes had been stained years ago to a mellow oak color, which complemented those parts of the house made of yellow brick. Although her father had been dead for five years now, there was still a brass plaque attached to the lamp post in the front yard close to the street. It read: Dr. Alan Patterson, M.D. At one time, she and her father had planned for the day that plaque would also have her name on it. Dr. Wendy Patterson, M.D. Alas, fate—and a two-timing boyfriend—intervened.

If Wendy were alone, she probably would have wept. As it was, Diane was already slipping on her coat while Wendy parked in the driveway behind Aunt Mildred's green Camry, fifteen years old but only thirty thousand miles. Wendy knew because

Aunt Mildred had told her so in a recent phone conversation.

Parked behind the Camry was a vintage sports car, a Triumph, with a license plate that read "iSamba" and a plate surround proclaiming, "I'd rather be dancing." The mysterious Raul's vehicle, Wendy surmised.

Grabbing their duffel bags, she and Diane made their way up the brick sidewalk, which had heaved a little here and there—that should be repaired before someone tripped and fell. Otherwise, the hundred-year-old house looked in good shape, especially with the beautiful Della Robbia wreath on the door and a matching garland around the fanlight window and door trim.

She could have rung the bell. Everyone in Bell Cove had one of the trademark Bell Forge doorbells. But it was her house. So, she just opened the door and stepped inside.

At first, no one noticed her and Diane standing in the entryway. A vacuum was running upstairs. Loud Latin music was blaring from her dad's old stereo system in the front parlor. A petite, gray-haired lady with a walker was dusting some of the side tables. Her aunt Mildred and a handsome older man—Raul?—were on their knees attempting to roll out the large Persian rug onto the bare wood floors. At the far end of what would have been the second parlor, divided by pocket doors which were now open, a man in a wheelchair was polishing silver. And in the middle of all this, a woman of advanced years, but beautifully built and coiffured, was waltzing by herself, arms extended, as if she had a partner.

The song ended and in the brief silence before the next song came on, Wendy called out, "Aunt Mil," and, at the same time, upstairs a male voice exclaimed, "Oh, shit! The vacuum died again."

Everyone on this floor turned to glance her way, except the dancing lady, who kept on dancing, as the next song came on, "Livin' la Vida Loca." The Crazy Life.

Oh, yeah!

Aunt Mildred and her male companion rose to their feet. He went over to turn off the music, while Aunt Mildred rushed toward her, arms outspread in welcome. "Wendy, honey, we weren't expecting you till tomorrow."

They hugged warmly, both speaking at the same time.

"Oh, it is so good to have you home, baby girl."

"I was able to leave a day early. It *is* good to be home. What is that wonderful smell?"

"Raspberry shortbread sandwich cookies, of course."

Wendy's favorite. She hugged her aunt again. Then, with an arm over her aunt's shoulders, Wendy re-introduced her to Diane. "You remember my friend and housemate, Diane Gomulka, from Washington State. She's in the WEALS, like me. You met her two years ago when you came to visit."

"Welcome, welcome!" Aunt Mil gave Diane a hug, too, then mentioned to Wendy, "I thought you were bringing some fellas with you."

"They'll arrive tomorrow. And another female friend might show up here later this week."

"Good, good," Aunt Mildred said, and then with a decided nervousness, she began to introduce her around the room. The lady with the walker was Gloria Solomon, who had been the town librarian for many years; she'd shushed Wendy more than once for talking during "silent time." And the man polishing silver was Harry Carder, a widower, who had been a financial consultant or something with the bank; his wife, Julia Carder, had been Wendy's dentist growing up. Aunt Mildred whispered to her that Gloria and Harry were supposed to have departed, at least for the holidays, but plans changed suddenly which she would explain later.

The dancing lady was a new arrival to Wendy's house, Claudette Deveraux from New Orleans. How and why she was here would also be explained later.

A short, pudgy man in khakis with red suspenders over a red-and-green plaid flannel shirt came bopping down the stairs, having heard the commotion. He was bald as a cue ball. No surprise that he introduced himself as Elmer Judd. "No, not Elmer Fudd, Judd. J. U. D. D." He rubbed his bald head and said with a laugh, "You could say I fulfilled the expectations of my birth name." Elmer was a former veterinarian from Hatteras. Which accounted for the mixed-breed dog the size of a pony which came bounding down the steps after him, followed by a bulldog and a Pekinese. They all decided to sniff various body parts on the new arrivals.

"You promised to keep the dogs out of the way, Elmer," Wendy's aunt chastised the little man.

"Sorry. I didn't think Wicked Wendy was coming till tomorrow," he said, then winked at Wendy. "Just kidding. Mildred has been ordering us about all week because the house had to be perfect for Wendy. Anyways, meet my family—Duke, Prince, and Earline."

"I never, ever called you wicked," her aunt said.

Wendy just laughed. "I never thought you did."

Then the last introduction took place. "Wendy, this is my close friend Raul Arias, from Spain. Raul, this is my precious niece, Wendy."

A man of medium height, maybe five ten, with perfectly groomed, white, wavy hair stepped forward. "Senorita," he said with a deep Spanish accent, kissing her hand. "You are as beautiful as your aunt said."

He kissed Diane's hand, as well, and to her, declared, "Ah, a blonde. I am, what you say . . . a sucker, for blonde women." He gazed adoringly at her aunt's reddish-blonde locks.

Wendy and Diane rolled their eyes at each other, after which they took their duffel bags upstairs where Wendy settled her friend in the bedroom next to hers. While Diane went off to shower, after which she planned a walk to explore the town, Wendy went back downstairs to talk with her aunt. Even though she hadn't had much sleep in the past twenty-four hours, she was too amped up to take a nap.

The house was built in a sort of modified Colonial Revival style, very symmetrical in appearance with six-over-six windows, often paired together, giving the interior a light airy atmosphere. A wide center hall divided all three floors, what would be considered wasted space in today's home designs, but a blessing for ventilation during the hot summers. Downstairs there were two large parlors and a dining room on one side, and, on the other, what used to be her father's waiting room, consulting room, and examination room, behind which was her mother's small sewing room which had been converted to a sickroom when her illness progressed. The kitchen and a breakfast nook occupied the entire back of the house. French doors in the dining room and kitchen led to the wide porch that covered three sides of the house. It was a home made for families, which the original owner, Ephraim Thompson, had in spades—eight children in all. But unfortunately her mom and dad were unable to have more than one, which they later discovered was due to her illness.

Wendy found Aunt Mildred in the kitchen, thankfully alone. Probably deliberately so, to give them a little privacy.

Her aunt smiled warmly at her and said, "I have ginger tea made. Would you like a cup?"

"Sure."

Aunt Mildred had introduced her to ginger chai tea when she moved in after her sister-in-law's death. She used to travel to Durham to obtain the special tea in one of the Asian markets, but nowadays it was available everywhere, even in tea bags.

When Wendy was feeling lonely or homesick back in Coronado, she often made herself a cup of the soothing brew.

Wendy sat in the chair of the alcove facing the bay. There wasn't much of a beach here, and the view was limited by the dunes, but she loved it nonetheless. Home.

Aunt Mildred carried a tray to the table holding a china teapot, two cups and saucers, all in the Royal Albert Scottish bone china pattern of dogwood flowers, and a plate of raspberry shortbread cookies. Without asking, she placed the latter in front of Wendy and began to pour the tea into the two cups, adding a spoonful of honey and one cube of sugar in each, no milk.

Taking a bite, Wendy pretended to swoon. "Um, my favorite!"

"I know. They were your daddy's favorite, too. Our mother used to make them at Christmastime every year, when we were in Scotland, then later when we immigrated to the United States, and settled in Kearny, New Jersey, where there was an enclave of Scottish immigrants. I was only five years old and your father was seven. Mama made shortbread throughout the year, but the raspberry ones were reserved for holiday treats. Your daddy used to sneak some from the cookie jar to take to his room. I suspect Mama knew but never said anything."

Wendy had heard this and many other stories of their childhood together, countless times, but she never tired of hearing them. "You miss Daddy, don't you?" she asked, reaching a hand across the table to squeeze her aunt's hand.

"I do. It got to be unbearably lonely here in this big house without him and . . ." She glanced pointedly at Wendy. ". . . and you."

"Oh, Aunt Mil, I'm sorry that I haven't come back more often. It was selfish of me. Especially when Daddy was alive, I should have—"

"No," her aunt interrupted her. "You have your own life. I didn't mention that to make you feel guilty. It was more to answer the question that I know is foremost in your mind. What is that old lady doing with all these people in my house?"

"Aunt Mil! This is your house, too. I've told you repeatedly to think of it as your home. I don't begrudge you any guests. I do wonder, though, about . . . well, why so many, and why they live here and not in their own places. None of them are indigent, as far as I can tell." She shrugged. "I mean, do *you* need money? Have you done this out of financial necessity?"

"Not even close! I have my pension and social security benefits. Plus, I have an impressive nest egg. No, money isn't a problem. And before you ask, I'm not losing my mind, either." She sighed deeply and began to explain. "If you've never lived alone, you can't understand how lonely a person can be, even in the middle of a crowd, even in the middle of a small town with so many caring people."

Or in college when your heart is broken. Or in the Navy in the midst of boot camp. Or WEALS where teammates are like sisters. Even on dates with one man after another, never any real relationships. The loneliness never goes away. No, Aunt Mil, don't think for one second that I don't understand.

Sensing her thoughts, her aunt smiled sadly and continued, "It started about two years ago. Joy Lowry was my first housemate."

"The bookstore lady? Why would she move in here? She lives in that big blue oceanfront mansion with the widow's watch cupola on top that resembles an ice cream cone."

"Lived, not lives," her aunt corrected. "Joy's husband, Bill Lowry—remember him, the insurance agent, who always drove the latest model red Mercedes—ran off with his twenty-year-old secretary. Can you imagine? Joy was left to prowl around alone in that big house, which she wanted to sell, but she didn't want to leave Bell Cove."

"So, you invited her to move in here with you."

"Yes. A temporary arrangement. Later, she married the new vicar of St. Pete's over in Nags Head. In fact, lots of my housemates have found love while living here. Which of course has caused some of the busybodies in this town to think we have shady doings going on here." She arched her brows at Wendy as if wondering if she'd heard those rumors.

Wendy admitted nothing. "How many housemates have you had over these two years?"

"About fifteen, but never more than three or four at once, and usually they leave in a few months. I do apologize for there being so many here now. Gloria was supposed to go into one of those assisted-living places, but there was no room available at the last minute. And Harry—poor soul—should be at his son's place in Seattle for the holidays, but the ungrateful boy decided to spend Christmas skiing in Aspen with his family. They didn't invite Harry to accompany them, not that he would have wanted to go, being in a wheelchair and all.

"Claudette is our latest addition. I don't know a lot about her background, just that she arrived in town in the fall, driving a fancy old car with Louisiana plates. It's parked over at Gus's garage because we don't have room here. It's a big 1960s Mercedes convertible that Raul says is worth about fifty thousand dollars. She was staying at the Bell Breakers Motel for more than a month when it closed for the season. Then, three days ago, she showed up here, asking if we had room. As long as she blends in, I figure she's all right." Her aunt looked to her for approval. Which she did not need.

"How do you manage the sleeping arrangements? The stairs must be an issue for some of them, like Mr. Carder in his wheelchair."

"Actually, it's not a problem. Gloria is in your mother's sickroom converted to a guest room on this floor, for when her legs are weak. Most often, she's okay with walking unaided. Plus, I've pushed some of the furniture in your daddy's office to one side and installed a cot for Harry. Eventually, he'll move in with his son, I'm sure. But don't worry, I haven't gotten rid of any of Alan's medical things. I've left them there for you."

"I really should clear out those rooms."

"Your father wanted everything to stay the same until you came back and . . ." Aunt Mildred fumbled for the right words, then raised her chin and finished, ". . . and took over his practice."

"Oh, Aunt Mil, it's too late for that."

"It's never too late," her aunt protested. "It was always your dream. Do you like being in WEALS as much as you would being a doctor? I mean, do you intend to stay in the Navy forever?"

"Probably not, but, even with my four years of pre-med, it would mean another six years at least of medical school and internships and residencies. I'm thirty years old."

"Thirty years young," her aunt insisted. "If you really want it, you could still do it."

She was right. And Wendy *was* getting burned out by some of the missions she'd been on lately. As recently as last week, she'd been considering a change. But medicine? "No, medicine is no longer an option for me. Besides, I like what I'm doing, and I'm good at it, Aunt Mil. Really good. My current contract is up in June, at which time I will probably re-up for at least another year or two. Whatever I decide to do in the future, it will probably be related to the skills I've learned in the Navy."

"But you always wanted . . . if it were not for . . . oh, sweetheart, I hate that all your dreams were ruined."

Wendy shook her head. "Don't feel bad, Aunt Mil. I've come to realize that medicine was just a girlhood dream, one I fell into, more to please Daddy than myself. Of all the regrets in my life, that isn't one of them."

"You mean, like, one door closed, another door opened?"

"In a way." Feeling the need to change the subject, Wendy said, "Back to your housemates . . . how about Raul? Where does he fit into this mix you've described?"

"Forefront," Aunt Mildred said without hesitation, but blushing. "I've only known him for a few months, but he's added so much to my life . . . to many of the lives around here. He has a joy of life that's infectious. In his love of dancing, but in so many other ways, too. He's working on a book that will probably take him back to Spain sooner than later, but in the meantime . . ." She shrugged. "I'm enjoying myself."

"Go you!" Wendy said. "Wish I could say the same."

"Oh, sweetie, I had hoped that you'd found someone special by now. Is it . . ." She paused, as if hesitant to say what was on her mind. "Is it still Ethan?"

"Definitely not," Wendy said, probably too quickly, "but the scars run deep." She was the one who hesitated now before revealing, "I met him on the ferry this afternoon."

"You did? Yikes! That must have been a shock for you, after all these years of avoiding any mention of him."

"It was, and it would seem I've missed some important details by insisting on that rule. Poor Dad. I can't tell you how many times he seemed to bite his tongue for fear of saying the wrong thing."

"Like what?"

"Like Beth Anne having died."

"Yes. Very sad," her aunt said.

"What happened?"

"MS. They discovered she had it while she was pregnant, and it just got progressively worse after that."

"Oh, my God! And her daughter? Does she have the same thing? I wondered about the little girl in the wheelchair, but I never suspected anything like this."

"You mean Cassie? No, she doesn't have MS. Just some kind of congenital hip problem that will eventually be handled with a hip replacement. They don't like to do those on children until they're sixteen or something. Growing bones and all that."

Wendy tried to imagine how Ethan would have handled all these issues at the time. And since then.

"So, Cassie was in a wheelchair today? That's not usually the case. More often she uses crutches, or just limps along. I believe she was scheduled for some rehab at the hospital in Hatteras today. They must have worked her especially hard and wanted her to stay off her feet for the rest of the day."

Wendy was not surprised that her aunt knew all

these details. It was a small town, after all. Everyone knew everyone's business, and not always in a bad way. Her aunt, and others in the community, had probably been over there offering to help wherever they could.

"Did you say that you talked to Ethan?"

"Not exactly talked, more like we snarled at each other. I'm still floored about what you've told me about Beth Anne and the child. I hesitate to ask what else I've missed over the years."

"Well, you have two weeks to catch up, honey."

"One more thing. What's with that billboard on the edge of town? 'GET GRINCHED! WELCOME TO BELL COVE!'"

Aunt Mildred laughed. "It's the funniest thing. The town was a little short of money for street lighting, and someone suggested a novel method for raising funds. Ironically, they're raking in cash like crazy as everyone votes against someone else to avoid being the winner themselves. And I must say, I never saw so many cheerful people, not even at Christmastime. Sickeningly sweet, some of them are." She went on to explain the details of the competition.

Wendy was smiling as her aunt finished. "And Ethan is on this list?"

"At the top."

As Wendy finally agreed to rest for an hour or so—dinner wouldn't be served until six thirty . . . clam chowder with corn biscuits—she imagined Ethan as a grinchy man. That's not the way she remembered him, but then he'd been a boy of eighteen back then. The man she'd met on the boat today . . . was he grinchy?

Absolutely.

Wendy suddenly sensed a bit of grinch in herself. She knew where she was going to be spending twenty dollars tomorrow . . . for a good cause. Maybe fifty.

Chapter 6

A *what* kind of love? . . .

*E*than was eating a big fisherman's breakfast—two eggs, bacon, corned beef hash, home fries, four slices of toast, and coffee, lots of coffee—when his grandmother started in on him. He rarely ate lunch once he was on the go, and his work was strenuous, especially this time of the year. Food was energy. But he wasn't sure his digestion could take all this intrusion into his private space.

It was a sign of how buzzed the old lady was over the latest bee in her bonnet (her expression, not his) that she didn't even object when Harvey came sneaking into the kitchen from the sunporch where he'd been banned for punishment. He'd gotten loose yesterday and hightailed it (literally) next door to "visit" the neighbor's poodle. The neighbors were not happy, having already suffered the consequences of one of Harvey's previous visits, him being of mixed breed and a big galumph of a beast, at that. Being a responsible pet owner, he'd had the old boy fixed since then, but apparently neutering doesn't completely wipe out the sex drive in some cases. Besides, there can be non-sexual reasons for males to hump, his veterinarian, Jake Mellot, liked to tell him, always with an annoying grin, daring him to explain. Ethan couldn't imagine what reasons and refused to ask.

His grandmother also hadn't mentioned the two cats in the kitchen, one on top of the fridge, and the other shedding hair all over the rug in front of the sink. The rescue rabbits in the hutch out back were a sore point with her, too, but nothing she could complain about since he and Cassie handled their care.

Ethan loved animals, as did his daughter. Not so much his grandmother.

"Wendy is back in town. It's time you mended fences," she pointed out, not for the first time since he'd entered the room or numerous times over the past few days.

After twelve years of Wendy's name being taboo in this house, suddenly I'm being bombarded. Ever since she made peace with Mildred Patterson. Wendy this. Wendy that. Mildred said that Wendy . . . I wonder if Wendy . . . Bet Wendy looks different now that . . . blah, blah, blah. If she wasn't my grandmother, and if I didn't owe her big-time for all she does for me and Cassie, and, yeah, if I didn't love the old bat, I would tell her to fuck off. Instead, he remarked, "What fences? I don't have any fences."

"Boy, your fences are a mile high and stone-hard."

He gritted his teeth. "Mind your own business, Grandma."

She hated when he called her Grandma, much

preferring the more endearing Nana, but she didn't react to the jab this morning, having other, more important things on her mind. *Like interfering in my life.* "Boy, it's time for you to talk to the girl about what happened and get some closure so that you can move on."

I'm hardly a boy, at thirty, and Wendy is certainly no longer a girl. That ship sailed a long time ago. "I already talked to Wendy on the ferry, and, for your information, I got closure twelve years ago. Furthermore, Nana, I have no intention of moving anywhere. Let's drop the subject, please." He glanced pointedly at his daughter who loved to eavesdrop on adult conversations.

Cassie, who had been pretending to nibble on a buttered English muffin, dropping little bits for Harvey, but was following the conversation with too much interest, asked, "Is she the lady with the short hair, Dad? She's pretty."

"Wendy has short hair now?" his grandmother inquired. "Ah!" she added, as if that change of hairstyle was meaningful.

It was.

"Mom told me about Wendy," Cassie said.

Ethan and his grandmother both stared at the little girl who sipped at her cup of hot chocolate, knowing full well she had their attention by dropping that bombshell. The little imp!

Harvey's big tongue flicked out and he scarfed the last of her muffin. The big imp!

"What did Mom say, sweetheart?" his grandmother prompted before he could cut short this line of conversation. Apparently, she hadn't noticed Harvey's slick move.

"Mom said that Dad loved her, but not like he loved a girl named Wendy. She told me to never settle for any kind of love, except the Wendy kind. It's in that journal that she gave me to read when I was twelve years old. I'm almost twelve, you know. So peeking is all right."

Ethan inhaled sharply. That damn journal Beth Anne had always been writing in! He should have read it before handing it over to Cassie. "Oh, princess!" he said. "I'm sorry she burdened you with that."

"No, no!" Cassie shook her head. "Mom wasn't being sad or anything. It was when she was telling me all the life lessons she would miss giving me when I'm older. Like, study hard and find a job that makes you get up every morning with a smile."

That isn't too bad. In fact, it's excellent advice. Wish I felt that way about tree farming, the actual growing, not the business. But poor Beth Anne! Even though she had never mentioned it, he knew that she had followed news of Wendy's career, and for some reason thought that if she did something more interesting than being a wife and mother he would suddenly love her more.

"I thought you were going to wait for a guy just like PopPop," Ethan said.

Everyone in town knew the story of Samuel Rutledge and Eliza Metz, and no one romanticized it more than his grandmother Eliza who had pictures of the two of them all over the place. And no one relished the stories of their legendary love more than Ethan's daughter. Instead of bedtime stories, she was always begging Nana to tell her about the first time she met "that mountain boy," or how he proposed, or what their wedding had been like out on the beach.

"Can't I have both?" Cassie asked, as if he'd asked a dumb question. "Anyhow, Mom had lots of lessons to give me. They're in the journal. Be kind to everyone, even people you don't like. That was another one."

Even better, though I have trouble following that rule when it comes to that annoying Baxter. And, Nana, truth to tell, when she's on a nagging streak.

"Don't have sex until I'm sixteen, or until I'm ready."

"Whaaat?"

His grandmother barely stifled a smile, probably at his discomfort, not at Cassie's precocious words.

"And don't settle for a lukewarm love, aim for a Wendy kind of love."

Harvey spread-eagled himself on the floor, under the table, and let loose with a low dog moan, as if he knew all about love.

A Wendy kind of love? Ethan put his face in his hands for a moment. Then he looked directly at his daughter. "I loved your mother, don't ever think that I didn't." *Loved, never in love, but she doesn't need to know that.*

"I know," Cassie said.

"After all, without her, I wouldn't have you, and I love you bunches. That's the best kind of love."

"I know." Then, unaware of the shock she'd created, Cassie asked, "Can I be excused? I want to go into the Christmas shop with Nana today. Is that okay?"

Just like that, the subject was no longer of any interest to the little girl.

Suddenly, he noticed her attire for the day. A pink sweatshirt with silver sparkly snowflakes in the form of a tree, over darker pink sweatpants, and her pink boots. In her hair, which she insisted on caring for herself, there was pinned a sprig of holly attached to a headband, which was . . . what else? Pink. She looked like a pink elf, perfect attire for the Holiday Shoppe. *Or. . . . Oh, no!* He would bet his last dollar that Zach Stanton was on the schedule today. He was about to object, not liking the idea of his young daughter having a crush on an older man . . . sixteen years old! Girls her age should be interested in Barbies, not Kens. Not that Zach was any kind of Ken with his tattoos and one earring. But his grandmother kicked him under the table, a silent caution to not overreact. He knew she was right, forbid a kid something and they wanted it even more. So, all he said to Cassie was, "As long as you don't overdo."

Cassie got up and walked out of the kitchen. No need for crutches today. She only limped slightly. *Please God, let her improvement continue*, he prayed. The cats followed after her, but Harvey stuck around, still hoping for some scraps.

Once they were alone, his grandmother pointed

a spatula at him. "Like I said, closure. I'm not getting any younger. I won't always be around, you know."

"If you're planning on kicking the bucket, please don't do it today. I have too much to do without having to make funeral arrangements."

"Very funny. Maybe I want to get a life for myself. Maybe I want to sign up for mambo lessons. Maybe I want to get myself a Latin lover."

His mouth dropped open. "You're kidding. I hope. Or maybe mambo lessons would do you good. Better yet, get yourself a boyfriend. Get two. It might improve your mood and stop your nagging."

Under her breath, his grandmother said, "I'm not the only one that needs to get laid."

Sometimes his grandmother went too far. Ethan said the bad words he'd been holding back, under his breath, followed by, *A Wendy kind of love.* Those words would stick in his craw for a long time now.

As if she hadn't shocked the pants off him, his grandmother was off on another tangent. "By the way, I heard on the radio this morning that Frank Baxter is leading the contest for best grinch. You've dropped to third place. Moving into second is Gabriel Conti, the architect who inherited his family's factory here in Bell Cove. Apparently, he made a remark to a Durham newspaper, something to the effect of, 'Who needs bells today, anyhow? You can buy them at Walmart for a dime a dozen.'"

At least she was off the subject of closure. "That

doesn't bode well for our committee meeting with him this afternoon."

"I wondered why you were wearing a shirt and tie."

He figured it was the least he could do to make an impression, though his appearance wouldn't matter diddly-squat to a big shot like Gabriel Conti, who thought quality bells could be bought at Walmart. The Durham architectural firm he was a partner in was in the media all the time for the famous buildings it designed around the world. Gabe probably forgot they'd even met as teenagers. "We were supposed to get together last week, but he canceled at the last minute. I heard he met with the real estate developer, though."

"It'll be a cryin' shame if they close the factory down."

"We're trying our best."

"If bells aren't selling, it's too bad they can't find another business to take over."

"If Conti would give us time, we might be able to lure a suitable enterprise here."

"Maybe that's what the excess money from the grinch contest could be used for. A Bell Cove Development Authority or whatever you call those committees that try to entice businesses into their communities with tax incentives and stuff."

He just gaped at his grandmother. *What does she know about development authorities? And another committee? Not for me! And just how much damn money does she think this crazy contest is going to make?* Instead of snapping at her, like he was inclined to do, he said, "It's hard to attract new business, with Bell Cove being so inaccessible."

"Bell Forge managed with barges off that back dock harbor."

"Pfff! Have you seen that thing lately? The wood is rotted out and would crumble under the weight of a two-ton church bell."

"It could be rebuilt," she started to say, then, at his scowl of disbelief, she added, "by a motivated buyer."

"And where would we find one of those?" he scoffed.

She shrugged. "Maybe it's time for a Christmas miracle."

He laughed. "Yeah, that's what I'm gonna be praying for . . . a miracle of the bells." He was kidding, of course, but the light in his grandmother's eyes—the same blue as everyone's in the Rutledge family, including his and Cassie's—made him regret his hasty words.

Especially when she said, "Hmmm."

He knew, he just knew, that not only was this town going bonkers over a grinch contest, but they would now be praying for a bell miracle.

Personally, Ethan was praying he could make it through the holiday this year. *A Wendy kind of love.* The words kept drumming in his head. He reacted the only way he could, by muttering, "Bah! Humbug!"

"What did you say?" his grandmother asked.

"I said, 'Merry Christmas! It's off to work I go. Ho, ho, ho!'"

"I think you've got elves and dwarves mixed up."
That wasn't the only thing he was mixed up about.

Fancy meeting you here, Mister Crab . . .

Wendy spent the next morning with Aunt Mildred finalizing sleeping arrangements for her
friends who should be arriving that afternoon. A
cleaning lady, Sally Davis, came in once a week
to help her aunt, but the third floor hadn't been
touched in years.

Sally was up there now mopping the old oak
floors to a high sheen with Murphy Oil Soap, the
not unpleasant scent of which drifted all the way
down to the kitchen where it warred with the delicious aroma of homemade marinara sauce. Wendy
and her aunt were in the laundry room folding the
third batch of bed linens and towels. If the weather
was warmer, the sheets would be hanging outside
on the clothesline, and the doors would be open to
the bay breeze, adding yet another scent to the air.

Elmer was making lasagna for dinner with toma-
toes canned from his own garden, taken over recently by the new owners of his home which had
been sold out from under him by an unscrupulous
family member. The issue was currently slogging
through the mud of the state court system. He was
being aided by Harry, whose wheelchair fit perfectly under the low island where he was chopping onions, mushrooms, and garlic. Gloria was

perched on a stool—no need for the walker today, apparently—making an arrangement of holly, pine-cones, and a fat clove candle for the dining room where they would be eating that night, with all the extensions added to the table for the first time in years.

Wendy could hear some jaunty Christmas music coming from the front parlor where Raul was ap-parently teaching Claudette how to do the Carolina Shag to "Jingle Bell Rock," while the New Orleans native was showing him how to shake a leg with a Cajun Two-Step. How they were doing that with the rug down, she wasn't sure. Maybe they were out in the hall.

It was organized chaos, which Wendy didn't yet understand. For now, she was more concerned with the logistics of having anywhere from ten to fifteen people residing in this house for the holidays.

With Gloria in her mother's sewing/sickroom and Harry next door in her father's office made into a temporary bedroom, it meant that her aunt and Raul shared one of the five bedrooms on the second floor, she was in her old room, and Diane in the second guest room, which was separated by a Jack 'n Jill bathroom. The new arrival, Clau-dette, had been using the second guest room, but would be sleeping on a pull-out sofa downstairs with Gloria for the time being. Elmer occupied the first guest room on the second floor. The old mas-ter bedroom hadn't been used since her father died, but Wendy wasn't so sentimental that she would mind one of her SEAL friends using it. A change of linens and quick dusting was all that was needed there. If Delphine should show up, she could take one of the twin beds in Diane's room.

In addition to the small shared bathroom, there was also a large bathroom on this floor with an old-fashioned claw-foot tub, alongside a more modern shower stall put in when Wendy was a kid. The first floor had a half bath. Wendy wasn't sure how that worked for the handicapped two down there, and she wasn't asking. There was also a full bath on the third floor, with two bedrooms, once intended for servants, and a large school/playroom.

The basement was half finished with paneling, used occasionally for parties by Wendy and her friends when she was growing up. Now it was a junk room with old furniture and boxes stored to the ceiling. Not a mess she wanted to tackle during this trip.

Wendy really needed to think about getting rid of this big elephant of a house, with all this space. It was something she would discuss with Aunt Mildred before she left. When her father was alive, he liked having those three rooms on the first floor for his home medical practice, and he had been a big man in stature who relished what he called "breathing room."

One thing was certain; she wouldn't sell if her aunt wanted to stay here. Money wasn't an issue for Wendy. At least not at the moment.

About noon, Wendy showered and changed to black leggings and a fluffy soft, white cashmere mock-turtleneck sweater. She was going to meet her friend Laura Atler for lunch at the Cracked Crab. Before going outside, where the temperature had dropped to a low thirty degrees, which had everyone wishing for a white Christmas, even if only flurries, she grabbed her mother's old red coat from the hall closet. She buttoned it and pulled the collar up, relishing the feel, almost as if being enfolded with maternal warmth.

I'm becoming way too sentimental. That's what comes from returning home. She sighed and went out, telling her aunt she would be back about three or so. Diane had taken the rental car that morning to the Graveyard of the Atlantic Museum on Hatteras Island where she planned to spend a few hours.

Laura was already at the restaurant when Wendy arrived fifteen minutes later after her brisk walk to town. She knew because she'd gotten a text message a few moments ago. The bell tinkled on the door when she entered, but the hostess was missing from the entry area, probably showing someone else to a table.

Wendy walked up to the reception desk to get a closer look at the big Mason jar sitting there with a poster behind it listing all the nominees thus far for Bell Cove Grinch of the Year. An amazing twenty-two names and twelve thousand dollars had been raised thus far, the proceeds to go for street lighting and other civic projects. Wendy recognized some of the names, including Ethan who was now number four. At the top was Gabriel Conti, whom she'd never met but assumed was one of the founding bell factory family members. But wait, she had met him long ago when she was a teenager and he'd sometimes visited his grandparents here during the summer months. But then, Wendy had eyes for Ethan only. Plus, she was often away being a swimming instructor at summer camps.

Looking around to make sure she wasn't noticed, she wrote Ethan's name on two of the slips of paper and dropped a ten-dollar bill in the jar. Immature? Yes. Satisfying? Hell, yes!

Laura was sitting at a table near the back of the restaurant, which was surprisingly busy for this time of the year. If the delicious aromas of seafood coming from the kitchen were any indication, she could tell why.

They both laughed when Wendy took off her coat, revealing her white mock-turtleneck, and she noticed that Laura was wearing an almost identical one under a Christmassy green pantsuit. Some things never changed, apparently, including their shared taste in clothes.

After Wendy explained that Diane wouldn't be joining them, having opted for the touristy day, she and Laura hugged warmly, each commenting on how good the other looked. Laura was a beautiful blonde, one of those women who came late into their beauty. Growing up, Laura had always been a little too pudgy, or suffered from acne, or hair issues, or chronic shyness. Now, she was petite, with clear skin and to-die-for long platinum tresses styled into a mass of waves. She couldn't be too shy anymore if she was editor of the weekly newspaper where she probably had to do a lot of the interviewing herself.

Even though Wendy hadn't come home much over the past twelve years, she'd kept in touch with her best friend by phone and email. Time didn't matter with "sisters at heart," which they had always proclaimed to be.

Tony Bonfatto, the owner of the Cracked Crab, came over to hand them menus personally. After introductions and some small talk, during which Wendy could tell that he had a thing for Laura, they placed their orders. Wendy would have a soft crab sandwich on a fresh-baked roll with a side of coleslaw, and Laura opted for lobster bisque, with a small baguette. Diet sodas for them both.

Before he left, Tony reminded Laura, "Remember the committee meeting over at the forge at two."

Laura nodded.

The forge—Bell Forge, Wendy assumed—was located about five miles south of the town, beyond the Rutledge Tree Farm.

Wendy arched her brows at Laura after the restaurant owner went back to the kitchen to place their orders.

Laura understood Wendy's silent question. "We're on a committee of the town council, going to try to persuade the owner of the bell factory to keep it going. And, before you get any ideas, Tony is just a friend."

"Uh-huh," Wendy said, unconvinced, at least from Tony's end. The waitress brought their drinks and arranged some silverware before Wendy continued, "Anyone else special?"

"No one since I broke my engagement to Dane."

Wendy arched her brows again.

"Turned out Dane was a dog. A horndog."

"Enough said!"

"How about you?"

"No one special for me, either. A few possibilities over the years, but nothing lasting more than a few months. To tell the truth, I've been too busy for commitments of any kind."

"Yeah. Me, too."

She and Laura looked at each other and burst out laughing. The too-busy-for-love excuse was bachelor girl bullshit, and they both knew it.

"Maybe we're destined to be spinster ladies, as Aunt Mildred calls modern females who choose not to marry."

"Yuck!" Laura said. "So, what's going on out at Chez Geriatrics? Oh, that was mean!"

"Yes, it was," Wendy said, biting her lip to keep from laughing.

"How is your aunt, anyway?"

"She's fine, as far as I can tell, but you were right to warn me. I appreciate that."

"So, dish," Laura encouraged.

"She's been lonely, and sensing other lonely folks of a certain age around her, she's invited them, or they invited themselves, to live with her, temporarily. I don't have all the details yet, but it seems tame enough."

"Even the shady dance club with the Julio Iglesias lookalike?"

Wendy smiled at that description, but had to admit that Raul did look a bit like the Latin music artist, albeit with white hair. "I haven't seen much of the dancing yet."

Laura leaned across the table and half whispered, "Do he and Aunt Mil sleep together?"

Wendy leaned forward a bit, too, and whispered back, "Yes."

"Hard to picture two old people doing the dirty, huh?"

"That reeks of ageism," Wendy said with mock primness.

"Don't tell me you didn't think the same thing."

"I did feel a bit uncomfortable last night when she and Raul went off to bed together. In fact—and if you ever repeat this, I swear I will hunt you down and hurt you, and believe me, we WEALS have secret torture methods—I saw him pat her ass when they were walking down the hall." It reminded her a little of the time she'd seen Eliza Rutledge pinch her husband's butt all those years ago.

"That's kind of cute, actually." Their orders arrived, and they ate silently for a few moments, relishing the delicious food, before Laura asked, "So, are you going to let me interview you for a feature story?"

"No."

"Please. Pretty please. I want to get a face-to-face color story on what it's like for a hometown girl to go off and be a female warrior against terrorism."

"It's been done before, honey."

"Not about you, and not in my paper."

"I can't, Laura. That's all I need is for some terrorist getting my name and address and coming after me."

"Then, how about those SEALs you're bringing

here as houseguests? It could be anonymous. I wouldn't have to use names or pictures, or maybe shadowy images. Any hunks in the bunch?"

She had to think for a moment. She'd become so used to her SEAL buddies, on missions and on the base, knowing way too much about them, some of which was not so attractive (like belching on command, or body odor after a day in the field, or watching them hit on women, or worse yet, cheat on women) that she didn't see them the way other people did. "I suppose they are good looking. JAM—Jacob Alvarez Mendozo—used to be a priest, or in a seminary at one time. Merrill 'Geek' Good is a genius, graduated from college when he was sixteen or near to. Aside from being a world-class battle strategist, he's also an inventor. Made millions, they claim, from something called a penile glove. Don't ask. And K-4, that's Kevin Fortunato, joined the SEALs when his wife died of cancer."

"Holy moley, girl! A priest, a sexy tycoon, and a grieving soldier widower! You've given me fodder for a year of stories."

Wendy just smiled, not about to prick Laura's balloon by informing her that SEALs, especially active ones, did not speak about their work or their lives, especially to a newspaper reporter. Public exposure was taboo, as she'd already mentioned to Laura in terms of terrorists. But besides that, seasoned soldiers did not like to talk about their work.

"Why didn't they travel here with you?"

"They decided to go to New Jersey first. There's

some kind of treasure-hunting company that's for sale, and they're thinking about buying it, I guess. Or exploring some possibilities for the future when they eventually retire. Special forces men, and women, burn out after a while, as you can imagine."

"Good grief! Another story angle. Hunky treasure-hunting SEALs!"

Wendy reached across the table and squeezed her friend's hand. "It is so good to see you."

"Likewise," Laura said, squeezing back. "Does that include you? Are you ready to give up the web-foot warrioress life?"

"I don't know. Maybe." She told Laura then about the recent death of their teammate and how it was affecting them all. "Maybe we just need a little R & R to re-energize."

"That's what we do best here on the Outer Banks, rest and relaxation," Laura said. "Can I ask you one thing?"

Uh-oh! Wendy sensed by the way Laura bit her bottom lip with nervousness that she was not going to like this question.

"Do you still love him?"

Wendy flinched, as if she'd been sucker punched, which she had been a few times during Hell Week, before she'd learned to duck and cover, or to give back as good as she got. She couldn't be mad at Laura for her blunt question, though. That's what friends did. Shared their innermost thoughts. And she sure as hell didn't need to ask who Laura meant. Ethan, obviously.

"How could I? It's been twelve years. He betrayed me in the worst way a man can to the woman he presumably loves."

"He was a boy, and you were a girl," Laura pointed out.

"A moot point. Ethan slept with another girl, got her pregnant when we were supposed to share some corny forever kind of love." Despite herself, Wendy felt tears well in her eyes. That's what being home, being here in Bell Cove did. That's why she'd avoided it for twelve years.

"Yeah, he did, and he paid for it. He never loved Beth Anne. You know that. Eighteen-year-old boy, mad at his girlfriend for making other plans for the weekend, goes to a party, drinks a little beer, and succumbs to the temptation of a willing partner. It happened only once." Laura held up a hand to halt the protest Wendy was about to make. "I'm not saying he wasn't wrong. He screwed up. Big-time. But, Wendy, your breakup was a kick in the guts to not just the two of you, but the whole town. If you two, who practically glowed when you were around each other, couldn't make it, then maybe there was no such thing as real love. Your refusal to come back here . . . it was like you broke up with the whole town, not just Ethan."

"That's a whole lot of guilt to lay on me. I was young, starry-eyed in love, and I was crushed."

"I know, I know. And believe me, I'm not defending Ethan. The jerk! I've let him know what I think of him from the get-go. And, no, I'm not saying that you should have hung around and worked things out, like some folks said."

"People said that?"

"Yeah, but don't be too hard on them. I know it's a town full of busybodies, but that's what small towns are like. For good and bad. Good, because people really do care, and bad, because some are just plain snoopy. I'm of the first persuasion, and I'm just saying . . . is it really over?"

"Dead and buried," Wendy said without hesitation.

"Well, speaking of the corpse . . ." Laura said.

Wendy turned to see Ethan walk into the restaurant. He hadn't yet spotted her and Laura at the far end of the dining area but was headed toward Tony, who was speaking to some customers at a nearby table. A light blue dress shirt and tie were visible under his open, black cashmere overcoat, the blue of the shirt making the color of his eyes stand out even more against the framework of dark lashes. If he'd looked hot in a work jacket and jeans yesterday on the ferry, he looked hotter than hell in professional attire. And Wendy wasn't the only woman in the room who noticed his sexy good looks.

"Hey, buddy, I just dropped Cassie off at a friend's house for the afternoon," she heard him say to Tony. "Want a lift to the forge for the meeting?"

Wendy arched a brow at Laura. "You didn't mention that Ethan would be going to your meeting, too."

"Oops."

"Sure," Tony said to Ethan. "Maybe Laura will

want to ride with us." He made a motion with his head toward their table.

Just then, Ethan noticed her, and before he could catch himself, he recoiled.

He recoiled!

But then, his lips parted, and his eyes—those beautiful summer-sky eyes—held hers for a long moment. And, for just that blip of a second, they were teenagers so much in love that it hurt.

Wendy might have made a low moan, out loud, or maybe it was a silent moan. She was too stunned to be sure.

Laura said, "I hate to tell you, Wendy, dear, but you are glowing."

"That's just blood rushing to my head."

"Uh-huh." Then, in a low voice, Laura began to sing the lyrics to that old Whitney Houston song, "I will always loooooove you . . ." It had been their song. It had been playing on his car radio the night that they first made love. It had been the kind of song that, no matter where they were, or how public the setting, when it came on, they stopped and looked at each other.

Wendy hated that song.

Laura had a really good voice, but at the moment Wendy could barely hear her for the loud pounding of her traitorous heart. Apparently, her feelings for Ethan weren't as dead and buried as she'd thought they were.

Chapter 7

I'm sorry, so sorry . . . oh, hell, Brenda Lee
said it much better than he ever could . . .

*D*amn!" Ethan muttered. "Damn, damn, friggin'
damn!"

He had known that he would run into Wendy
while she was in town, but still he was unprepared
for the assault on his senses when he saw her in the
Cracked Crab. Blindsided without armor.

"What? What's up?" Tony asked, not understanding. He was fairly new to Bell Cove, or at least he
hadn't been around back when . . .

"Nothing," Ethan snapped, so abruptly that Tony
raised his brows.

Instead of making a teasing remark, as he usually
did, this time about him turning into the grinch,
Tony just gave him a questioning stare. When
Ethan didn't respond, Tony shrugged. "I'll go get
my coat from the office and we'll head out. Could
you ask Laura if she wants to come with us? If I ask,
she'll probably say no, just because she thinks I'm
hitting on her."

Which he usually was. Tony had been batting

zero in his attempts to date Laura, and, ordinarily, Ethan wouldn't mind doing him this favor. But now? With Wendy there? Oh, man! He turned to tell Tony that he would wait in the car out front, but Tony was already gone.

With a deep inhale and exhale of surrender, he stepped forward and spoke to Laura, who was putting on her coat. "Hey, Laura. I was in town dropping Cassie off at the Hendersons' and thought I'd stop to see if Tony wants to ride with me to the meeting. You want to come with us?"

"Okay. Wait a sec while I go to the ladies' room. Gotta refresh my makeup to impress Mis-tah I-hold-the-future-of-this-hick-town-in-my-hands Conti."

He laughed and said, "Sure," but what he thought was, *Oh, shit! Laura's got her attitude on.*

"Good seeing you, Wendy," Laura called back to her old friend. "Remember, *The Bell* party on Friday night." Laura waved and left.

Leaving Ethan alone with Wendy. Well, alone in the middle of a restaurant, but with them, that had never mattered.

That was then, and this is now, he reminded himself.

Yeah, right.

Ethan smiled then when he noticed the red coat she was wearing. "Still channeling Little Red Riding Hood?" He remembered how she cherished that old coat of her mother's after she died. He remembered how pretty she'd looked in it. Still did.

Now that he'd gotten over the shock of her short

hair, he liked it. The way it cupped her head with reddish-brown curls acted as a frame for her face's smooth skin and perfectly formed features. Except . . . wait . . . was that a thin scar that ran from beneath her left ear, under her chin, and towards her windpipe? She hadn't had that or any other scars when he'd known her and every part of her young body. Holy crap! Had someone tried to slash her throat?

But then, he had to remind himself that this was only one of the many things that would be different about her now. After all, she was a trained female Navy SEAL now. She'd always been physically fit, an Olympic-level swimmer and diver, and she had taken some karate self-defense classes, but she had a different kind of physique now, and she carried herself differently. Harder. More sharply honed. Hell, she probably killed people. Bad people. The Wendy he'd known wouldn't kill a mouse. She hadn't owned a weapon or had the skill to use one, not even a can of frickin' Mace.

All these changes! Because of me? Or maybe this is the real Wendy I never knew.

"Yeah. Old habits and all that," Wendy said, knocking him out of his trance.

For a moment he didn't understand what she meant, but then he realized that she was reacting to his Red Riding Hood remark. Had she taken it as a criticism? He hadn't meant it that way.

Damn! I'm like a teenager tripping over my own tongue.

She was gathering her purse, taking out a bill to

leave on the table for a tip. Obviously, she was in a hurry to leave. With her face flushed to match her coat, she looked as panicked as he felt, or maybe it was just anger, old and new.

He should say something to cool the air. "So, how's it feel to be back home?" *Could I sound any more lame?*

"Good and bad." At least she'd paused in her leave-taking and was looking at him. Closely.

He waited for her to elaborate. *Come on, Tony, how long does it take to grab a coat?* "Oh?" *Another lame remark!*

"The good? I love the Outer Banks, you know that."

So, why have you stayed away? was his unspoken question. "You used to," he conceded.

She didn't respond to that jibe, except for a lifting of her chin which further exposed the scar, but went on. "The bad is that it's not the same here without my dad. Plus, it's been an adjustment with all those people in the house. You've probably heard the rumors about Aunt Mil."

"I don't pay much attention to gossip. My grandmother was over there last week, the first time she and your aunt have spoken in twelve years. Said that the people she met seemed nice."

"What? Twelve years? Are you kidding? They were best friends."

He shrugged.

"How *is* your grandmother?"

"Nana is as crotchety and as interfering as ever."

She laughed, although he could tell that her mind was still snagged back there on a twelve-year spat between the old ladies. "Crotchety equals grinchy in my book. Surely she's not on that list of nominees."

"She actually is. One vote from a difficult customer. But mostly, she's just grumpy with me."

They exchanged a smile, and it was nice. Friendly. But then, he recalled his daughter's words of that morning, *a Wendy kind of love*, and knew that he and Wendy would never be friends.

"You're frowning," she pointed out. "Something I said?"

"Nah. Just a lot on my mind." *Where the hell was Tony?* Now, Laura, he knew, was probably pulling a deliberate ploy to make him squirm. She'd had it in for him ever since . . . well, for a long time.

"Is it your daughter? Aunt Mil told me that she has some physical problems, and I noticed the wheelchair yesterday."

He stiffened. No way was he going to discuss Cassie with this woman who probably thought he'd been carrying a torch for her all these years, that he regretted everything that had happened with Beth Anne. How could he, when that one-night stand had resulted in his precious little girl? "Cassie is fine. It's just a busy time of the year for me, with the tree farm, and then this business with the bell factory." He shrugged.

She didn't look convinced.

"Look, Wendy, this is really awkward, and it shouldn't be. We have a history. Big deal! I don't love you anymore, in case you're thinking that I've been pining away over you, and—"

"Pining?" she sputtered with a laugh. "What kind of word is pining?"

It was the kind of word his grandmother would use. He should have laughed, too. Instead, for some reason, her laughter ignited a spark of bitterness that he must have been harboring all these years because he added, "—and you sure as hell never loved me."

He immediately regretted his words when he saw the hurt in her eyes, those beautiful brown eyes flecked with gold that were glistening now with tears . . . tears he'd caused.

"Don't . . . you . . . dare . . . say . . . that!" she half whispered.

"Ah, Wendy," he said, and pulled her into his arms, right there in the middle of the Cracked Crab restaurant. She fit just right, like always, with her face tucked against his neck, smelling of lilies of the valley, or some summery flower. Then, when she lifted her face to say something, he almost kissed her. It was a reflex, something he'd done so often over so many years.

But not lately.

Not for twelve years.

Have I lost my mind?

He jerked back, dropping his arms, and murmured, "Sorry," before turning, about to walk away.

That apology covered a whole lot of sins. He hoped.

But then, none of that mattered because three men walked into the restaurant, causing a stir. Everyone in the place turned or craned their necks. It was almost as if a bomb of silence hit the place, causing a momentary lull. No clatter of silverware. No shouting of orders. No hum of conversation.

The three men, who stood in the dining area, scanning the crowd, did not wear uniforms. Nor did they sport military haircuts. But it was as clear as the skies on an Outer Banks summer that these were lean, mean fighting machines of Uncle Sam. Maybe special forces. Probably Navy SEALs, he concluded when one of them spotted Wendy and waved, calling out, "Hey, Flip."

She smiled as if she was about to be rescued by Uncle Sam's finest.

Rescued from what?

Me?

That is just great!

The background Christmas music changed from "Jingle Bell Rock" to "Deck the Halls."

He would like to deck something.

He had no idea what the "flip" reference was, but assumed these must be some of her houseguests. A Hispanic man with a ponytail, a baby-faced stud with the body of an extreme athlete, and an Italian- or Greek-looking guy who probably posed for statues on the side.

Shiiit!

Wendy met them halfway, giving each a warm hug of greeting. He couldn't help but overhear their conversation from several feet away, even though the diners and wait staff resumed their business, only half eavesdropping.

"Hey, guys! I wasn't expecting you today," Wendy said.

"Drove all night. Geek is a maniac on the highway," the Hispanic one told her.

"How would you know, Jam?" Baby Face/Geek countered. *Jam? The guy's name is jelly? And the other one is a geek?* "You slept the whole way from Jersey. Your snores sounded like a foghorn when we crossed on those ferries."

"Those ferries! Man, they get old fast," contributed the Italian/Greek military god. "Is that linguine with clam sauce I see that lady eating over there? Or how about the smell of that pasta sauce? I'm starving." He sniffed the air which was redolent of seafood and garlic and rich red sauce.

"You better not order Italian, if you're going to eat here," Wendy advised. "We're having lasagna for dinner. By the way, how did you know I was here?"

"Stopped by your house. Met the senior squad. They were doing the Watusi. Man!" Baby Face/Geek winked at Wendy.

For some reason, that wink really irritated Ethan.

"Yeah, we know about the lasagna," the Italian/Greek put in. "Elmer Fudd made me give his sauce a taste to see if it had enough Parmesan. Guess he figured that my being Italian made me an expert. It was gooood!"

That settled it, as far as this guy's nationality. Italian. And what was that about Elmer Fudd? Oh, he must mean that little bald guy who recently moved into the house.

"Babe," the Hispanic jam dude said to Wendy, "those churches out there on the square are seriously amazing. I can't wait to explore."

Ethan was even more irritated at the endearment and wondered why a Navy SEAL would be so interested in churches.

"Forget the holier-than-thou crap, Father Mendozo. I can't wait to get in some winter surfing," Baby Face/Geek said.

"You'll freeze your balls off, idiot," the Italian said.

"Yeah." Baby Face smiled as if that were a good thing.

Ethan found himself studying the three men, wondering which, if any of them, was Wendy's lover. Considering the way times had changed—the way Wendy had changed—maybe they all were. There was a thought to pierce his heart.

Just then the two churches and the town hall clock did their bell thing, tolling once, twice, in succession, each a different tone thanks to the Bell Forge craftsmen.

The three men stopped talking and listened. Then, as one, they said, "Cool!"

On that note, Ethan left.

Wendy never even noticed.

Fatherly advice . . .

Wendy watched with a heavy heart as Ethan walked away.

This has to stop.

Now!

I've come too far to let a man . . . any man . . . that man . . . turn my life upside down . . . again.

She settled the guys in at the restaurant and told them she would meet them back at the house. Before she left, JAM squeezed her arm and asked in a soft voice, "Is he the one?"

"The one what?" she replied, walking toward the door, not bothering to wait for his answer. Behind her, she heard him say to the other two, "Yeah, he's the one."

JAM caught up with her outside the restaurant and said, "I'm not really hungry. Mind if I walk with you?"

She shook her head.

At first, they just walked in silence. Here and there, people would recognize her and shout out.

"Hey, Wendy! Merry Christmas! Glad to see you home."

That was Mr. Baxter from the hardware store. Lordy, what was he doing with that hairstyle?

"Merry Christmas, Wendy! Are you coming to the bell concert?" Mrs. Jeffers, the church bell choir director at St. Andrew's, asked.

"Wouldn't miss it," Wendy said, remembering how she'd played in the handbell choir from a very young age. It was a rite of passage for all children in Bell Cove. How proud she'd been at her very first recital when she'd successfully completed her first public tremolo, the gentle swaying of a bell, being careful to rest the bell on her shoulder when not playing. How proud her parents had been, sitting in the front row. Mother in her red coat, Daddy in his favorite tweed jacket and Christmas bow tie.

Francine Henderson waved from the front display window of her beauty shop, Styles & Smiles. Wendy had known Francine all her life, although she was a few years younger. At first, Wendy was puzzled by the odd orangish tint to the skin of two older women with gray-blue "helmet" hairstyles who walked out, announced by the distinctive tinkle of the doorbell—every home and business in Bell Cove had its own unique doorbell sound—but then she noticed the poster taped to the glass door which read, "Spray Tans, Reduced Price Today."

She and JAM exchanged glances and smiled.

All the streetlights were shaped like bells, as she'd told everyone back at the Wet and Wild on that fateful night. They hung from highly polished brass poles, tied with red ribbons. In the gazebo in the center of the square, a perfectly shaped Fraser Fir with fairy lights would draw carolers at nighttime. A donation from Rutledge Tree Farm? Probably. At least it wasn't one of those Charlie Brown lookalikes, though who was she to judge?

JAM watched everything with interest, and people watched him . . . a stranger to this small town. And an interesting one, at that. He wore a lined windbreaker with the U.S. Navy logo on the back over faded jeans and flat-heeled boots. Black hair was pulled off his Hispanic-featured face.

"Let's go in," he suggested when they came to Our Lady by the Sea Catholic Church.

She hesitated, not having attended church much in recent years. "Sure," she said, and was glad she'd agreed once they entered.

It was a beautiful church, especially at Christmas-time with dozens of poinsettias adorning the steps leading up to the altar and sprays of evergreens attached to the ends of all the pews. Two large Christmas trees stood at either side of the communion rail, behind which was a large Nativity scene with painted statues of Mary, Joseph, the Wise Men, and shepherds, minus the Christ child which would be placed in the manger at Christmas Eve Midnight Mass. Up above, in the loft, the choir was practicing for the upcoming services, a clear-toned, poignant version of "Silent Night." Candles burned on side altars honoring various saints, filling the air with a heavy scent of cloves and a foreign essence, as only church incenses seemed to do. What were the spices that the Wise Men had carried? Frankincense and myrrh. Could it be a combination of those? Probably not.

Wendy sat on a bench at the back, watching as JAM walked up to the rail, knelt, made the sign of the cross, and bowed his head. What a strange contradiction he was! A former priest—or at least a seminarian at one time—who was a fierce, focused warrior when in battle. She wondered—but would never ask unless he volunteered, for fear it would sound judgmental—how he came to join the special forces, after being in such a seemingly pacifist place.

When a young priest came out of the sacristy, he paused and stared at JAM for a moment, perhaps recognizing a kindred spirit. Then he approached JAM, who stood, and they conversed quietly for a few moments, after which they shook hands, and the priest blessed him by making a cross in the air in front of JAM's face.

"I love churches," JAM said as they walked out. "The look of them, the smell of them, the feel of them. Big, small, all denominations. No matter the architecture. But especially the old ones with stained glass windows and wood that reeks of ancient mysteries. Whether a person believes in God or not, they can't deny the peace of a church, the sense of welcome and open arms." He glanced at her to see if she shared his opinion, not at all embarrassed by his long discourse which had been a little bit preachy. That's how JAM was, open and honest, always.

"Do you ever regret leaving the church?" That question didn't seem quite so intrusive as her earlier wondering about the dichotomy of peacemaker/killer.

"Oh, I've never left the church. Just the priesthood. No. No regrets." He paused then before asking, "How about you, Flip? Regrets? Do you wish you hadn't come back here?"

They were walking as they talked, headed out of the town center, toward the residential area. She thought before answering. "No, I don't regret coming home. It had to be done. Too many loose ends that I've ignored for years."

He nodded, as if he understood.

"Trite as it may sound, I need closure," she continued. "About so many things."

Another nod, but then he asked, "Including Tall, Dark, and Broody back there?"

"Oh, yeah."

He arched a brow.

She thought about saying nothing, but then she gave him a brief version of their history leading to their breakup and Beth Anne's pregnancy, concluding at the end, "Perhaps I was a bit hasty in the way I left Bell Cove twelve years ago, without getting all the details. Not about what had happened. No, that had been crystal clear. But I suspect that's the reason for Ethan's bitterness toward me, that I didn't give him time to work things out. Why should I have? The jerk!" She sighed deeply before summing up the situation, from her viewpoint. "Ethan and I had been a couple practically from kindergarten. We loved each other. Deeply. I know, everyone thinks their love is the best, the most unique, but ours truly was. Everyone remarked on it. But then, like I said, Ethan got a girl pregnant the summer following our high school graduation. End of story."

JAM pretended to be playing the violin. "So, he fell in love with someone else. Happens all the time, Flip. To both men and women. That's what country music is all about, 'he done her wrong' songs. Nothing new."

"No, I'm not making myself clear, apparently. It wasn't like that for Ethan. It was a one-night stand following a party. He didn't love Beth Anne, at least he hadn't back then, but he was going to marry her to give the baby a name. 'A horrible, stupid mistake,' he said in apology to me, but not to worry, the marriage would be a 'technicality.' Seriously, that's what he'd said it would be. Marriage as a temporary solution that would be corrected in nine months, give or take."

"Dumb schmuck!" JAM concluded.

"Yep," she agreed, although she kind of resented JAM classifying him as such. "The shotgun wedding, without the weapon . . . the old-fashioned notion of 'having to get married.' I probably could have forgiven the lapse in judgment, but the marriage . . . ?" She shook her head vehemently. "Never."

"Now that's where I disagree, with you and my own church. Unlike the old days, priests today are told to discourage couples from marrying just because the woman is pregnant. I, on the other hand, know what it's like to grow up illegitimate, and, when a child is involved, I vote for doing what's best for the kid."

Wendy wasn't about to get involved in an argument about marriage and children. And, actually, she wasn't sure she disagreed with JAM. "In the end, all our plans went up in smoke. We had planned to attend UNC that fall, he in a pre-veterinarian program, me in pre-med. We would be married the summer following our sophomore year and continue our studies through med schools. Eventually we'd come back to the Outer Banks to practice. Have three children . . . two girls and a boy. And live happily ever after. Instead, I ran away and never looked back, well, hardly ever. So much for all our beautiful plans!" She laughed, or tried to.

"Silly girl!" He looped an arm over her shoulder and tugged her close for a hug. "Don't you know that the only time God laughs is when He hears us humans talk about *our* plans?"

"What does that mean?"

"It means that nothing happens to us in this world except what God plans for us. Doesn't mean we have no choice, but the Great Master Planner has the last word. I know, that sounded really preachy."

She laughed because that's just the word she thought of earlier. "Yeah, it did."

He shrugged. "You can take the boy out of the choir, but you can't take the choir out of the boy."

"Are you really the guy who supposedly spent three days of your last liberty in a Tijuana motel with Salina Gonzalez, the Spanish soap star?"

"What's your point?"

She shook her head, as if he were hopeless, and laughed. "Honestly, are you saying everything that happened with me and Ethan was meant to be?"

"I have no idea. And who am I to stick my nose into your private affairs?"

"Yeah, right. Like your nose isn't already dripping wet!" She elbowed him to show she hadn't been offended. "Give it to me straight."

"You asked for it. 'In for a penny, in for a peso,' as my Nonna used to say. I haven't done any counseling for years, but if I were foolish enough to tell you what to do, there are things I would want to know first."

"Like?"

He proceeded to shoot out one question after another:

"Did he ever try to make some other arrangement with this woman regarding the baby?"

"Are you sure the girl was pregnant at that time?"

"Did he try to find you after you left?"

"How soon did he marry?"

"Was he married in the church?"

"Did he ever get a divorce?"

To each of his questions, she replied, "I don't know."

In conclusion, he said, "Someone needs a little closure."

"Jeesh! That's what I told you to begin with. Some priestly advisor you are!"

"I'm better at giving advice as a SEAL."

"And what advice would that be?"

"Fuck the guy's brains out for a day or two and see what happens."

At least she was laughing by the time they got home.

Chapter 8

Where's there a cave when a
grinch needs one? . . .

*E*than didn't talk much on the short trip to Bell Forge. At first.

Luckily, Laura and Tony didn't question him about his black mood.

Unluckily, all they wanted to talk about was that stupid grinch contest.

"Did you guys see the NBX *Morning Show*?" Laura asked from the passenger seat in his Lexus. "Our grinch contest was the highlight segment."

Ethan hadn't, but he'd heard about it. All morning.

—On the radio coming back from the mainland, where he'd overseen another load of bundled trees going out on a sweet reorder from the DixieMart chain.

—When he'd stopped at Gus's Gas & Goods for a cup of coffee.

—At his local tree lot, where he'd helped his workers unload another two hundred and fifty trees from the mainland farm.

Business was booming, he was busy, and he

didn't have time, or the interest, for all this crap. Not that anyone asked his opinion on the subject. If they did, he'd probably earn another vote.

Tony, who was in the backseat, leaning forward between the two of them on propped elbows, said, "Yeah, I saw it, Laura. You looked great in the interview, especially when you talked about the history of Bell Cove, and how it was important to maintain the town's historic integrity, like the bell street lighting, with proceeds from this contest. Was Sam hitting on you?"

"A little, but you're right. This is a great publicity stunt for Bell Cove."

That's exactly what it was—a stunt!—if you asked Ethan. Which nobody did.

"My phone's been ringing all morning," Laura told them excitedly. "Media wanting to schedule interviews. People asking if we're planning any special events around the grinch crowning on Christmas Eve. We should call for an emergency council meeting ASAP to plan some activities."

I'll match your ASAP with my NCIH, as in No Chance in Hell! No more council meetings before Christmas!

"Right," Tony, the love-struck suck-up, agreed. "And, if we're going to be bringing more tourists into town . . . the kind we like, the day-trippers who spend the day, spend money, and then go home . . . all the businesses in town should offer things related to the contest. Like, I could add a new menu item. Whoville Crab Hash, for example. Or Cindy Lou Bread Pudding."

That was all the incentive Laura needed to go off

on a tear. "Maybe Monique's Boutique could get in a special order of grinch-type clothing. And Bob's Butcher Bin would do a bonanza in business if it advertised Christmas Roast Beast. Frank could change the sign on the sleds he's selling at his hardware store to be grinch sleighs, or something. And I bet someone," Laura looked pointedly at Ethan, "could whip up some grinchy mistletoe wreaths."

I wouldn't, but my grandmother probably would. And what is grinch mistletoe anyhow? The kind that made a person kick someone, instead of kiss them? Ethan felt like he'd fallen into some Wizard of Oz garden hole of craziness, or rather a Whoville garden hole of craziness. *At least it's taking my mind off Wendy. For the moment. Still, I wonder if she stayed to have lunch with her Navy buddies. I wonder what she thought of me. Hell, I wonder if she's thought of me at all these past twelve years. Should I call and ask her to meet me for a drink or a cup of coffee? Not to start something . . . hell, no! Just to clear the air and all that. Be grown-up about what happened all those years ago. Maybe even—*

Laura jarred him out of his straying thoughts by asking, "So, Ethan, do you think you'd be able to duct tape some reindeer horns on Harvey for the parade, like the Grinch did with that dog, Max, in the book?"

"What? Are you serious? What parade?"

"Just thinking out loud here, Ethan. Be a team player. Get with the program. About Harvey . . . ?"

"The only way Harv would let me near him with duct tape is if I give him endless biscuits. Even then, there better be some hoochie mama poodle with loose morals around. Harv has a thing about poodles," he said, then suggested, "Here's a thought. You two looney tooners with all these great ideas could get Francine to offer green spray tans, instead of that yammy orange."

Laura and Tony missed his lame attempt at sarcastic humor, which was evident when Laura eyed Ethan in an alarming way and observed, "Good idea, Ethan," and Tony said, with a laugh, "Or maybe *our* grinch could be orange."

"You two are nuts. First, I am not going to be named this town's Grinch of the Year, even if it costs me a thousand bucks. And second, I wouldn't let Francine near me with a spray gun if my life depended on it."

"You're brilliant, Laura," Tony said, totally ignoring what Ethan had just said. "This could be really fun."

"I know what fun is. This is not fun," Ethan interjected. "Excuse my language, but this a fish fuck waiting to happen."

"I think that's supposed to be a goat fuck," Tony corrected.

"Since when did you become the dictionary police?" He glared at Tony, who just grinned. Obviously, friendship meant nothing when sex, or the possibility of sex, was on the line.

"So many possibilities!" Laura cooed. "But there isn't much time. This is Wednesday. Only five days until Christmas Eve."

"Is it possible to make this happen on such a tight time line?" Tony asked.

"We'll make it happen," Laura assured him. "Let's plan on a council meeting tonight."

Ethan groaned. He wasn't going to any more meetings this week. It was too much, just before Christmas. He was about to say that, but Laura was off to the races.

"Tony, you call Doreen and set up the meeting, and you know what? I just decided. I'm going to put out a special issue of *The Bell* tomorrow. I'll probably have to stay up all night to pull it off, but it will be worth it. Oh, man! News about the grinch events. Wendy back in town. Hunky SEALs invade Bell Cove. The forge factory update. It will be my best edition yet. Maybe even earn me a prize in the state newspaper competition this year."

"Oh, look, he's already there," Tony said.

Tony was right, Ethan noted, as he drove his car into the Bell Forge parking lot, which was three-quarters empty, even on a workday. Gabriel Conti, dressed in a camel-hair overcoat over a dark suit and tie, stood staring up at the mansard roof on the brick building. Of average height—about five ten or so—he had black hair that would probably be curly if it wasn't styled so short, what they used to call a razor cut. He was clean-shaven, but with a dark stubble already at this time of the day. Probably a twice-a-day shaver.

"Gabe, long time, no see," Ethan said, walking forward with an extended hand.

They shook, and Gabe said, "Ethan, how you been? Holy crap, it must be fifteen years since I saw you last. It was that summer we sailed till our skin blistered from so much sun."

"Yeah, as I recall, you were trying to impress Rita Dorset, the lifeguard over at the golf club."

"And you had eyes only for some girl named Winnie."

Ethan didn't bother to tell Gabe that it had been Wendy, not Winnie. "Hey, my sympathies on your grandfather's death. I would have attended the funeral, but my daughter was having some medical issues at the time."

"You have a daughter?" Gabe smiled, as if that were some great achievement.

It was. To him. "I do," he said. "How about you? Married? A family?"

"No, and no."

"We'll have to get together and catch up sometime soon. In the meantime . . ." Ethan motioned for Laura and Tony to join them. "This is Gabriel Conti, whose great-great-grandfather and his brothers built this place."

"That would be three greats," Gabe corrected with a smile. "Great-great-great-grandfather Salvadore Conti."

"Right," Ethan said. "And, Gabe, this is Laura Atler, editor of *The Bell*, the local newspaper, and Tony Bonfatto, owner of the Cracked Crab restaurant."

They all shook hands and remarked on the

weather, which was getting colder by the hour with an overcast sky. They might very well get a dusting of snow tonight.

It was clear by the way Gabe was staring at Laura, and she was stealing looks at him, that there was an instant attraction going on. Much to Tony's chagrin.

Ethan couldn't remember the last time he'd felt that way on first meeting a woman. Well, unless you counted a woman you'd met again after a dozen-years-long separation.

I am not going there!

"I noticed you looking over the building as we drove up," Laura remarked.

"Yeah. It's a beauty, isn't it? They just don't go to this kind of trouble with factories today."

Gabe would know, being an architect, but as a layman, Ethan could appreciate its aesthetics, too. The simple, utilitarian brick of the long, rectangular structure was softened by the gleam of old copper on the flat portion at the top of the pitched slate roof. Not to mention the leaded windows and the double doors of the entry, which were unusual arch shapes with carved wood surrounds.

"And it's still basically sound, too. Imagine the abuse it's taken over the past hundred years . . . wind, salt, water, storms."

Like Ethan's tree that just went on forever. Still standing after all this time.

Hmmm. Is it a promising sign that Gabe admires the structure?

Laura must have thought the same thing because

she said, "Sounds like you don't want to see this family heirloom torn down."

Gabe laughed. "Family heirloom? I wouldn't go that far. More like a family albatross. I take it you've read the article in the Durham paper. But wait. Ethan said you're with the local paper. Are you the newshound responsible for that contest naming me some kind of grinch monster? My mother heard about it all the way in Italy."

Laura blushed.

Now there was a sight, Ethan thought. Laura Atler embarrassed! She could sling arrows of sarcasm at him like a trooper, but be taken down by a mere zinger from a stranger.

Coming to her defense, like an Italian stallion warrior knight, was Tony, who said, "Laura isn't the only one responsible. The whole town council voted to have the contest. It's all in fun."

Ethan would have liked to say that he never voted for any contest, and it was debatable about the fun of it, but he didn't want to make Tony look bad.

Gabe turned to Ethan and grinned. "I hear you're right up there near the top in terms of grinchiness. Wonder how much it would cost to put you firmly over the top?"

"Don't you dare. Keep in mind, I might have a little extra cash handy, too, for a good cause." Ethan pretended to give Gabe a devious look.

"Hey, hey, hey! The rules of this contest bar any ballot stuffing," Laura said.

"There are rules?" Ethan inquired. "That's news to me."

"Anyhow, I was misquoted in that newspaper article." Gabe held up a hand to prevent Laura from asking what he meant by that. "But I'm not a sentimental idiot, either. Family heirloom or not, whatever I decide about this building will be based on the bottom line. It pays its way or goes its way. Furthermore, anything I say here today is off the record. I better not be reading a twisted version of my words tomorrow in the local rag."

Any attraction Laura might have been feeling toward Gabe immediately disappeared. The look she cast his way now was one she might give to a cockroach, or a slimy developer.

In order to soothe the rising tempers, Ethan changed the subject. "You know, Gabe, I always wondered why your ancestors chose a remote portion of a barrier island to build their forge. The temperatures here in summer are brutal; imagine forge workers in the pre-air-conditioning days. Plus, it must have been a bitch to get all these bricks and slate tiles out here."

Gabe nodded. "Survival, pure and simple. They originally settled in Chicago where not one, but two of their factories burned down. Arson. Keep in mind, in the early 1900s, millions of Italian immigrants entered America, and prejudice then was high against any foreigners, but especially those dark, hairy characters who were deemed natural-born criminals. There were even studies, believe it or not, that supposedly proved Italians were little more than primates genetically inclined to violence. That's why the three brothers sought out a piece of land remote enough to build their own community, despite all the hardships in getting building materials here."

"I didn't know that," Laura said, even as she typed away on an iPad Mini.

Gabe glared at the device.

"My ancestors faced the same prejudice," Tony said, drawing Gabe's attention away from Laura's note-taking. "They lived in the tenements of Little Italy, fifteen people to a room sometimes. Beaten to a pulp if they went out on the streets alone at night, for no reason other than they were 'wops.'"

Gabe nodded his understanding and looked toward Ethan.

Ethan shrugged. "My family probably came over on the *Mayflower* and remain dumb tree farmers to this day."

They all laughed at that and went inside.

"I'll show you around. My manager is out sick today." Gabe let out a snort of disgust. "That's a lie, actually. I fired Jackson's ass first thing this morning after looking over the books last night. No, he didn't embezzle money or anything like that. He just hasn't done a damn thing to generate any cash for more than a year and a half, ever since my grandfather first got ill. He single-handedly dug a grave for this old company which had already been floundering."

That sounded bad. Really bad for Bell Forge's future.

"And, no, Lois Lane, that is not for publication," Gabe added.

Laura made a low growling sound but said nothing.

"The days of sitting on a good reputation and waiting for customers to come to you are long gone," Gabe went on. "Bell Forge doesn't even have a frickin' website, let alone a sales force or a salesperson to solicit new orders. Believe it or not, my ancestors who started this company—the three brothers—knew that, even back then. One of them was an artisan, designing the bells. Another was the workhorse, the guy manning the bellows of the forge. And the third, and probably most important, was out drumming up new accounts."

Ethan understood exactly what Gabe was talking about. While he'd never had a real interest in growing trees, he'd discovered over the past twelve years that he had a knack for business. He'd managed with home study and an inborn gene for wheeling and dealing to turn his family tree farm into a multimillion-dollar enterprise, complete with a small but efficient managerial and sales staff on top of the farm workers. Thus, his contracts with several nationwide chain stores, like DixieMart, Landscape Depot, and Starr Foods. "I have a stockbroker friend on Wall Street who told me one time that his company gets tons of applicants from Harvard Business School types, but what they really want are good used-car salesmen."

"Right. It's all well and good to have a finely crafted product, but if no one knows about it, big deal!" Gabe was one disgusted puppy. "I blame myself for not getting involved earlier. I mean, the situation with Whitechapel closing last year is a perfect example. We should have had someone over in London, trying to pick up their accounts. For that matter, who the hell makes all those Salvation Army bells? And has anyone thought about meeting with the Pope? They've gotta buy a lot of bells in the Vatican, wouldn't you think?"

It was steaming hot inside the building, even though only one of the two forges was firing; so, they all took off their coats. Laura took off her suit jacket, too, and Gabe didn't bother to hide his appreciation of her shape in a figure-hugging white sweater. And Laura noticed Gabe noticing her, if the wink she gave him was any indication.

So, Gabe and Laura were off to the flirtation races again. Which could be a good or a bad thing in terms of their negotiations. Ethan wasn't able to object. He'd never been attracted to Laura himself. Probably because she hated his guts. Or because he couldn't look at her without thinking of Wendy.

Aaarrgh! Wendy again!

Gabe led the tour with more knowledge about bell making than Ethan would have expected. It wasn't the first time Ethan had been here. In fact, all schoolkids in Bell Cove did at least one Bell Forge field trip. But he hadn't been here in years.

"You're lucky. They're about to cast a large, rather ornate bell for St. Mark's College in Atlanta," Gabe told them. "This part is exciting and dangerous. Make sure you put on those hard hats and goggles while the molten metal is being poured. But the part I like best is when they begin to rub the ash off the cooled bell, and you see the bronze emerge with all the etched details. It's always a surprise. Like opening a Christmas present."

Gabe might not have gone into his family business, but he clearly loved parts of it, nonetheless. Like Ethan and the tree farming, in a convoluted reverse sort of way. Ethan had hated tree farming, but had been forced into it, and now he loved it . . . at least the business end of it.

Maybe this meeting wouldn't be hopeless after all.

At the end of the tour, they went into the office, Gabe behind the desk and the three of them in folding chairs.

"Here's the deal," Gabe said. "The forge sits on a five-million-dollar property. Yeah, that's what the Benson group has offered. It would be a teardown, for them."

The three of them were shocked into silence for a moment. They'd known that Outer Banks property was valuable, but not that valuable. For just a brief blip of a second, Ethan wondered what his five acres would be worth. A fortune.

"Add to that a factory with a specialized product that is no longer viable in today's market. A money pit of colossal proportions."

Laura had tears in her eyes, which Gabe noticed. He and Tony were feeling a bit deflated, too.

"I understand your feelings," Gabe said, pushing a box of tissues toward the edge of the desk nearest Laura, "but I can only afford to take the tax loss for so long before throwing in the towel."

"Aren't there any alternatives to a firm like Benson's, which you know will subdivide and commercialize?" Laura asked, swiping at her eyes.

"There might be. I have a real estate company looking into other businesses that might fit into this space. And I haven't given up on bell making entirely, but it would require a total refab of the company's operation, an adaptation to today's market."

"What can we do?" Ethan asked.

"Your town—the council, or some redevelopment body—could put out feelers for someone interested in taking over the building."

"But for five million dollars!" Laura exclaimed. "No one except greedy developers with plans for condos or strip malls or boardwalks would be able to come up with that kind of cash. The bloodsucking creeps!" You could tell by the glance she gave Gabe that she put him in that same sleazeball category.

Gabe glared right back at her.

So, they were back to combatants, not potential lovers.

Oh, well!

"How much time do we have?" Tony asked.

"Let's meet again next week after you've all had a chance to digest what I've told you. I'm going to be in town through the holidays, staying in my grandparents' place." He groaned. "That's another thing. I've got to go through that big white elephant of a place to see what can be done. What a mess!"

"You would sell Chimes?" Laura asked, aghast. Chimes was the name given to the white-shingled

Conti mansion on a man-made bluff facing the ocean, once home to the three Conti brothers, only one of whom had a wife. Probably another multimillion-dollar property.

"Why not?" Gabe asked, cocking his head to the side. "No one's living there. It's too big for one family. Besides, it's kind of ugly architecturally."

Laura inhaled sharply. "It's beautiful, and it's a historical treasure. I might not have a fancy degree in architecture, but I recognize beauty when I see it. Try to sell that house as a teardown, Mister Conti, and I'll see you in court."

Ethan wanted to warn Laura that this animosity was no way to win Gabe over to their side in saving Bell Forge.

But Gabe just grinned at Laura and said, "Game on."

Chapter 9

Good friends, good food, booze . . .

The conversation around the dining room table that evening was wild, to say the least. Maybe it was the wine, or the bourbon in the dessert, which was aptly called Boozy Bread Pudding, or just the Christmas spirit, but everyone was feeling a little more relaxed and cheerful than usual.

Wendy and her aunt sat at either end of the long table, to which an extension had been added, with Aunt Mildred's five houseguests on one side, and Wendy's four Coronado friends on the other. While they ate Elmer's delicious lasagna with a green salad and warm garlic bread, washed down with a bottle of red wine . . . or two, or was it three? . . . which Geek and K-4 had purchased after their lunch at the Cracked Crab, the subject matter went all over the place. Starting with sex. Yes, sex!

"Is it true what they say about Navy SEALs in bed?" Gloria, the longtime librarian, asked out of the blue. Aunt Mildred had warned Wendy that Gloria was in the beginning stages of Alzheimer's and had good days and bad. She was going into an assisted-living facility as soon as a room was available after the holidays.

"Absolutely," JAM, Geek, and K-4 said as one.

"I only ask because I read a book about SEALs one time. Apparently there are females, called SEAL groupies, who follow them around, just for that purpose. They're called by the insulting name of frog hogs."

JAM, Geek, and K-4 cringed.

JAM responded to Gloria's jab, which she really hadn't intended to be offensive, with utter politeness. "Ma'am, I never heard that term before," which was a lie, "and if I have any groupies, I don't know where they're hiding." He pretended to be looking under the table for hidden lurkers.

They all laughed.

"I don't know," Diane said. "In my limited experience . . ." She batted her eyelashes with mock innocence. ". . . that's just a *highly inflated* rumor started by Navy SEALs themselves."

"Ah disagree," Claudette said, to everyone's surprise. She hadn't talked much so far. And to speak up now on such an intimate subject! In her deep Southern accent, she told them, "Ah spent an evenin' one time in a Nawleans hotel with a Navy SEAL who had the stayin' power of a Chattanooga race horse. He was Cajun, as well, so, that might account for it."

Whoa! This is getting a little out of hand.

Instead of being embarrassed, the other senior citizens at the table offered their opinions. The consensus seemed to be that older folks could get away with saying whatever they wanted, just because they had those years behind them.

"Personally, I always thought brokers did it with more *interest* than the average fellow," Harry contributed while he worked on his second helping of bread pudding, not even bothering to look up. "My wife, Julia, on the other hand, knew the *drill* better than I did." Julia had been a dentist.

"Ha, ha, ha. On the other hand, there's something to be said for short men." Elmer snapped his suspenders and winked. "Short in height, long in . . . well, you get the drift."

Wendy and Diane exchanged grins. Who would have thought!

But then, Wendy's aunt added to the madness. "I always believed that a man who danced well could do other things well. You know, the moves, the rhythm, the energy."

Raul just bowed his head in acknowledgment of the compliment.

Oh . . . my . . . God!

JAM, Geek, and K-4 were enjoying the hell out of the discussion without saying anything explicit themselves. But they were thinking it, all right. If they let loose with their opinions, the remarks would be crude, to say the least.

Wait until this group found out about Geek's invention, the "penile glove." They would probably want a demonstration, or be checking it out on the Internet later tonight.

"And you said we would be bored," K-4 reminded Wendy.

Throughout the meal, everyone spoke of Christmas traditions in their families, or special things that had happened in their lives during the yule season. It was the first Wendy had learned that JAM had been raised in an orphanage, where Christmases had been rather bleak.

Geek, on the other hand, came from a wealthy family who often spent Christmases on the ski slopes of Aspen or the Swiss Alps.

"My wife and I were so poor the first few years we got married that we spent the whole day of Christmas in bed because there was no heat," K-4 said.

"Yeah, that's your story," Geek teased.

"And I'm sticking to it." K-4 grinned.

"How did your wife die, Kevin?" Aunt Mildred asked, refusing to use their SEAL nicknames.

"Cancer."

Several of them, including Wendy, nodded at his answer, having had personal contact with the Big C.

"When I was six, our dog, Betty, gave birth to a litter of six puppies on Christmas Day. There was dog shit and piss everywhere. The best Christmas ever. It was probably when I first got interested in becoming a veterinarian." Elmer sighed at the memory.

Which made Wendy recall how Ethan had dreamed of becoming a vet someday. There hadn't been an animal he didn't love, from birds to Bassets.

"Well, I win the prize for best Christmas stories," Diane declared. "It's how I got my SEAL nickname of Grizz. I was home alone when I was eighteen because my family was off to church, but I had the flu. While they were gone, a huge black bear managed to get into our garage and went on a rampage. To the shock of my dad and brothers, who fancied themselves big game hunters, I shot that beast right between the eyeballs, and we ate bear meat all winter."

"Is bear meat edible?" Aunt Mildred asked.

"Sure, and if cooked properly, it's as good as venison or any other wild game."

"In the South, we're known to cook everything but the toes on any animal, and even those in certain parts of the bayou," Claudette told them. "Mah daddy was especially fond of possum, bless his heart."

Wendy went into the kitchen and brought back a fresh carafe of coffee for those who'd had enough of wine. "Okay, guys, tell us about your meeting with the Jinx folks," she said, then added an explanation to the others. "There's a treasure-hunting company for sale in New Jersey called Jinx, Inc., named after its original owner, the Jinkowsky family. The guys stopped off there yesterday to look it over before heading down here."

"Very interesting," Geek said. "Jinx makes the distinction of being a treasure-hunting company, not just a shipwreck salvage company. In other words, they search for all kinds of things, from lost Nazi loot to gold mines, and, yeah, sunken ships."

"You wouldn't believe some of their finds," K-4 exclaimed with excitement. "Pink diamonds from some Atlantic shipwreck. Spanish coins buried by a famous pirate in a Louisiana bayou. Recovered stolen artwork. The walls of their warehouse and display cabinets are loaded with evidence of their successful projects. It's like a freakin' museum."

"Not all their ventures have been successful," JAM cautioned. "Treasure hunting is like high-stakes gambling."

"JAM is right," Geek said. "It can cost millions to engage in some of these searches, especially the deep-water shipwreck ones, that on top of all the hoops a company has to go through with state licensing and potential lawsuits from foreign countries claiming the ships and their contents belong to them, even though they've made no effort to recover them for centuries. Finders Keepers doesn't apply anymore in the Law of Finds."

"On the other hand, the rewards can be monumental, even if you give the other country their twenty-five-percent cut," K-4 argued. "Do you know, there are still three million shipwrecks sitting on the bottom of the world's oceans and seas? And that's no bullshit—the statistic comes from a United Nations study. Three million! Of course, only about three thousand of those have the potential for big bucks. Still . . . three million!"

"Sounds like you've decided," Wendy remarked to K-4.

"Doesn't matter how I feel. I'm not the one with deep pockets," K-4 said. "I'm due for renewal this summer, though."

Everyone looked at JAM and Geek.

JAM put his hands in the air. "Don't look at me. I'm no millionaire. Besides, I'm not ready to quit the teams. I have another year to go on my current contract. Maybe later. Just not yet."

Which left Geek.

"I'm thinking about it," Geek said. "I re-up in May . . . or not. I've been in about fourteen years now. That's a long time in special forces."

"Those of us who grew up on the Outer Banks have been hearing about shipwrecks and salvors all our lives. The good and the bad," Aunt Mildred interjected. "There must be a dozen companies with licenses for wrecks off our coast right now."

"And occasionally one of them hits the jackpot. Like that recent 'Pulaski' discovery," Elmer pointed out. "That's what makes all the others keep trying."

"I went to that Graveyard of the Atlantic museum today," Diane told them. "You guys should definitely visit if you're seriously considering this venture. K-4, you mentioned the huge number of shipwrecks still sitting on the ocean bottoms around the world. Well, get this: there are three thousand shipwrecks still uncovered off this coastline alone. Makes even the most cautious person get the fever."

"Why is this particular company wanting to sell out? Jinx, did you say? Isn't that an ominous name?" Harry asked.

"Their headquarters on Barnegat Bay is about to be demolished as part of a federal wharf restoration project," Geek told them, "which won't be finished for five years. In the meantime, they need to find another site, temporary or permanent. They've decided to just sell."

"Jake and Ronnie, the owners, are thinking about getting involved in some small private casino in the Poconos," JAM added.

Harry frowned. "If there's no building to sell, what would potential investors get for their money?" Harry had been a financial consultant at one time; so, his viewpoint was valuable.

"Goodwill. The company name, its reputation, past and existing accounts," Geek explained.

"Plus a big-ass salvage boat, don't forget that," K-4 said with a laugh. "I mean, we're talking a huge boat that sleeps eight and has all the latest technology for exploring and recovery."

"I think the most interesting thing, and this is rather ironic with us being here on the Outer Banks, is that they have a salvage permit with the state of North Carolina, obtained before this whole issue of wharf redevelopment came up in Jersey. It's for a site five miles out in the Atlantic where a trio of Portuguese ships supposedly went down in 1862. Called the Three Saints . . . the *St. Martha*, the *St. Cecilia*, and the *St. Sonia*. Cool, huh?"

"So, you could conceivably establish a new head-quarters for Jinx anywhere, even here on the Outer Banks," Wendy mused.

"I suppose so," Geek said. "But like I mentioned, shipwreck salvaging is only one of their services. And who knows where the next project would be located?"

"Are you going to do it?" Diane asked, her question addressed to Geek, since he was the only one with the cash to do it, unless he took in other investors.

"I don't know. A lot to think about." Geek took a sip of wine and leaned back in his chair. "Like JAM, I'm not sure I'm ready to give up the teams. Still, I am thinking about it. I brought a pile of paperwork with me to sift through."

"You should talk to my daughter, Bonita, when she comes for the Christmas Day Open House," Raul said then. "Bonita is some kind of oceanographer—or a marine archaeologist, I am not sure which—in Ocracoke. She has worked with some of the Outer Banks shipwreck salvaging companies."

"That would be great," Geek said.

Wendy was staring at her aunt. That was all very interesting about Raul's daughter, but what was that about an open house?

Her aunt understood Wendy's unspoken question and said, "I decided to resume the annual Christmas Day Open House this year, like your mother and father used to hold. I sent the invitations out weeks ago, before you decided to come home. I hope you don't mind."

Did she mind? Not really. It was just a surprise. They'd stopped the ritual party a year before her mother died, when she'd gotten too sick to organize even family meals, let alone a community event. And that's what the Patterson open houses were, open to everyone in town. From noon to four p.m., giving families a chance to open gifts that morning and then go to church services, with plenty of time afterward to hold their own feasts at home later that day or early in the evening.

Christmas Day might seem like an odd time to hold a party, but originally, when her mother and father had started the tradition, it was because they'd wanted people with no families around to have a place to go and celebrate. *Shades of Aunt Mildred?* Wendy mused. But what had happened was that everyone came, even if only for a half hour. It had become a means for all the townsfolk to enjoy the day together.

"Are you sure you're up for that? I mean, it's a lot of work. As many as fifty or sixty people could show up, as I recall."

"We'll all help," Elmer said, and the other seniors nodded and offered enthusiastic encouragement to Aunt Mil.

"Hey, I can be the bartender," K-4 said.

"I make a mean Santa's Wild-Ass Elf cocktail," JAM said, waggling his eyebrows. "Very festive."

"Did you know that the word *cocktail* was first used in the early 1800s, referring to any drink with sugar, water, and bitters?" This from Gloria, ever the librarian. "It was called a 'bittered sling,' which came from the German word *schlinger*, which means to swallow quickly."

Everyone gaped at Gloria. She was a walking encyclopedia.

"Are you sure? In Nawleans, we're told that the cocktail was invented in a French Quarter pharmacy where it was served in an eggcup, which

is called a 'coquetier' in French and later became
Americanized to the word *cocktail*."

Everyone gaped at Claudette now. She hardly
talked at all, but then the most amazing things
popped out of her mouth.

Before you knew it, someone would be saying
cocktail came from the Latin for you-know-what. If
F.U. were here, it would have been said by now.

JAM waved a hand in the air. "Hey, in Mexico, we
say the cocktail was named for an Aztec princess,
invented by some lonely vaquero, or something."

They all laughed then.

"So, it's only seven thirty," K-4 said, glancing at
his watch. "What say we go pick up a Christmas
tree? Wendy? You said you wanted us to do it tomorrow, but why not tonight?"

Wendy wasn't about to chance another meeting
with Ethan, but she didn't mind them going. In
fact, she'd appreciate it.

So, the three SEALs and Diane went off to Rutledge Tree Farm, while Aunt Mildred cautioned, "I
do not want one of those Rutledge Trees. I want a
regular tree," which led Wendy to explain the history of the Rutledge Tree, after which all four of her
guests said, "Cool!"

Wendy and Aunt Mildred rolled their eyes at
that and went up to the attic to gather the boxes of
Christmas tree decorations while the other seniors
cleared the table, did the dishes, and made room in
the front parlor for the tree. It took three trips for
the two of them to carry all the boxes downstairs,

and by then Raul had put some soft Christmas music on the stereo and lit the logs in the fireplace.

"I like your friends, Wendy," her aunt said while they were carrying down the last load.

"I like yours, too," Wendy replied.

Her aunt beamed. "I am so glad. I was worried that . . . well, I was worried."

"What? That I would kick them out, and you with them?" Wendy teased.

"No, of course not. Well, maybe," she admitted. "If you disapproved, I would have had no choice but to ask everyone to leave."

"Now, stop right there. You don't need my approval for anything, Aunt Mil. I told you that before."

Not totally convinced, her aunt smiled softly. Wendy suspected that her aunt was worried about what would become of the house, if Wendy wasn't coming back here to live, eventually. That was a decision they would make together, but this wasn't the time for that discussion. She squeezed her aunt's hand in reassurance.

The guys and Diane were back an hour later with a huge, ten-foot, perfectly-shaped Fraser Fir, which almost met the ceiling once it was in its stand and topped with the ratty old angel that had graced Patterson family trees for fifty years. Because of the chipped paint on its china face, which gave it a perpetual wink, Geek said it should be called a Fallen Angel. They also bought a three-foot Rutledge Tree for the kitchen, where the seniors decided it should have culinary type ornaments . . . a.k.a. dried fruits left over from a fruitcake baking project last week, along with strings of popcorn alternated with cranberries. The ugly little tree looked almost pretty.

Around eleven, her Coronado buddies, including Diane, decided to go to The Live Bass, a local bar they'd passed on the way to the tree farm, for a few beers. Wendy opted to stay home, despite their entreating her to come along. They even invited the seniors to come, which pleased them to no end, but they, too, declined, it being past their bedtimes.

Once her guests were gone and her aunt and the rest of the seniors had gone to their respective rooms, Wendy put another log on the fire, turned off all the lights, except those on the tree, and let herself remember. Standing before the tree, she examined one ornament after another.

First, there were some miniature Bell Forge commemorative bronze bells, including her favorite, for 9/11, featuring etched twin towers. The Pope Francis visit to America. Virginia Dare and the Lost Colony, which was supposedly on the Outer Banks. The Wright Brothers' first flight from Kitty Hawk. A dozen commemoratives in all.

Then, she examined the vintage glass ornaments passed down through the family, those that survived clumsy children handling them over the years. Only seven of the original two dozen remained, and a few of those had flecks of paint missing.

Her childhood handmade efforts had all been collected and stored for her. They were on the tree, too. K-4 had gotten a big kick out of the cardboard reindeer with five legs that she'd made in kindergarten.

But then there were those with special meaning. The bright red tin apple purchased the year her parents took her to New York City, a.k.a. the Big Apple, to see the Rockettes' Christmas show. She'd been about seven and for a long time after dreamed of becoming one of those beautiful dancers.

One year her mother got inspired to make a whole army of stuffed mice cloth ornaments, complete with clothing and tools of their trade. A Mr. and Mrs. Santa Claus, he carrying a sack of toys, she with a baking tray of cookies. A farmer and his wife, he with a shovel in hand, she with a basket of vegetables. An Amish man and woman in black garb, he with a flat-crowned hat and suspenders, she with a white apron. A Scotsman with a bagpipe, wearing a kilt. A skier and a golfer. A physician complete with tiny stethoscope (her father's favorite, especially since that particular mouse had ginger-colored hair). A soldier and a sailor. A policeman.

Originally, her mother had made them to give to the church to sell at its summer bazaar, with a duplicate set for her own family. She probably could have sold them in one of the local stores, but she'd lost interest in making any more. The illness had already set in.

And then there were the special ones. The ones Ethan had given her, knowing how much she loved Christmas and tree decorations with a provenance. She wouldn't have put these particular ornaments on the tree, but Geek had already opened the box, and she hadn't wanted to call attention to her distress.

She smiled at the cardboard heart cut out of a valentine. It was signed in pencil by Ethan, except it was spelled ƎTHAN. They'd been in first grade at the time. In return, she'd given him five Necco candy conversation hearts from her lunchbox that her mother had packed for her that morning. Ethan told her years later that he'd eaten four and saved the one that said XOXO.

The starfish was purchased for her by Ethan on a tenth-grade field trip to Myrtle Beach. He'd bought it for her in a shell shop, along with a bead bracelet. Somewhere in the attic, if it hadn't been thrown away, was one of those hokey, boardwalk photobooth, period costume pictures of Ethan dressed as a riverboat gambler with a mustache and her as a dance hall girl.

A meticulously hand-carved blue spruce tree, about three inches tall, had been made by Ethan in the high school wood shop the Christmas following his fifteenth birthday, a simulation of the blue spruce tree the two of them had planted out on the family's local tree farm. His father, who had been experimenting for years, mostly futile attempts to raise evergreens on the Outer Banks, had been delighted at Ethan's interest. Little did he know, he and Wendy had planted the tree, which they called their Forever Tree . . . (*yeah, hokey, but then, they were only fifteen, and in luuuuve*) . . . with the idea that by the time it was full-grown, it could be their Christmas tree the first year of their marriage.

They'd babied that seedling with fertilizer, netting for protection from the sun and wind, bug repellants, and lots of love. And it grew. Very slowly, but by the time of their high school graduation, it had been four feet tall. But it had survived. A miracle, his father had said. Probably the fertilizer, his grandmother had proclaimed. But she and Ethan had known why the little tree survived. Their love.

The blasted tree was probably dead by now.

Back to the tree in front of Wendy. There were so many keepsakes-turned-ornaments that tugged at her heartstrings, but the one that made her heart ache was the miniature lighthouse Ethan had given her to mark the place where they'd first made love. Her father and Aunt Mildred probably thought it was just a souvenir from visiting the Bell Cove lighthouse before it closed. She and Ethan had known it meant so much more.

She swiped at the tears that slipped from her eyes and determined to toss all these items in the trash before she returned to California. But just then, the house phone rang in the hall. In the distance, she could hear the town clocks tolling the hour. Who would be calling at midnight?

If it was the guys or Diane, they would have called her cell phone. But maybe something had happened, and it was the police, or a hospital calling. She rushed to the vintage telephone chair stand in the hall, sometimes called a "gossip bench," to pick up the cordless before it awakened others in the house.

"Hello."

A moment of silence. Then a male voice said, "We need to talk."

She put a hand to her chest, as if that could still her wildly beating heart.

"Meet me tomorrow at four."

"Where?" she asked, although she knew—she just knew—what he was going to say.

"The lighthouse."

Chapter 10

Oh, how clueless some men could be! . . .

*E*than couldn't sleep at all that night.

So, he got up at five and prepared to fly over to the mainland tree farm, earlier than he'd originally planned, but that would give him plenty of time to be back by four. An opportunity had come up suddenly for him to purchase a hundred acres of adjacent land, which he'd been after for the past year. If this transaction worked out, he could double his production and profits within five years. Plus, he could diversify with some new species adaptable to a warmer climate. *Shades of my father and grandfather!*

Which was one more reason why he should move to the mainland. But his grandmother wouldn't budge, no matter the incentives he offered her.

"I'll build you a new house, with all the amenities."

"I like my house, and what's wrong with the amenities here? The stove cooks, the fridge freezes."

"You'd have free time to go back to your painting."

"And what good would that do me? I paint Outer Banks lighthouse scenes."

And so, he stayed. He owed his grandmother too much for all she'd done for him, caring for Beth Anne and Cassie. Hell, she'd cared for him, too, when he'd been a walking zombie for months there, back when . . .

Which brought him to the reason for his sleep-lessness. Wendy. He wasn't sure what he hoped to accomplish by meeting with her. He must be a glutton for punishment. But, no, it was just the op-posite. Time to end the punishment with a shot of hard-reality closure. Just like his grandmother kept hammering away about.

It's not like he hadn't thought about Wendy over the past twelve years, but somehow he'd managed to push the memories to the background. The crushing hurt of her leaving had slowly morphed into a mere sore spot when he'd allowed himself to think about her at all. But now, since she'd come back, it had become an open, festering wound. So much guilt! So much bitterness! So many ques-tions!

It had to stop.

Sure, he could ride it out. She'd leave again in an-other week or so. Then, he could go back to the way things were.

Or could he?

It didn't help that those buffer-than-Rambo Navy SEAL buddies of hers showed up at the tree lot last night. And they'd been nice. Dammit. It would have been better if he could picture her with a bunch of brain-dead apes. Instead, they'd been articulate and friendly, although the female with them kept giving him the stink eye, as if she knew something about him.

All was quiet in the house when he left. His grandmother wouldn't get up till seven, then would go in to the tree lot to open up at nine.

When he got to his office on the mainland, he took some ribbing over the grinch contest, news of which continued to spread, mainly due to daily reports being given on NBX's *Morning Show*. The subject even came up at his meeting later with the irascible old man, Jeb Parkins, farmer-turned-real-estate-magnate (*picture Beverly Hillbilly in a Walmart suit*), who did, in fact, sell Ethan the land he wanted, for more than it was worth.

Once they'd settled on an amount, Jeb added, "Let's put another thousand on top of that and I'll donate it to that grinch thing over at Bell Cove." Parkins winked at Matt Holter, Ethan's lawyer and best friend, who came to the negotiating session with him, having already been on the mainland this week on a court case. Parkins's wink conveyed where that thousand bucks would go. Two hundred votes. For guess who? Not Matt.

"How about we put another thousand on that," Ethan suggested through gritted teeth, "and you don't step foot in Bell Cove for the next month or so?"

"Why would I want to step foot in Bell Cove? I'm off to the Bahamas once your check clears."

"Oh?" Ethan gritted his teeth even tighter at the implication his check might bounce. "Bet the missus is packing as we speak."

"The missus died three years ago, ya fool. I'm going with my main squeeze, Suzie Q here."

Ethan and Matt both gaped for just a second at the young legal aide, Suzanne Ellison, taking notes for Parkins, him being too tight to hire an actual lawyer. Her face bloomed with color but she didn't deny the old man's claim.

After the meeting, Ethan asked Matt, "Do you think he's serious?"

Matt shrugged. "Could be."

"Why would a young, good-looking woman date a man old enough to be her grandfather? I mean, he has dentures and wild hairs sticking out of his ears."

"Welcome to the real world, my friend. Money, money, money."

"And notice I said 'date.' I don't even want to think about him naked and making his moves." He shivered with distaste. "Some things aren't worth the money."

Matt laughed. "Sad to think that the old man is getting more action than you and I these days. Unless . . . I've been out of town all week, but I hear Wendy's back in Dodge." He raised his brows in question.

"And you think she's suddenly hopping in my bed? More like the shoot-out at the OK Corral since she's been 'back in Dodge.'"

"You've got your Old West towns mixed up, pal," Matt pointed out with a laugh, then asked, "That bad?"

"Not yet, but it probably will be." He wasn't about

to mention his meeting this afternoon with Wendy. Matt would say he was a fool. He was.

"She used to consider you irresistible."

"My irresistibility factor has dropped to about zilch."

"And how about hers?"

"Don't ask."

Matt just grinned. He'd been around back then. He knew Ethan almost as well as he knew himself. No fooling him.

"Word is that Wendy has a hot babe as a houseguest. And here I was hoping we could double date."

"What are you, like, fourteen and horny?"

"Thirty and horny."

"I know the feeling. Maybe we ought to follow Parkins's cue and get ourselves a money honey. Slam, bam, it's been swell, ma'am. No commitment. No hassle."

They both actually seemed to consider the idea for a moment, then laughed, and at the same time, said, "Nah!"

Matt went back to the Rutledge Trees office with Ethan and waited while he outlined to his staff all they would need to do to prepare the newly purchased fields so they would be ready for a spring planting. After that, he and Matt flew back to the Outer Banks, then hopped in Ethan's pickup for the ride to Bell Cove.

Matt went off to his law office, and Ethan decided to do some last-minute Christmas shopping. The town bells rang out the hour. Only two. He had plenty of time. Most of his holiday purchases had been made on the Internet, but he liked to spend his dollars locally wherever and whenever he could.

His first clue that something was amiss came when he went into Monique's Boutique where he was picking up a coat he'd special ordered for his grandmother. It was the kind of thing she'd never buy for herself, even though it was nothing fancy. A long, cashmere belted coat in a shade of blue that would match her eyes. He'd noticed her looking at it in Monique's window, but when he'd checked last week, discovered they would have to order it in her size.

"So, is it true you're buying more land on the mainland so you can close your business here?" Monique, whose real name was Molly O'Brien, stood glaring at him with her hands on her ample hips. She'd moved here five years ago and had always seemed a friendly sort. Not so friendly now!

"Huh?" Ethan said. At the same time he noticed the coolness of Monique's voice, he saw the grinch contest jar on the counter with the poster showing his name had suddenly jumped sky-high.

How did word of his business across the sound travel so fast? And how did the story get so twisted? Probably Baxter. Or maybe that contrary old fart Parkins. Ethan wouldn't put it past either of them.

"No, I am not moving, Monique. And I have no plans to close my business here." Not immediately anyhow.

"Well, I'm glad to hear it," she said, unconvinced. But then she relented and showed him the coat.

"It's beautiful. I know Mrs. Rutledge will love it. Should I gift wrap it?"

"Please. I'll pick it up in a half hour." He inserted his debit card into the chip reader on the counter and punched in his PIN number. When the transaction was complete, he said, "Pass the word if you can, Molly. No move by Ethan Rutledge."

"Got it," she said.

But it was probably too late.

Next, he stopped at The Book Den where the new owner, Clare Hunter, was behind the counter ringing up an order while an assistant was waiting on another customer. It was one of the Navy SEALs that Ethan had met last night, the Hispanic one, except now he was sporting a black eye.

"Hey," the guy said, coming over to shake hands. "Christmas shopping?"

"Yeah. For my little girl. What's with the shiner?"

"I ran into one of your locals at a bar last night, and he took exception to my ethnicity, and my hairstyle."

"That's why I stay away from bars late at night," Ethan said with a laugh. "It was probably Stoney Adams. He usually manages to piss off one newcomer to town per month."

"Well, it earned me a spot on your town's grinch list. Near the bottom, with only ten votes, not like you raking in the big bucks, but who would waste fifty dollars on me?"

"It's for a good cause," Ethan said, repeating the lame mantra everyone chanted his way whenever he asked the very same question. "Where's the rest of your gang?"

"Flipper is helping Aunt Mildred and Elmer Fudd make fudge for some church bazaar or something. Grizz is hibernating with a good book. Geek and K-4 are jogging."

Ethan must have looked puzzled because the SEAL laughed and explained, "Nicknames. We all get them during Hell Week. Wendy's is Flipper because she swims like a fish. Grizz shot a bear one time. Merrill is Geek because he would be the first to admit that's what he is. And Kevin Fortunato is K-4 for obvious reasons. And me, JAM for Jacob Alvarez Mendozo."

Good thing he'd reminded him of his name, which Ethan had forgotten. But that was way more info than he'd wanted and he certainly hadn't meant to ask about Wendy. But Flipper? He smiled.

Clare came over then, and Ethan introduced her to Jacob Mendozo as a Navy friend of Wendy Patterson, whom Clare had yet to meet. The two of them—JAM and Clare—immediately began talking about California where Clare had a sister, and about how JAM had always thought it would be cool to run a bookstore in a small town like Bell Cove. Clearly, there was an instant attraction going on, so Ethan sidled away.

And, yes, he had to think that this guy must not be Wendy's lover if he was looking at another woman that way. But then, maybe he was a hound.

Or maybe that's how they did things in California. Not that it was any of his business.

With a grunt of disgust, he moved to the tween section of the bookstore. Cassie was an avid reader, and if he let her, would probably be devouring novels way too adult for her still-childish mind. She loved *Harry Potter* and the *Narnia* chronicles, and had reread them several times, but she still liked books like *Anne of Green Gables*, and even *Winnie the Pooh*, which he supposed had a message for kids of all ages, even adults. He wouldn't let her buy the *Twilight* series. Not yet. He also bypassed the huge display of *How the Grinch Stole Christmas* books, which she already had. However, against his fatherly misgivings, he purchased the three *Hunger Games* books.

He noticed the ladies coming out of the hair salon still sported an orange skin tone, but it was lighter now, more like a rutabaga than a yam. Francine must still be fine-tuning her machine. Who knew what would be next in her produce line? Squash?

Too late he realized that he should have avoided this side of the square because he was in front of *The Bell* newspaper office where the windows were plastered with upcoming events. Apparently the town council had been busy little bees at the emergency meeting he'd missed last evening.

He thought about going inside to ask Laura what was up, but then through a small section of the window not covered with "latest news" he saw Gabe Conti inside leaning against the counter talking with Bell Cove's very own Katharine Graham, a.k.a. Laura Atler. That was either good news or bad news, that they were chatting each other up, but he wasn't sticking around long enough to find out. Instead, he put a dollar in the vending machine and took out a paper to read later.

By the time he got back to his truck, a half-dozen people had stopped him on the street to ask about his dumping Bell Cove for the mainland. Another half dozen just gave him dirty looks. And Ina Rogers stepped on his toe with her walker in passing. He was pretty sure it was deliberate.

He drove out to the tree lot where both his grandmother and Cassie were working. Cassie was behind the counter on a high stool, chatting up customers, under orders not to put too much strain on her hip by walking around if she wanted to be well enough to participate in all the holiday events the next few days. His grandmother manned the register, and three high school boys, including the infamous Zach the Teenage Heartthrob, took care of customers out on the lot.

"How did it go?" his grandmother asked.

"A done deal. But how did word spread so fast? Have you been talking?"

"Me?"

"Well, someone must have mentioned my meeting with Parkins today. Now, everyone's voting me top grinch because they think I'm closing shop here."

"Don't blame me. Maybe people are voting for you because you deserve the honor. Did you ever think about that, Mr. Scrooge?"

"Huh? What burr's got under your saddle?"

"Nana's upset because Maybelle Foster was in this morning and bragged about all her Christmas shopping being done, the gifts wrapped, the tree decorated, and Nana hasn't even had a chance to make any of her homemade Christmas cookies yet."

"Buy the damn cookies from the supermarket. Who needs homemade?"

"Bite your tongue, boy."

"Go to the church bazaar then, and buy a whole table of homemade goodies."

"And let everyone know I was too lazy to make any of my own?" His grandmother looked at him as if he'd lost a few screws.

"We're not moving, are we, Dad?" Cassie asked, giving a quick glance out the door to where Zach was carrying a bound tree to someone's car.

"No, sweetheart, we're not moving." *Anytime soon.* To his grandmother, he said, "I'm going home to change clothes and make some calls. I'll be back in a bit. And, honestly, if you're feeling overwhelmed, take tomorrow off. That high school girl, Pastor Morgan's daughter, has been wanting extra hours."

"Okay," his grandmother said, but she would probably work anyway, even if she called in Sally Morgan. She added, "Make sure I left the Crock-Pot on low. We're having chili for dinner."

Even with all these stops, Ethan was a half hour early for his meeting. The lighthouse section of the beach probably wasn't the best place to be meeting Wendy, but he hadn't wanted their conversation to be in the public eye, more grist for the mill. If the town gossips had him closing his business and moving lock, stock, and barrel to the mainland, he could only imagine what they would do with an image of him and Wendy together, the Sweethearts of Bell Cove, second in legendary love only to his grandmother and grandfather. They'd have him chucking this burg again, but this time on his way to California where he would be a househusband to a female Navy SEAL, or else become a SEAL himself.

As if!

He was probably worrying about nothing. Wendy probably didn't even remember that the lighthouse was where they had first made love. Sixteen years old and steaming with testosterone and hormones.

He got out of his pickup and turned up the collar on his jacket before walking across the sand. The temperature wasn't that low today, but the breeze off the ocean made it feel like a nor'easter blowing in.

The weather further reassured Ethan that Wendy wouldn't have a problem with this meeting place because it had been a hot summer evening when the big event had taken place. Back then, the lighthouse had already been closed for a year, in need of repairs, which it still needed. Maybe he could suggest some of the grinch money go toward its restoration.

In any case, after that first time, they'd made love whenever and wherever they could, which hadn't been easy in such a small town, with his father and grandmother always around, or Wendy's father and aunt. That expression, "Where there's a will, there's a way," could have been written about them, though. The attic bedroom of the Patterson house on those rare occasions when no one was home (*and almost got caught more than once*), the barn that still stood back then on his grandmother's property (*the straw rash on both their butts had been like a badge of honor to their fool minds*), a bath stall at the pool (*whoever said public sex was a turn-on didn't understand teenage anxiety*), a utility closet at school (*with the smell of industrial-strength disinfectant being forever after associated in his mind with sex*), on the dunes at night (*Can anyone say sand fleas?*), in the cabin of a rented powerboat (*Try fitting a six-foot-two male onto a five-foot cot!*) . . . oh, the risks they took! But not where protection was concerned. He had always been meticulous about using a condom until Wendy managed to get a prescription for birth control pills from a doctor over on Nags Head.

Too bad he hadn't been as careful with Beth Anne. The reason, pure and simple, had been alcohol. That's why he'd never overindulged since then, in booze or casual sex.

He tried to see in the salt-crusted window of the lighthouse, to no avail. There probably wasn't even any furniture in there anymore, and if there was, it would be rotted with damp and mold.

He heard a car engine and turned to see Wendy pull into the parking area in her aunt's old green Camry. He remembered when Aunt Mildred had bought that car and been so proud of its pretty green color, which she'd claimed matched her eyes.

Once the engine was off, Wendy got out of the vehicle and began to walk toward him. She wore her mother's red coat, buttoned the whole way up against the chill, and her short hair blew every which way with the wind.

If I could turn the clock back twelve years, her eyes would light up on first seeing me, instead of gazing at me with suspicion, even fear. She would run full speed, arms spread wide, and I would catch her and twirl us both in a circle, her long hair making a reddish-brown spiderweb around our faces. Pure joy! Just at being with each other! We would get dizzy with the spinning and fall to the ground where I would nuzzle her neck and inhale the sea-salt scent on her skin. Then I would kiss her hello.

She tripped and said a foul word under her breath. Nothing joyful there.

When she got close enough to hear him, he started to say, "The reason I wanted us to meet was . . ."

But she spoke at the same time. "The reason I agreed to meet with you was . . ."

They both said as one then, ". . . closure." And laughed because they had always finished each other's sentences. Some things didn't change.

But then he discovered that Wendy's idea of closure was different from his.

She reached out and slapped him across the face, hard.

Chapter 11

*Heaven laughed the day man
invented the word "closure" . . .*

"Oh. My. God!" Wendy put a stinging palm to her chest and stared, appalled, at the rising marks on Ethan's cheek. "I am so sorry, Ethan. I never intended to do *that*."

Ethan stared at her, equally shocked, but then he yanked her into his arms and kissed her, hard. Then soft. Then hard again, before putting her away from him and shaking his head with disbelief. "I never intended to do *that*, either. I swear I didn't."

They gaped at each other.

She pressed her fingertips to her lips, testing for bruises, or just to check whether he'd actually kissed her. If you could call it a kiss! More like a reciprocal slap!

Then they both burst out laughing.

"Well, now that we have that out of the way," Wendy said with a calmness that surprised her because inside her emotions were roiling.

What would he do if I put my hand to his face and

*traced the red finger marks I raised? Would he turn his
mouth against my palm the way he used to? Would the
tip of his tongue tickle the skin and raise goose bumps on
other parts of my body?*

*Or maybe he would trace my lips which he'd just
kissed so hard, in anger. Then softer, in apology? Then
hard again?*

His emotions must be conflicted, too.

"Can we start over?" Ethan inquired, smiling
sadly.

She flashed back to the present with his words.
Surely, he didn't mean . . .

Without waiting for a reply, he said, "Forget that
bad start there. I'm glad you came, Wendy."

*Oh, so that's what he meant. Not that I would want
him to mean it any other way.*

"I know this isn't an ideal meeting place, especially with the chill factor, but I didn't want the
gawkers-turned-gossipers to have a field day. Damn,
I'm rambling like an idiot, aren't I?"

She nodded her understanding, of both the need
for privacy and of his nervousness, and motioned
for them to walk, in the opposite direction from
the lighthouse. The brief dart of his gaze toward
the old structure told her loud and clear that he remembered as well as she did what had happened
there. On the other hand, he was a guy, and guys
weren't sentimental about such things.

Although the view off the barrier islands was
spectacular, there were no nice beaches on Bell
Cove, and this section was no different. Some
sand and sea grass and occasional scrub pines, but

mostly rocks. Luckily, they both wore flat-heeled boots and were able to manage the uneven terrain. It was cold so close to the water with the wind biting the bare skin of her face, but her mother's coat was warm, and, frankly, she felt a bit overheated with nervousness. Ethan was dressed for the weather, too, in a drab green parka over an ivory, cable-knit sweater and jeans. Whether he was overheated or not didn't bear thinking about.

"You first," Wendy said. "You've implied that I deserted you twelve years ago without giving you a chance to plead your case."

"I'm not sure that 'pleading my case' is the right term. There was no excuse for what I did, but it's what happened afterward that knocked me flat. Call it an eighteen-year-old's delusion, but when I confessed my sin, I thought you and I, together, would be able to weather the storm."

"Are you mocking me when you use the word *sin*, like it was no big deal?"

"Huh? I said sin and I meant sin. Not in the church sense, but in a wrong I did you. Hell, Wendy, don't get your feathers all ruffled over semantics or we'll never move forward."

Her feathers got further ruffled at his mentioning her feathers, but she managed to tamp her temper down. "You expected me to stay in the same town where a woman—a girl, really—was growing bigger and bigger with your child?"

"I don't know. I wasn't thinking. It's just that all my life, till then, it had been you and me. A couple. I foolishly thought our love could weather any storm." He stumbled over the word *love* as if he wasn't sure it was the right one to describe their teenage emotion. "I sound like a friggin' Hallmark card."

Yeah, he does. In an adorable way. But no, no, no. I will not let him distract me. "Ethan! Beth Anne had already moved into your house. That was more than a storm. That was a tsunami."

"She moved into our house because she had nowhere else to go. Her parents kicked her out when they learned of her pregnancy. You remember how religious the Collins family were and how strict they were with their kids?"

Actually, she didn't remember the Collins family, at all, and she'd barely known Beth Anne in high school. In those days, all of Wendy's attention was focused on Ethan, or her swimming, or her best friend, Laura. That was it.

"I don't mean to be callous, but why couldn't she have gone to one of those agencies that help pregnant teens?"

He raised his chin defiantly. "It was my baby, Wendy. I had an obligation."

She shrugged. In truth, she wouldn't have expected any less of the boy she had loved back then. And, yes, she had loved him, no matter how he tried to color it now. "So, our parting was predestined from the moment you got the news from Beth Anne."

"No! Not at all! My family would have helped Beth Anne through the pregnancy. We didn't have to marry. I could have still gone to the university to begin my studies. I know, I know, it sounds naïve now, but I truly believed you and I, together, could make it work with . . ." He let his words trails off.

"With love?" she jeered. More Hallmark wishwash, in her opinion. "So, how soon after I left did you marry Beth Anne?"

He rubbed a hand over his face for a moment before looking at her, directly, and admitted, "One month."

She gasped, never expecting it had been so soon. And, for a guy who claimed marriage wouldn't have been necessary, why had he done it at all?

"At Beth Anne's first prenatal visit, it was discovered that she had the beginning stages of MS. Some forms of the disease are more virulent than others, and one thing that can trigger acceleration is stress. Even pregnancy itself can be a stress factor. The doctors recommended abortion, but Beth Anne was adamant about having the baby. She figured it might be her only chance. As a result, she spent most of the pregnancy in bed or in the hospital."

"And that's why you never went to college?"

He nodded.

"I pictured you there, at UNC. With Beth Anne. Living in married housing or something. The perfect little family."

He made a scoffing sound. "Never left Bell Cove."

"And the baby? You said your daughter doesn't have MS, but is her handicap related to Beth Anne's condition?"

He bristled.

Something she'd said must have hit a sore spot.

"Cassie was born with some hip complications. They can be corrected with surgery, and she's already had six of those, but the problem is that she's a growing child, her bones are still developing. It's best to wait till she's sixteen, or reached her full growth, before doing a full-blown hip replacement. After that, she would ideally need only two or three more operations over a lifetime. Otherwise, she can lead a normal life. I don't like to think of her as handicapped." He glanced over at her sheepishly, realizing he'd probably overreacted by over-explaining.

So, that's how she'd offended him, with the word *handicap*? "Sorry. I didn't mean to be insensitive. It's obvious how much you love your daughter, Ethan."

"I do. More than I ever imagined caring for another human being."

Including me? she wondered, but what she said was, "Even having to give up your dream of becoming a vet?"

He combed his fingers through his hair, which was damp from the mist off the water, while he sought the right answer. "The thing about dreams is they're not real. I probably wasn't meant to be an animal doctor, and I would have discovered that along the way if Cassie hadn't come along."

"You're not saying that you shifted your dream to that of your father and grandfather?" That was too much of a stretch for Wendy to accept. Growing up,

Ethan had hated tree farming, and especially the obsession the males in his family had with developing an Outer Banks Christmas tree.

"Hardly. I still hate digging in the dirt, mucking about in fertilizers, picking off bugs, the constant pruning, but I discovered that I have a knack for business and sales."

"Actually, I knew that, as of this morning. Based on something Aunt Mil said, I googled 'Rutledge Trees' on the Internet. Very impressive stats! Plus, the rumor mill has it that you just bought a lot more land to increase production."

"The rumor mill! Remember what Nana used to say about gossip? The Devil's Radio," Ethan said with a shake of his head. "Now it's your turn to bare all."

As they'd been walking along the shore, every little thing Ethan said or did evoked a memory.

The way he combed his fingers through his hair, short as it was, when at a loss for words. He'd been doing that for as long as she could remember. Kindergarten, even, when she'd asked him if she should color the sky blue or gray on her picture. He'd been so cute back then, shy, inclined to blush when singled out by of all things, a girl! He still was. Cute. Well, more like handsome now. As for blushing, yes, there was a slight flush at his inadvertent use of the words "your turn to bare all," which was exactly what he'd said that first time they'd made love.

He'd taken off all his clothes, and although they'd

been "making out" every which way but actual intercourse, driving each other crazy, for more than a year, it was the first time she'd actually seen him in the buff. At the time, his saying it was her turn to bare all had seemed like the sexiest, coolest thing in the world.

But she knew what he meant now, and it had nothing to do with sex.

"I was shocked and devastated, Ethan. In retrospect, I could have handled things better, especially in how my behavior affected my dad and Aunt Mil. My only excuse is that I was eighteen and emotional."

"Where did you go?" he asked and took her hand to steer them around a large piece of driftwood and back the way they'd come. When he didn't let go but instead laced his fingers with hers, she should have objected. But it was probably just a reflex action and her calling attention to it would make it seem as if his touch bothered her.

Which it did.

Funny how couples today don't appreciate the sensuality in little things, like holding hands. They are always in a hurry in this fast-paced digital world where speed is king. Maybe that's why my relationships since Ethan have been unsuccessful. I haven't found a good handholder. There's something to be said for just the press of a large male palm against a smaller, softer female one. The slow slide of skin surfaces, causing nerve endings to stand to attention. Then, fingers spreading and sliding into nature's intended slots, male and female. Finally, the

press of two hands into one fist. It was a slow dance,
when done properly. A preamble to more intimate things.
But, oh, the joy of just holding hands!

"Wendy? I asked you where you went when you
left Bell Cove," Ethan reminded her.

She shook her head to clear it of wandering
thoughts. "At first, I went to my mother's stepsis-
ter in Maryland. I don't know if you remember, but
Lizzie Samuels came to Mom's funeral, the first I'd
known she even existed. She was a lot older and
they'd never been raised together, but anyhow, I
just showed up on Aunt Liz's doorstep in Annapo-
lis, and luckily she took me in until I could decide
what to do."

"I looked for you, but no one would tell me anything. In fact, your dad threatened to get a restrain-
ing order if I didn't stop bothering him."

"I didn't know that, but then I warned Dad and
Aunt Mil to never mention your name or I'd cut
off contact totally." She thought for a moment. "It
sounds so melodramatic now, but it was the only
way I could move forward back then. Maybe if my
mother had been alive, she could have talked some
sense into me."

"Still, you must have landed on your feet. You
went to college. Not UNC, but at least you got an
education. What I don't understand is why you
didn't continue on to med school, instead of joining
the Navy. I mean, really, Wendy, you, a soldier?"

"You'd be surprised." She made a fierce fighting
face at him, which caused him to laugh. She liked
that she could make him laugh when he was in

such a serious mood, especially after she'd practically decked him with that slap. "I really floundered in college, in pre-med. I discovered that I really didn't like all that science. In fact, I hated it, and for the first time began to question my medical vocation. It was the Navy that came to me, not the other way around. Well, the Navy special command in Coronado that encompasses SEALs and WEALS. They recruited me for the program. It was my swimming that got me noticed."

"They do that?"

"Sometimes. They look to Olympic and college athletes who excel in skills that would do well in their programs. In my case, swimming and diving. I was still doing that on a competitive level."

"Yeah, I know. Flipper."

"Where'd you hear that?"

"Your friend, JAM. Met him in the bookstore earlier."

She considered asking what else JAM disclosed but set that question aside for now. "At the time WEALS came shopping, I was undecided about what direction I wanted to head next, and a friend of mine was trying out." She shrugged.

"And you like it?"

"Most of the time."

He cocked his head to the side and studied her face.

"We lost a teammate recently. A suicide bomber in Baghdad."

He squeezed her hand and stopped to stare at her. "Now, see, that's what I'm having a hard time

accepting. I'm the reason . . . my stupidity . . . is
the reason you're in such a dangerous line of work.
What a fucking nightmare! How do you think I'd
feel if you had been the one at the receiving end of
that explosive?"

"Not as bad as I would be feeling," she joked.

"Not funny, Wendy. Not funny at all."

"Take it down a notch, Ethan. What you did was
stupid, and it's all on you, but what I did from then
on was my choice, my responsibility, not yours."

"Sorry," he said.

"Me, too," she said.

At the same time, he dropped her hand and used
a finger to trace the scar that ran from her ear to
her windpipe. It was barely noticeable anymore.
Hardly anyone mentioned it, but he had apparently been more observant than most folks. "Did
you get this in action?" he asked in a voice husky
with emotion.

"I did. No biggie!" Although, yes, it had been a
big deal at the time.

He motioned with his head for them to resume
walking, but instead of taking back her hand, he
tucked both of his into his parka pockets. It was
for the best that he kept his distance, she realized.
She'd been liking his hand-holding too much.

"So, are you happy?" he asked.

"Yes, mostly. And you?"

Instead of answering directly, he said, "My little
girl is the best thing that ever happened to me. She
makes up for any regrets I might have ever had."

Wendy felt a twinge of hurt at his words. Time was, she was the best thing that had ever happened to him. How pathetic was that of her! Jealous of a little kid!

They'd arrived back to where they'd started, and the sky seemed suddenly overcast. To her surprise, snowflakes began to fall softly. Big fluffy puffs of white that would dissolve on hitting the ground, but were so beautiful in the air. She raised her face upward, then smiled at Ethan, as they both said, "Fairy snow!" It was a name they'd given this kind of phenomenon as kids. Another shared memory.

"So, is this how closure looks?" she asked him, as they stepped onto the short wooden stairway leading to the parking area. She opened the door to her car but didn't get in yet.

He leaned against the back door and stared at her. "I don't know. Here's the kicker, and I know I shouldn't tell you this, but what the hell! My little girl told me something yesterday that knocked me for a loop. Her mother apparently advised her that when she grew up she should never settle for anything less than a 'Wendy kind of love.' It was one of a bunch of life lessons Beth Anne wanted to impress on Cassie before she passed on. They're all recorded in a diary."

"Oh, Ethan! I'm not even sure what that means." But she did. In her own way, she'd been holding up an impossible threshold for all the men she met, waiting for an "Ethan kind of love."

"I thought I hid my bitterness from Beth Anne

all those years. I thought I loved her, in a way. I certainly wasn't the walking wounded, as far as I know."

"Oh, poor Beth Anne!"

"I don't like the bitterness that seemed to consume me since you sashayed back into town. At least, I thought that's when it started, but now I know it must have been festering under the surface for twelve damn years."

She didn't like the sound of that "sashayed," as if he was judging her, but she picked her battles and asked, "And so you sought closure with this meeting today? Is the bitterness gone now?"

"Yeah. I think so." He glanced at her. "Was bitterness your issue, too?"

"A little. More hurt than bitter, I think. So, yeah, the air is cleared in that regard."

"So, we're good?" he asked, reaching out to flick a snowflake off her nose. Or maybe he just wanted to flick at her, a playful jab, to show they were good, now.

She, on the other hand, couldn't stop staring at the ones caught in those sinfully long black lashes of his.

He knew, or he used to know, how much she admired and envied his lashes. In fact, he'd used them to his advantage on occasion, lowering them to half mast, ever so slowly, then back up, high. Now, noticing her regard, he blinked rapidly to get rid of the flakes. Nothing flirtatious or enticing there!

Still, she was entranced. That was her only excuse for revealing, "Do you know what JAM suggested

I should do to attain closure? Screw your brains out, except he was a little more explicit."

Ethan did one of those slow blinks, then let out a choked laugh. "I didn't know *that* was on the table."

"It's not," she said.

But she was wishing it was. Oh, yes, she was.

Chapter 12

*He was thinking about screwing, but
it wasn't a hardware issue . . .*

The next day, on Friday morning, only four days
till Christmas, another emergency meeting of the
town council was called, and Ethan couldn't duck
this one.

"Either show up, or I'll have your mutt arrested
and quarantined by Bill for the holidays," Doreen
threatened.

Bill Henderson was the sheriff/police chief/dog
catcher for Bell Cove and vicinity, and he also happened to be Doreen's son-in-law.

"On what grounds?"

"Trespass. Stalking. Humping a poodle. You
name it."

Doreen wasn't usually so crude. Maybe he should
nominate her for the grinch contest, or threaten to.
*On the other hand, if I alienate her, she would probably
cast more votes my way. Damn! I'm becoming just as
monkey-ass crazy as the rest of this town. Being nice
when I don't want to just to avoid winning some damn
contest.*

"Have the Levys complained again?" he asked, more politely than he was thinking.

"The Levys are always complaining."

"What's the big deal? Harv's been snipped."

"Yeah, but just because a dog's been neutered doesn't mean it isn't inclined to make the moves, like it used to. Do I need to explain that to you?"

This was not a conversation he wanted or needed to have with Doreen. "This is blackmail."

"So sue me."

Be nice, Ethan. Be nice. That's my new mantra. He gritted his teeth and said nothing, which meant he was going to the meeting. Which would be a useless effort, if Doreen only knew. Ethan couldn't seem to concentrate on anything. Wendy's words kept lurking in the back of his brain:

Screw my brains out? For closure?

Oh, boy!

When he got to the town hall at nine o'clock, all the bells were ringing at once. A miracle of the bells, you could say. Or else, Frank Watson, the tuner over at Bell Forge, might have been cajoled to work on them, again.

All the other members of the council were present when he sat down at the conference table. He wondered what threats Doreen had used on the others. In front of each chair was a folder, and, inside, yep, an agenda. And a Revised Calendar of Events for Bell Cove Christmas, 2018.

He rolled his eyes. In the past, they hadn't needed any frickin' printed schedule to announce the same old/same old events. Christmas Bazaar

at Our Lady by the Sea. Festival of Food at St.
Andrew's. The children's bell choirs performing
at both events. The Bell Ball. The Christmas Eve
Candlelight Bell Walk throughout town, complete
with folks in period Edwardian costumes, caroling and ringing handbells. That was followed by
Midnight Mass with full vocal and bell choirs.
Christmas Day services at St. Andrew's, featuring the children's bell choir. Often people attended
events at both churches, regardless of their religious preferences.

But now . . . Oh, Lord! There were all kinds of
new activities planned.

"What are you griping about now?" Laura asked.

*Be nice, Ethan. Remember, that's your new mantra.
Niceness.* "What is all this stuff? A parade with
floats and antique cars. What floats? Who's doing
all this work? And the only antique car I know of
in Bell Cove is Sam Wheeler's rusted-out Camaro,
but that hardly qualifies as a vintage worthy of a
parade.

"And, holy hell! A grinch crowning at the Whoville dance. What dance? What crown?

"And TV coverage of all Bell Cove events, with a
live mic next to the Nativity scene in the gazebo.
The rest of the world is taking down Nativity
scenes to be politically correct, and we're going to
start one?"

He looked at Laura and she just smiled. "All that
and more, sweetie! It'll be great fun."

Yeah, just swell.

"By the way, Ethan, you're gritting your teeth."

He bared his teeth at her to show he wasn't actually gritting.

She just laughed.

Being nice is harder than it looks, he decided. "Look, I'm all for raising funds for a good cause, and even for promoting the town to increase business, within some limitations. I don't even care if it's hokey as hell. But this is all happening too fast without any planning or regard for efficiency. It feels like you're throwing a wad of pasta against the wall to see what sticks and what just makes an ungodly mess all over the floor."

"What about pasta?" Tony asked from Ethan's other side. "Did you hear about the green pasta we're serving on Snarky Sunday?"

"I'm offering a special on Reuben's Great Masterpiece sandwiches at The Deli on Snarky Sunday," Abe interjected. "I ordered in forty pounds of fresh sauerkraut. Sure hope we get the crowds we expect, or I'm gonna be stuck."

Sally Dawson from the bakery, Jeremy Mateer from The Cove general store, Frank Baxter from Hard Knocks, and Doreen from Happy Feet Emporium all mentioned their special efforts related to the grinch contest.

And apparently his grandmother had offered to sell something called Whoville Mistletoe Balls.

He didn't want to think about the connotation that might be put on those offerings. "Kiss My Balls" came immediately to his cynical mind, but

that's what happened when a person tried too hard
to be nice. It wasn't natural.

On and on the festive suggestions went.

And all that time, he kept thinking, *Screw my
brains out.*

When the meeting was finally over, he had a
world-class headache, and it was only eleven a.m.

"Are you coming to *The Bell* party tonight?" Laura
asked as he stood, gathering up the paperwork, so
he could leave and pick up Cassie at her children's
choir practice. Well, actually, he had another hour
yet. Maybe he'd go out to the lot and check out
those balls.

"I don't think so." Forget about going to the lot.
He just wanted to go home and think about, *Screw
my brains out.*

"Gabe will be really disappointed."

"Huh? Why would Gabe care if I attend your
newspaper party?"

"Because we're holding it at his house?"

Ethan plopped back down into his chair and just
stared at her. "When did all this happen?"

"If you'd stop skipping special meetings of council, you'd be better informed." She smirked at him.

He just stared her down until she gave in and
explained, "I talked Gabe into letting us rent his
house for our annual party. Plus, he's letting us run
a few tours of the old place over the next few days
to raise more funds for our community redevelopment fund. It's where the grinch crowning and
dance will be held, too. I convinced him that all
these things would show his goodwill toward Bell

Cove and, in return, the house will be cleaned up a bit to show to Realtors if he still decides to sell."

"I'd like to have been a bee on the wall when all this convincing was taking place," he remarked.

She smacked his arm and said, "Get your mind out of the gutter."

The gutter was right. *Screw my brains out.*

"So, are you coming?"

I'd like to, he thought, but that wasn't what Laura meant, of course. "I don't know. I'm not much for social drinking."

"That was a long time ago, Ethan. Get over it!"

"I wasn't referring to *that.*"

"Everyone will be there. Don't you want to see what the inside of that mansion looks like now? The bathroom with the gold-plated taps in itself is worth a look-see. Plus, it's another chance to work with Gabe and maybe influence the fate of Bell Forge."

He knew now how Laura had convinced Gabe. She wore a person down.

Still, he resisted.

Until she tossed in the final zinger.

"Wendy will be there."

It wasn't surprising what phrase went through his mind then.

Christmas visitors are the best kind . . .

Cassie paid Eddie Van Hoy, the cab driver, six dollars and fifty cents, including a tip, for her fare, then hitched her backpack over one arm and carried her crutches in the other, before turning to the rough brick sidewalk leading to the Patterson house. Eddie, who also delivered groceries for the Shop-a-Lot and prescriptions for the pharmacy, watched her till she got to the door, as she'd known he would, him being a nice old man, a friend of her grandmother's. She waved that she was all right, and he could leave.

Propping her crutches beside the door, Cassie rang the doorbell. She loved that every house in Bell Cove had a different sounding chime. This one went bing-bing-bing, bing-bing-bing, bing-bing-bing. Theirs at home sounded more like ba-dinnnng, ba-dinnnng, ba-dinnnng. Her friend Marsha's was the coolest of all: bong, bong, bong!

The door opened almost immediately, and Cassie was assaulted by the sound of loud music and the smell of fresh-baked cookies or cake, something buttery and sweet. Cassie recognized the woman standing before her from the ferry a few days ago. It was Wendy Patterson.

She was shoeless, wearing white socks, gray yoga tights, and a *Winnie the Pooh* sweatshirt that said, "A bear, however hard he tries, grows tubby without exercise."

Cassie smiled. Winnie the Pooh was her favorite storybook character. "You're Wendy Patterson, aren't you?"

"Yes, I am. And you're Cassandra Rutledge, aren't you? Can I help you? Did you come to see my aunt?"

Cassie shook her head. "I came to see you, Miss Patterson."

Wendy blinked with surprise. "Well, come in, then. And you can call me Wendy. Miss Patterson makes me sound old." She made a funny face that sucked in her cheeks and puckered her forehead.

Cassie laughed and stepped inside where a lot of old people—some really old like her great-grandmother, and others as old as her father and Wendy here—were sitting around by the Christmas tree or in front of the fireplace where a huge fire was blazing. A couple were playing cards. There was even dancing at the one end, to "Survivor," of all things. Who knew that old folks listened to Beyoncé, let alone knew the moves?

"Aunt Mil, we have a visitor," Wendy said to an older woman who was coming from the kitchen, which could be seen at the end of the long hallway. Cassie remembered Miss Patterson, who had been the music teacher at her elementary school until she retired when Cassie had been in first grade. She wore a white ruffled apron over a red sweater and red plaid pants.

"Cassie! How nice of you to come visit! Is your grandmother with you?"

She shook her head.

"Your father?"

"No. I came alone, Miss Patterson. In a taxi."

The older Miss Patterson exchanged a look with Wendy, then said to Cassie, "Come along to the kitchen, honey. We're just about to have a cup of

ginger chai tea with cookies. And you can call me
Aunt Mil, just like Wendy and her friends do."

So, two people who didn't want her to call them
"Miss," a sign of respect Nana had drummed into
her. Cassie stored that knowledge away to think
about later.

In the meantime, no one had ever offered Cassie
a cup of tea before, let alone tie tea, whatever that
was, and it made her feel grown-up, and that
maybe she wouldn't get in trouble for coming here,
without permission.

Wendy helped her off with her coat, but Cassie
held on to her backpack as she braced her crutches
against the wall.

"Don't you need those?" Wendy asked.

"No. My dad makes me take them everywhere
for Justin, but I don't always need them."

"Justin?"

"Just in Case," Cassie replied.

Wendy laughed.

It pleased Cassie that Wendy got the joke. Not everyone did. It also pleased her that Wendy didn't
remark on her limp as they walked down the hall,
or slow down as if Cassie couldn't walk as fast as
anyone else.

Cassie got another shock when she entered the
big kitchen where there were even more people.
A half-dozen men and women were arranging
all kinds of cookies in foil pie tins, pulling plastic
wrap up into big twists, which were then tied with
red and green curly ribbon.

"Those are donations for the church bazaar," Wendy explained. "I notice you're wearing pink again today."

"Uh-huh," Cassie said, looking down at the pink fuzzy sweater she wore over white tights with her pink Uggs. "Pink was my mom's favorite color. Once I even put her pink flannel nightgown over my pajamas to help me sleep."

"I know exactly how you feel. I lost my mother when I was twelve years old, and I often wear her red coat. It makes me feel like she's hugging me."

Cassie was stunned that someone could explain exactly how she felt.

"You should wear blue sometimes, too, though. Like this color," Wendy advised, pointing to the blue background on the Christmas tablecloth featuring silver bells and green holly. "The exact same color of your eyes. It would make you look even prettier than you already are."

Wow! No one had ever told her that before.

Just then a bald man wearing red suspenders came in from the back door, followed by three dogs, a tiny Pekinese, a bulldog, and a big brown dog, all of whom headed immediately for Cassie.

She braced herself against the back of a chair as the dogs caught sight of her and came barreling toward her, immediately sniffing out the newcomer.

"Get those dogs out of here," Aunt Mil ordered from the counter where she was preparing a tray.

The bald guy came over to Cassie and said, "Don't be afraid, honey. Duke, and Prince, and Earline are saying hello. Dogs do that with their noses, you know."

"I wasn't afraid," she said, leaning down to pet each of them, "but sometimes I lose my balance if I get jostled."

"Me, too," he said with a laugh. "Can't tell you the times a dog knocked me to my bum and licked my face like a lollipop."

"Do all these people live here?" Cassie asked once she and Wendy were seated in a little window nook at the other end of the kitchen.

"No. Just Aunt Mil and a couple of her friends, most of the time. I'll only be here with my guests for the holidays."

"You'll be going away again, then?" she asked. That could be a problem for Cassie's idea.

"Yes. My work is in California." Cassie could tell that she wanted to say more, but Aunt Mil came then and handed out the tea, which was in pretty cups and saucers decorated with flowers. There was also a platter of cookies on a plate that matched the cups. Along with a bear squirt bottle of honey. Watching Wendy put two squirts of honey in her cup, Cassie did the same, stirred, then sipped. It was strange, but good, especially when she took a bite of cookie, too.

"Oh, you picked my favorite," Wendy said. "Raspberry shortbread cookies. Now, before we go any further, you need to call your grandmother or father and tell them where you are."

Cassie started to protest. She hadn't even had a chance to bring up the reason for her visit. And she'd only taken one sip of tea and eaten half a cookie. "But—"

"They'll be worried about you, sweetheart. I'll just go see if Aunt Mil needs help loading these cookies into the car."

Pulling her cell phone from her backpack, Cassie decided to call her father since he was the one who was supposed to pick her up. He answered on the first ring.

"Hello."

"Dad?"

"Cassie, where are you?"

She gulped before revealing, "I'm at the Patterson house."

"What?" he yelled.

She held the phone away from her ear for a moment.

"How did you get there?"

"In a cab."

She heard him mutter something under his breath that she was pretty sure were swear words.

"Why? Were you invited?"

"Not exactly. Dad, don't be mad."

"I'm not mad, princess, but I was worried when you weren't at the church when I got there. And you know better than to barge in on people."

"They don't mind. In fact, me and Wendy are about to have a tea party with ginger tie tea and cookies, and there are three dogs here named Duke, Prince, and Earline. And a bunch of people are making a gazillion cookies for the church bazaar. And did you know that old folks can dance to Beyoncé?" She stopped to catch her breath and added, "And Wendy wears her mother's red coat to remind her of her mother, just like I wear pink to remind me of my mother, but maybe I could get a blue sweater sometime, just for a change."

She thought she heard her father sigh. Then he said, "I'll be right over to pick you up."

"Okay, but . . ." She paused. ". . . could you maybe wait a little while before coming?"

When she clicked off the phone, Wendy came back and sat down next to her. "Is everything all right?"

She nodded.

"Cassie, I think I know why you came here to see me today."

"You do?"

"Uh-huh! Your dad told me what your mother said about a 'Wendy kind of love,' or some such thing. I just wanted you to know that it meant nothing, except—"

Cassie waved a hand dismissively. "That's not why I came."

"It isn't?"

"Nope." She leaned down and unzipped her backpack, pulling out a book with "The Pelican" embossed on its cover. It was her father's high school yearbook.

She could see that Wendy recognized the book, too, which only made her frown more with confusion. Cassie flipped the pages until she got to the photograph she wanted to show her. It was a half-page picture of a girl wearing a black one-piece bathing suit and a white bathing cap, caught in the midst of a perfect swan dive. The caption read: Wendy Patterson, First Place, State Diving Championship, third consecutive year.

"Can you teach me to do that?"

Chapter 13

Shagging down memory lane . . .

*I*t killed Ethan but he waited before rushing over, as Cassie had pleaded. So, it was forty-five minutes before he pulled up in front of the Patterson house. Only the father of an almost-twelve-year-old girl would understand his terror when he'd arrived at the church to find his daughter missing.

At least, it had stopped him thinking about, you know, screwing for closure. That is, until the object of his waking wet dreams stood before him.

Wendy was already opening the front door when he bounded up the sidewalk. Wearing white socks, gray, calf-length tights, and a *Winnie the Pooh* sweatshirt, she looked about sixteen years old. And sexy as hell!

Putting a fingertip to her lips, she motioned for him to follow her into the hallway and toward the open door on the left, leading into what used to be her father's reception room for patients. He probably would have followed her into a closet at that point, that's how pathetic he was becoming, but then he remembered the reason for this visit . . .

his daughter. Wendy wasn't beckoning him off for a little afternoon delight. More like an afternoon rude awakening, in the form of his daughter.

Speaking of whom . . .

He stood frozen in place for a moment, looking through the archway on the right, seeing Cassie at the other end of the living room. Because of the loud music, he remained unnoticed, so far. And he hadn't rung the doorbell.

Four couples—Cassie and a short, bald guy with red suspenders, Aunt Mildred and her Latin Lothario, Wendy's WEALS girlfriend from California and Gloria Solomon, the longtime town librarian, paired with two of the Navy SEALs—were all doing the Carolina Shag to that old Temptations song "My Girl." And they were good! All of them, including Cassie, who was laughing as she did the intricate steps. A half-dozen other seniors and guests sat about clapping and offering advice.

Was it like this all the time? Maybe the rumormongers were right about the goings-on here. Crazy town, for sure!

Ethan was about to step forward and stop Cassie. The rest of them could act as wild as they wanted, but Cassie might twist her hip the wrong way, and it would be weeks of rehab before she was walking normal, or semi-normal, again. Funny, though, her limp didn't show when she danced. He'd never realized that before.

Wendy stopped him by putting a hand on his upper arm and tugging him across the hall.

"But she might hurt—"

"She's fine. C'mon. Remember when we used to do that dance?"

"Oh, yeah." *I remember that and a lot more.*

"We did have moves."

Seriously? You expect me to react to that? He just grinned.

"I was referring to the shag," she chided him, but a cute blush tinted her face.

He could have pointed out that the word *shag* had more than one meaning, but he was being nice today. At least, that's what he told himself.

When she closed the door behind them, he saw that there were a number of boxes about, both here and in the adjoining examination room, visible through the open pocket doors. "Packing up?" he asked.

"Yes, and about time, wouldn't you say? The local clinic is going to take some of this stuff. The medical books can go to a needy doctor just opening a practice here in Bell Cove. And the rest, to a thrift shop, I suppose. Too bad I didn't get to this sooner, I could have donated a lot of it for the church bazaar."

"That sounds like you're planning to sell the house?" There was a slight buzzing in his head at the thought, though why, he couldn't imagine. It wasn't as if Wendy had been here much at all for the past twelve years.

"No, nothing like that. Not yet, anyhow."

The buzzing stopped instantly and relief flooded him. He would have to think about why, later.

"I've known for years that medicine isn't in my future. So, this is a first step in that direction."

He sank down into a low leather sofa and said, "About Cassie showing up here . . ."

"Right." She sat down next to him, but not too close, so that she could turn and face him. Reaching to the coffee table in front of them, she picked up an old Pelican yearbook.

"Strolling down memory lane?" he teased.

"No, Ethan. This is your yearbook, not mine."

"Huh?"

"Your daughter brought it here, with this page bookmarked." She handed it to him, spread open to a page showing Wendy in a bathing suit, performing her trademark swan dive that had won her three state championships.

"I don't get it."

"That's what she wants."

"I still don't get it."

"Cassie asked me if I could help her accomplish this."

He was still confused. "The body or the dive?"

"Probably both. You have to realize that Cassie is at an age where girls first start to be aware of their bodies, and Cassie has been forced to be more aware than others because of her hip issues. When she looks at that picture, the body posed in a perfect position to show muscle definition and body toning, well, to her that's an ideal she wants to reach."

"Cassie won't be having a permanent hip replacement until she's fifteen, or sixteen. Until then, *that*," he tapped the photograph, "would be an impossible dream."

"She knows that. She's a precocious little thing, isn't she? It's a long-term goal she's setting for herself, but something she wants to start working towards now."

"And you learned all that in . . ." He checked his watch. ". . . an hour and a half?"

She nodded.

He bristled. Why would Cassie confide in someone who was virtually a stranger to her, and not to him? And he didn't want to hear about any of those "girl talk" arguments. Hadn't he been the one who talked to her about sex and menstrual periods? Didn't he buy her a training bra for her nonexistent breasts? Hadn't he held her when she was sobbing over a remark Billy Sampson had made about "gimps"? He'd thought, until now, that there was nothing his daughter couldn't speak with him about. But then, she'd shocked the hell out of him this week with the "Wendy kind of love" remark, which she'd been keeping to herself for a long time now.

His hurt feelings must have shown on his face, or in his demeanor, because Wendy said, "Don't get bent out of shape. Cassie just thought I could help her. She didn't realize that I wouldn't be staying here in Bell Cove."

"Even if you were, I'm the one who knows Cassie's limitations. Swimming is actually good for her condition, but there are certain strokes that put too much stress on her hip, like a frog kick. She has to be careful."

"I understand that, but Cassie thinks you're too cautious."

He rolled his eyes.

"I know what you're thinking, but—"

"Wendy, you don't have a clue what I'm thinking." *About anything.*

"Okay, poor choice of words. Let me rephrase that. I know it's none of my business how you raise your daughter, but if you're willing, I could spend a day at the pool with Cassie before I go back to California. The health club in Sunset Dunes still has a high dive, doesn't it? Oh, don't go getting all frowny faced again. I wouldn't be putting her on a high dive. Just demonstrating."

"You would do that?" he asked, but what he was thinking was "frowny face"? Really, all this grinch crap was getting to him. Next he would be walking around with a loopy smile on his face, just to prove he wasn't a grouch. Jeesh!

"Sure."

"Why?"

"Don't be an ass. As a favor to an old friend."

Number one, yes, I am being an ass. A grinchy ass. Number two, "friend," my ass! "What would just one day accomplish? Wouldn't that set her up for disappointment? I mean, she might get attached to you, and, then, bam! You're gone. Again."

She narrowed her eyes at him. "That was a cheap shot."

"I've been burned, Wendy. I don't want my little girl to get burned, too."

"So much for closure! I got burned, too, you idiot!"

He put his hands up in surrender. "Listen, I appreciate your offer and your good intentions. I want my little girl to be happy. If you think one day in a pool with her would help, in any way, go for it."

"Thanks a bunch!"

Ethan couldn't seem to speak for tripping over his tongue . . . around Wendy, anyhow. "Can we start over?"

"I thought that's what we did yesterday."

"That was before you brought up 'screwing for closure.'"

Her eyes widened. "Is that what this is all about?"

"No!" He inhaled and exhaled before admitting, "Yes."

She smiled slowly and shook her head at him, as if he was hopeless.

He was—pretty much—when it came to her.

"So, friends with benefits for the week or so until you leave town?" he suggested, reaching out a hand to flick one of her earlobes, to show he was teasing. "Classic 'screwing for closure' method, if you ask me."

"Not a chance!" She laughed and smacked at his hand which had strayed to her nape.

He shrugged. "You can't blame a guy for trying."

"It's good to see you being so playful. I've hated how hostile you've been toward me. It's not right. Remember, Ethan, we were friends long before we were . . . anything else."

"I remember." *Everything.* "And you're right. Our kind of friendship was too special to lose. Hell, Wendy, I know you better than anyone in the world, or I did." He laughed. "Do you still sneeze three times in a row, never more, never less?"

She nodded. "And you always comb your fingers through your hair when you're nervous."

Like now. He deliberately folded his hands into a single fist on his lap. "You love broccoli. Yuck! But can't stand corn on the cob."

"Yep. Gets stuck in my teeth." She grinned, enjoying the memory game. "You could live on ribs with Maybelle's Southern Barbecue Sauce. And hamburgers, medium rare, with mushrooms and fried onions."

"Your pinky toe on your right foot is stunted."

"It's not stunted!" she declared with mock affront. "Just a little stubby."

He smiled. "Your favorite color is green. You wear a size eight shoe." *And you squeak when you're about to climax.*

She smiled back at him, and he suspected she'd just had a similar intimate reminder about him. Instead, she said, "It's good to just kid around like this with you. I've missed that."

I've missed you, he thought. *More than I realized. This is dangerous, dangerous territory. Quicksand for the soul!* Before he did something really stupid, like pull her over onto his lap and kiss her silly, he stood and held out his hand to her. "C'mon. Let's show those amateurs the way the shag should be done."

And that's just what they did.

The shag originated in the 1940s along the Atlantic Ocean strands between Myrtle Beach, South Carolina, and Wilmington, North Carolina. Perfected over the years, especially by teens with their beach music, it was like a jitterbug, but smooth, with no bouncing, the emphasis on the footwork. Every Southern boy and girl knew the basic steps.

To "Sixty Minute Man," he and Wendy demonstrated how the six-count, eight-step pattern could be perfected by two people who knew each other's bodies so well they anticipated and complemented each other's moves. They were laughing as hard as everyone else when the song was over. The best part was Cassie staring at him with wide open eyes and parted lips, totally impressed that her dad wasn't as much of an old fogey as she'd thought.

After that, Mildred went into the kitchen to get a tray of cookies Wendy was preparing for Cassie, along with some ginger chai, not tie, tea bags. Ethan talked a little bit with Harry Carder, the retired financial consultant, who'd given him much advice over the years in improving his business plan. Gloria Solomon, the longtime Bell Cove librarian, reminded him of how he'd had a passion for books about animals when he was young. He'd heard that Ms. Solomon was getting Alzheimer's, but she seemed okay today. After that, he walked over to the dining room table where JAM and one of the other SEALs, Geek he was called, were looking over some maps.

"Treasure maps?" Ethan asked, jokingly.

"Exactly. Geek is thinking about buying out a New Jersey treasure-hunting company that has the rights to salvage these three ships off the Carolina coast."

Ethan glanced at the maps and said, "I know those names. The Three Saints . . . the *St. Martha*, the *St. Cecilia*, and the *St. Sonia*. Seems to me there was some news story a year or two ago about the competition among various companies to get the licensing rights to this site. There was some ill-feeling from local outfits who felt they should have gotten favored treatment."

"Could be," Geek said. "Are you familiar with this section of the ocean?"

"A little." Ethan studied the map. "The shoals out there can be wicked under the best of circumstances, but during or after a storm, the shifting sandbars have sunk many a ship. Add to that, you have two strong ocean currents that collide near Cape Hatteras. As the ocean settles to its natural level, after a hurricane or even a regular nor'easter, no evidence is left behind. On the surface anyhow."

"The company in question does more than shipwreck salvaging. Treasure hunting of all kinds. But this particular project would be a start," JAM explained.

Ethan knew lots of shipwreck salvors. Mostly they were a crazy lot. Dreamers at heart. Gamblers to the bone.

"And you would operate out of New Jersey?" Ethan asked.

"Nah. We could locate a headquarters anywhere," Geek said.

"Even here on the Outer Banks?" Ethan asked, having a sudden inspiration.

"I suppose, but the land prices would be too high for purchase, and building rentals—especially a

warehouse on a harbor—would be cost prohibi-
tive," Geek explained.

"Not necessarily," Ethan mused.

The other guys, including K-4, the third SEAL,
and Wendy, who'd just come back from the kitchen,
all stared at him.

"Are you going to *The Bell* party tonight?" he
asked Wendy.

She hesitated, probably thinking that he was back
to the "screwing for closure" notion. "Yes."

"Good. Are you bringing your friends?"

She nodded, still not sure where he was going
with these questions.

"They need to meet Gabe Conti, owner of the
house where the party is being held. You remember him. He's the owner of Bell Forge now."

Wendy tilted her head to the side as she began
to understand the direction of Ethan's thoughts.
Laura must have explained some of Bell Cove's current worry over the future of the forge building. "Is
it possible?"

"Who knows? Worth exploring, though, wouldn't
you think?" Before Ethan left, he called Laura and
filled her in on his idea. She promised to come up
with a plan before this evening, one they could
broach with Gabe. The question was: Was Gabe
Conti a gambler?

All the way back home, Cassie chattered away,
happier than he'd seen her in a long while. He
wasn't sure what it was about the day that had
pleased her so. Maybe it was the Patterson house

itself. The atmosphere there was so loud and cheerful. Something that had been missing in their home for a long time. Oh, it wasn't that they were gloomy. It was just that Beth Anne had been sick for so long, and Cassie had been warned on more than one occasion to tiptoe, not stomp around, and to keep her voice down. Then, after Beth Anne's death, sadness had prevailed, with him off working most of the time, and, frankly, he realized now, becoming somewhat of a grinch.

Oh, Lord! For a brief moment, he'd forgotten about that stupid grinch contest. Served him right if he won the damn thing.

Cassie was talking excitedly now about the possibility of a trip to the pool with Wendy to get diving and swimming instructions. He kept warning her that the club might be closed over the holidays and that even if it was open some days, it might not be convenient for Wendy. There was no holding down Cassie's enthusiasm.

Everything was moving too fast, and not fast enough. He feared for Cassie getting disappointed. He feared for his rising hopes. There was a perfect reminder of why the best-laid plans often went awry sitting between him and Cassie on the bench seat . . . the high school yearbook that Wendy had handed him on the way out. He wondered if Wendy had looked inside the book at all that day after Cassie brought it there, other than the one page with the diving picture. Would she have seen the inscription on the inside cover?

Good luck, Ethan! Love you forever!
                                        Wendy

Yeah, right!
There was a flash to the past if he ever saw one,
not one Wendy would appreciate.

A novena for sex? . . .

Mildred went upstairs to her bedroom and closed
the door before taking out her cell phone and calling Eliza at the Christmas Shoppe.

"Ethan was here today," she said right off.

"He was?"

Mildred explained the circumstances of Eliza's
great-granddaughter and then her grandson showing up at her house today and everything else that
had happened.

"They actually danced together?"

"Yes. Nothing mushy like a slow dance. Just the
shag."

"Still. The very fact they could hold hands for a
dance is something."

"I agree, but the clock is ticking. We need to push
this thing along."

"How?"

"Well, the biggest problem as I see it is that there's
no place for the two of them to be together. *Together*
together, if you get my meaning. Not here with all
these people. It's like a zoo, if I must say so myself."

"And there's no hotel or motel nearby since the Bell Breakers Motel closed for the winter," Eliza pointed out.

"How about your place?"

"Cassie could have a sudden sleepover come up at one of her friend's, but what excuse could I have for being out of here?"

"Hmmm. Too bad you don't have a boyfriend!"

"Yeah. Maybe you could fix me up."

Mildred laughed. "Maybe, but not this quickly."

"I was just kidding. Listen, I'll think of some reason why I have to be away overnight. What else?"

"They'll both be at *The Bell* Christmas party tonight. The rest is up to them."

Eliza groaned. "Look how well that's gone so far."

"Let's pray, then."

"Praying for sex? Do you think that's a sacrilege or something?"

"Who cares!"

Chapter 14

Oh, the plans we weave . . .

Ethan noticed something strange when he was getting ready to go out that evening.

First of all, the house was unusually quiet, his grandmother having acted on a sudden desire to see the Winter Lights at the Elizabethan Gardens in Manteo with a few friends, an overnight trip that would involve some last-minute Christmas shopping in the morning. And she'd dropped Cassie off at her friend Melanie's for a sleepover.

When he'd gotten home from the Patterson house, he'd been surprised to find his grandmother in the kitchen with an overnight suitcase packed for herself and a sleeping bag with PJs and assorted toiletries laid out for Cassie. She'd been dressed in a blue pantsuit, the one usually reserved for church or weddings.

"Why, all of a sudden, are you taking off? It's not like you haven't seen the Winter Lights before."

His grandmother had put hands on both her hips and glared at him. "Didn't you tell me just yesterday that I should take time off?"

"Well, yes. I mean, of course, you should go if you want to. I'm just surprised."

"Maybe you're in for a lot more surprises," she'd snapped back.

"What's that supposed to mean?"

"Nothing."

"It meant something, for damn sure."

"Don't swear in front of your daughter."

Cassie, oblivious to their conversation, had been picking up the items that her great-grandmother had laid out on the kitchen table and putting them in her backpack, along with a *Winnie the Pooh* storybook that he hadn't seen since she was about five years old. And that friggin' yearbook, too! Why was she taking that? To show her friends?

Meanwhile, his grandmother had been on a tear. "You can make your own supper, can't you? Or will you be eating over at that newspaper party? No, they usually just serve picky food. Better make yourself a sandwich. You remember how to do that, don't you? I'm taking my Volvo, but don't you dare drive that truck to the newspaper party. Use your car."

"Why? What difference does it make what vehicle I use?"

"Don't argue. Just do as you're told."

"Huh?"

But that wasn't the strange thing that he was noticing now as he finished showering, his grandmother and Cassie long gone. The bathroom that adjoined his bedroom was sparkling clean, smelling of cleanser and air freshener, and newly laundered towels. There was some super fragrant Axe body spray sitting on the counter that he wasn't about to use; he'd bought it last summer to douse Harvey when he'd encountered a not-so-friendly skunk. No, good old Mennen Speed Stick deodorant would do him just fine.

Going into his bedroom, he noticed the smell of lemon furniture polish, and he saw that the coverlet had been turned down on the bed, showing the edge of what looked like ironed, crisp, white cotton sheets. Ironed sheets? Did people really iron sheets these days?

Now, he was no dummy. He paid a cleaning lady to come in every two weeks to help Nana with household chores, but he was pretty sure Alice had come a few days ago. And he could only imagine what Alice would say if she was told to iron sheets. What was his grandmother doing with this sudden cleaning urge? Was it one of those Christmas/Easter/Spring cleaning kind of frenzies that hit women sometimes? Or post-menopausal hormones? Or this stupid grinch business affecting her, as well as the whole town? Or . . . *oh, my God!*

She's setting me up.

My seventy-two-year-old grandmother is preparing what she considers the perfect sex den.

For me!

Like I can't make my own arrangements!

I'm thirty years old, not a kid!

Does she think I'm like Steve Carell in that movie, The 40-Year-Old Virgin, *and I don't know what to do?*

How embarrassing!

How adorable!
I could kill the old lady.
Or hug her.

Thus it was that he was smiling when he arrived at Gabe Conti's house an hour later. And, yes, he was driving his Lexus, not the pickup truck, which he much preferred. Well, it wasn't just his home situation that had him smiling, it was the whole transformation of the old Conti mansion and the stunned expression on Gabe's face.

There were about twenty cars there already, parked on both sides of the semicircle driveway. He parked behind Karl Gustafson's motorcycle. He could hear classical music coming from the open double front doors.

"Can you believe this?" Gabe asked, coming down the wide steps to greet him as he exited his vehicle.

They both stared up at the white lights that outlined every feature of the massive building, not to mention the single white candles that lit every single window. There were also live evergreen garlands around each window and door frame. Two twenty-foot Douglas firs, decorated with colored twinkling bulbs, could be seen through the large bay windows that framed both sides of the front door.

He wondered idly if he'd gotten that business.

"Let me guess? Laura?" Ethan said, biting his lip to restrain a smile.

"Yes! We've blown a fuse three times today, and I had to call in an electrician to install a new breaker. Time and a half."

"Well, it looks nice."

"Yeah, it does, but wait till you see the inside. She's like a bulldozer when she wants something. A velvet bulldozer. By the time you realize what's happened you've been flattened."

"You can always say no."

"Pfff! That's a word Laura doesn't recognize."

"There must be some benefits to you."

"There are," he admitted with a sigh.

He thought Gabe was going to say *friends with benefits*, which just showed where his mind was.

But instead, Gabe said, "Laura has been very helpful in assessing all the junk in this house, what to toss out, what to sell, and what to keep. You have no idea what a mess it is."

"A good mess or a bad mess?"

"Both, I suppose. The original house was built to accommodate the three brothers," he said, pointing to the central part of the mansion with the two wings extending out on either side. "My great-great-great-grandparents, Salvadore and Angela Conti, lived in the middle, and the bachelor uncles, Lorenzo and Tomas, lived in their own separate wings. What I didn't realize is that the uncles were collectors."

"Of what?"

"Lorenzo wasn't so bad. He collected pipes, the kind you smoke. Seven hundred and sixty-two. I would just toss them in the trash, but Laura says some of them are valuable. So, now I have to find someone who wants to buy them or sell them for me."

"You could probably list them on eBay. Or maybe

there's a pipe museum you could donate them to and take a charitable tax deduction."

"A pipe museum?" Gabe looked at him as if he was crazy.

Ethan shrugged. "I've heard of stranger things. Did you know there's a condom museum in Canada?"

Gabe shook his head at Ethan's sorry attempt at humor. "But that's not the worst part. Tomas was interested in big game, not hunting them himself, but collecting the trophies. The walls are covered with elephant tusks and zebra heads and a tiger skin the size of a small house complete with head and paws, and there's a ten-foot-tall gorilla guarding the fireplace. Half of them are probably endangered species . . . maybe not then, but surely today. If the news media finds out about this, my face will be plastered all over the place, like that doctor or dentist who killed an animal in Africa or somewhere, and ended up getting death threats."

"Whoa! You started with being the Christmas Lights King and moved on to America's Most Hated Man list. I thought you were supposed to be relaxing over the holiday."

"Tell me about it!"

They both burst out laughing then, knowing full well that when a woman was involved, men did the craziest things.

Just then Laura poked her head out the door. She looked like Santa's little hottie elf in a green velvet dress that was scooped low in front and ended about midthigh with a pair of four-inch black high heels that would be killer at the North Pole.

"Gaaabe," she said, "can you come help me with a little problem we're having in the kitchen?"

"Sure," he said, giving Ethan a wink to show that, despite his venting, he was more than okay.

To Ethan, she added, "Did you discuss our idea for the Bell Forge treasure-hunting venture with Gabe?"

"Um . . . not yet," Ethan said.

"What?" Gabe said.

"Nothing to worry about now, Gabe. Now, the garbage disposal is another matter." Laura batted her eyelashes at Gabe.

"I'm an architect, not a plumber."

As their voices faded and Ethan was left outside, gaping at the two of them, several cars pulled up. It was the gang from the Patterson house. Wendy, her California military friends, Aunt Mildred, and the other seniors. He smiled at Wendy and went over to help get Harry's wheelchair out of the back of the SUV.

This was supposed to be a casual event, and the men were dressed accordingly in slacks with sweaters, or dress shirts and sport coats. The ladies wore mostly pants and glittery tops.

If Laura had looked like Santa's hottie elf, Wendy was the Christmas Fairy in a shimmery sky-blue jumpsuit edged in silver braid. It was long-sleeved and the legs were full, but that was the only thing modest about the outfit. It came to a deep vee in front, hugged her waist and hips, and ended in strappy silver high heels which matched a silver chain loop belt.

It was the kind of outfit that gave a man ideas, and Ethan already had a few of those. Like that belt wrapped around a pair of wrists tied to a headboard, or a bare-naked body, except for silver stilettos, against crisp white sheets . . .

"Hello, Ethan, good to see you again," Aunt Mildred said, jarring him from his inappropriate reverie. "Is Eliza with you?"

"No. She went to Manteo to see the Winter Lights."

"Ah," Aunt Mildred said with a knowing little Mona Lisa smile.

"I have some good news," Wendy said, coming up to him. Even with the high heels, he still had a good three inches on her, but it put them on more level footing.

He grinned. He couldn't help himself. Images of an empty house, fresh pressed sheets, and other things came to mind. "Oh?" he said with as serious an expression as he could muster on his face.

"Get that look off your face, cowboy. I'm referring to the pool at Sunset Dunes Health Club. It's open tomorrow from nine to five, then Wednesday through Saturday next week."

"Don't blame me for ogling, Wendy. You can't dress up like Tinkerbell, all grown up and sex on a silver hoof, and expect a guy not to notice."

Her jaw dropped with surprise.

"But that is good news about the pool. Cassie couldn't stop talking about it on the way home this afternoon. So, tomorrow work for you?"

She nodded, hesitant now that he'd mentioned his attraction to her.

"It's a date then? If we leave about ten, we could have lunch and spend a few hours at the pool, or we could go there directly and have a late lunch."

"I wouldn't exactly call it a date," she was quick to clarify. "Not with the three of us."

"Did someone mention a three-way?" JAM said, coming up and throwing an arm over Wendy's shoulder companionably. "I'm game. We could make it a four-way, if you want."

"Get real," Wendy said, shrugging out from JAM's arm. "Both of you!"

"What? JAM was the one who suggested a four-some. I didn't mention anything about sex," Ethan protested, and recalled that JAM was the one who'd advised Wendy to screw his brains out, for closure. You couldn't hate a guy who thought like that.

"Yeah, but you were thinking it," JAM pointed out as Wendy huffed away and up the steps. They were both watching her butt as the blue fabric hugged her heart-shaped curves each time she raised a foot. "It's obvious every time you look at her, man."

"I'm that obvious?" Ethan felt like a teenager caught having illicit thoughts about a hopelessly out-of-reach cheerleader. Not that he'd ever had those about anyone else, not with Wendy around.

"Oh, yeah! But not to worry. Wendy changed her outfit four times before settling on that Tinkerbell Does the Christmas Tree Farmer space suit."

Ethan felt better.

A lot better.

He made her an offer she couldn't refuse . . .

Wendy couldn't keep her eyes off Ethan as he worked the crowd. This was the eighteen-year-old Ethan she had known—a boy—but all grown up and comfortable in his skin . . . a man.

There was a mixture of attire at this newspaper party, everything from slacks and sweaters to suits and ties, especially since some of the people came directly from work. Ethan was among the dozen or so men in the latter category. He wore a navy blue suit, the jacket open over a white dress shirt and red-and-blue striped tie.

She could see him now as the successful businessman he was, addressing people by name as he shook their hands, sometimes putting a hand on the shoulder at the same time. Those people he didn't know, he introduced himself to with a self-confidence she didn't recall seeing in him as a boy.

He threw his head back and laughed out loud at something being said in one group, then listened intently when someone was saying something to him, like Harry Carder, the retired financial advisor in a wheelchair who was residing temporarily in her house.

In her defense, Ethan was watching her, too. When his searching gaze would locate her across the room, he would either nod, or if he caught her watching him, wink at her. There was something hot and hungry in his scrutiny that made her feel hot and hungry, too. Once when he couldn't see her—she was just coming from the library—panic appeared in his eyes for a moment. Did he think she was going slip away from the party without saying her goodbyes? Why would she do that? Or even worse, skip town, again, without letting him know?

Wendy wasn't the only one following Ethan's progress, either. Women noticed him, and a few sidled up to him to get his attention.

Laura, who was passing with a tray of hors d'oeuvres for the buffet table, must have been thinking the same thing. "Still hot stuff, isn't he?"

"Does he date? Have someone special?"

"I have no idea. Whatever he does, he does off-island."

"I see you and Gabe are getting along well," Wendy remarked.

"I love his house," Laura said, gazing about the huge drawing room that easily accommodated the fifty or so people standing around sipping at stemmed glasses of wine, or munching on finger foods. The wallpaper and drapes and upholstery were faded and worn, but shabby chic in the soft lighting beside the beautifully decorated trees, probably the result of Laura's tasteful help.

"Yeah, but a house is still just a house, albeit a big one like this. What about the man?"

Laura's eyes twinkled mischievously. "I like him just fine."

"Poor Tony!" Wendy said.

"Hah! Have you noticed 'poor Tony' putting the moves on your friend?"

Wendy smiled, following Laura's gaze over to the

window seat alcove where Tony was sitting next to Diane. They were conversing enthusiastically on some subject, probably the bear Grizz had once killed and how one would serve bear meat in an Italian restaurant. Or maybe they weren't talking about that at all, Wendy mused, noting Tony's hand on Diane's knee, which was exposed by the short black sheath she'd bought that day in Monique's Boutique, a dress that would serve double duty at her cousin's upcoming wedding.

Laura took her goodies to the buffet table, then went over to join Gabe who was being hustled by Ethan and her SEAL friends regarding the treasure-hunting venture. Apparently, they'd come up with some crazy idea of saving Bell Forge by combining it with the Jinx company, whose name would be changed to Bell Forge Ventures. How the two would share one building was beyond Wendy, and she really had nothing to do with it; so, she circulated among the partygoers, many of whom she'd known all her life.

Ina Rogers, the longtime secretary at Our Lady by the Sea, was sitting in a wing back chair near the fireplace, a walker propped next to her. "Hello, sweetheart. It's good to see you back in Bell Cove."

Wendy hunkered down so that they were face to face. "You look just the same, Mrs. Rogers, except for that." She didn't mean her orangish skin color, although that was different, but, instead, pointed at the walker. "Anything serious?"

"Well, as serious as a double knee replacement can be. I'll be good as new in a few weeks."

"Are you still working at the rectory?"

"Absolutely. I keep telling Father Brad that I'll be there till the day I die. Which will save my family on funeral expenses. They can just bring the casket to the church, say a mass over my body, and cart me to the cemetery." She laughed at her own morbid joke.

"Father Brad? A new priest?"

"Honey, there have been eight priests assigned here since I was first hired as church secretary forty years ago. I like your friend, by the way."

"Which friend?"

"The Mendozo fella. He's come in to talk to Father Brad a few times. Seems they both went to the same seminary at one time."

"Really?" This was news to Wendy. She knew that the guys and Diane had been exploring the town a lot, usually on their twice-daily jogging runs, but this was the first she'd heard that JAM was visiting the church, other than the day the guys had arrived in town.

"Yes. I believe he's going to serve as deacon at Midnight Mass to replace Deacon Frank O'Malley, temporarily, as he goes to visit his daughter, Maura, in Miami. Maura just gave birth to twin boys."

Wow! Wendy thought. Not about the twins, but the fact that JAM was going to be a deacon, or that he was able to do so. Who knew? Yes, he had supposedly been in a seminary at one time, but she had no idea he kept up with the religious stuff. The public would love to learn about a Navy SEAL warrior with a spiritual side, but it would never happen.

Next, she talked with Francine Henderson, owner of Styles & Smiles, the local beauty salon. Francine was the daughter of Mayor Doreen Ferguson and wife of Sheriff Bill Henderson. Wendy had known both Francine and Bill in high school.

"Love your hair," Francine remarked, flicking the ends which she'd spritzed up this evening. "You should come in for a conditioning treatment. On the house."

"Thanks." *Not a chance! Not with the orangish tan you and Ina and a dozen other women in this room are sporting.* "Do you and Bill have any children?" Wendy asked.

"Two girls, eight and ten. How about you? Married? Kids?"

"No and no! Too busy!" *I can't believe I tossed that cliché out there.*

Francine leaned in closer and whispered, "I know you're in the Navy, but rumor is that you're one of those female SEALs. You can tell me."

Wendy issued a fake laugh and said, "I love rumors. I always learn the most interesting things about myself."

Francine blinked, not sure if Wendy was ridiculing her or agreeing that she was indeed in the WEALS. She smiled uncertainly.

Meanwhile a trio of high school students, two violinists and a flutist, continued to play soft chamber music. During a break, Claudette Deveraux, one of Aunt Mil's guests, sat down at the baby grand piano and, with an ease born of hours at the keyboard, began to play Christmas songs. No one minded that the piano was slightly out of tune, and in fact some gathered around to sing carols, including all the seniors. It was lovely, really.

"Wow! She's awesome," Wendy observed to Aunt Mildred. "Did you know she could play like that?"

Her aunt shook her head. "I had no idea. Claudette is pretty much a mystery, but she's coming out of her shell lately. When she first came to us, she was very quiet. And very sad about something."

Hmmm. Maybe she should ask Delphine, her other roommate, to check up on her while she was home in New Orleans. Too bad Delphine couldn't make it here after all! On the other hand, maybe that would be an invasion of privacy, not just to Claudette, but to her aunt, as well.

"It is so good to have you here, Wendy," her aunt said, a little tearfully, as she put an arm around her waist and squeezed. "I won't ask you to come home permanently, if you're happy in California, but I hope you'll come more often."

"I will, Aunt Mil. I promise."

From there, she spoke with Abe Bernstein from The Deli and complimented him on the *Diners, Drive-Ins and Dives* segment about his store. "Are you still making your famous Reubens?"

"I am, I am. And hoping to sell a ton of them over this holiday weekend with all the tourists coming in for the grinch nonsense."

"You don't approve of the grinch contest."

"Oy vey! I didn't mean to sound disapproving. Yes, it is a bit *meshuggeneh*, but in a good way. What do you think about my adding lox and bagels and cream cheese on Sunday morning?"

"Uh . . ."

"We don't have a huge Jewish population in Bell Cove, but perhaps the tourists would expect such things in a deli?"

"Or you could have your non-Jewish customers try something new," she offered. "Besides, the combination of bagels and cream cheese and lox is probably Americanized by now."

"You're right. Good to talk with you, Wendy. Drop by the store, and I'll give you something to nosh on, free, of course."

She'd run into Doreen Ferguson, the mayor, at her Happy Feet Emporium, where she'd bought her silver high heels this afternoon.

Doreen looked down at them now and smiled. "They're perfect with that outfit. What do you think of mine?" The mayor did a little twirl to show off her Christmas Tree dress.

And that was the only way to describe it. A Christmas tree adorned the whole front of the white dress, from the star at its top which pressed against her neckline, down between her breasts, spreading out in an ever-widening vee till it reached the calf-length hemline. The same was true of the back of the dress. Oh, and the trees were decorated with red and yellow lights.

"Very Christmassy!" Wendy observed. Just then, she noticed someone she knew well, or had known well, across the room, and she excused herself from Doreen.

Matthew Holter, Ethan's best friend in high school, had just come in and was listening to the carolers next to the piano. He was wearing a camel-hair jacket in a herringbone pattern over dark slacks with a white shirt and tie. Other than a slightly receding hairline, he looked pretty much the same as he had twelve years ago. Tall, wiry thin, overly serious. Sort of a good-looking geek.

"Matt! It's been way too long!" She went up and hugged him warmly.

"Ah, Wendy! Back at last!" He hugged her back, then held her away from him. "Whoa! Someone's out to break a heart tonight."

"What? You don't like my outfit?"

"Are you kidding? Every male in the room must have stood at attention when you walked in."

She laughed. "So, I hear you're a lawyer now. Married? A family?"

"Yes, I'm a lawyer. Was married but divorced three years ago. No kids, thank God! How about you?"

"Well, you probably know I'm in the Navy and a lot more, thanks to Laura's big mouth. I've never married or had any kids. Someday, maybe."

"But no one 'on deck' at the moment?"

"Nope." She smiled. "It's so good to see you."

He stared at her for a long moment, then said, "He's never gotten over you."

"Oh, Matt!" This was a subject she wasn't prepared to discuss. "He got over me a long time ago. He married, has a child, a whole new satisfying life."

"Yeah, right." Matt took a glass of wine off the

tray being passed around by a hired waiter. "Have you seen that damn tree lately?"

"What?" She was suddenly alarmed. Matt couldn't be referring to . . . oh, no!

"Just go look someday, that's all I'm saying." He squeezed her arm, and anything further he might have been going to say was forestalled by Diane coming up to them. Apparently, Tony had been called away to his restaurant for some kitchen emergency.

"Matt, I'd like you to meet my friend, Diane Gomulka from Oregon. Her nickname is Grizz because she's been known to shoot a bear or two. Diane, this is Matthew Holter, an old friend of mine. A lawyer."

Matt's eyes widened, taking in Diane's trim figure in the figure-hugging black sheath with the killer black strappy stilettos, and Diane wasn't unhappy with what she saw either.

As Wendy walked away, she heard Matt say, "The only bear I've ever come in contact with is a stuffed bear when I was a kid. Winnie the Pooh."

"My favorite," Diane cooed.

Wendy was feeling rather pleased with herself as she leaned back against the wall, alone for the moment, just staring around at all the familiar faces, and realized that she was enjoying herself. It really was good to be home. Peaceful.

But then Ethan walked up to her, leaned against the wall next to her and said, "Come home with me."

Wendy turned her head, inch by inch, without moving her body, to look at him. He was staring straight ahead, not even looking at her, but she noticed a tenseness in his jaw. "What's that supposed to mean?"

"Exactly what I said. My grandmother is out of town until tomorrow, and Cassie is at a sleepover."

Her heart was hammering so hard in her chest, she could swear there was an echo in her ears. But, no, that was the town clocks in the distance chiming the hour. Only ten o'clock.

Ethan turned then, and the blue, blue gaze stabbed her with its hunger. "I want to make love to you, Wendy. Come home with me."

"But . . . oh, Ethan, that would be such a bad idea. We live coasts apart. The past needs to be buried, not dug up again. So many things—"

He put a fingertip to her mouth to halt her further words. "No words. No what ifs and why nots. No thinking about the past or the future. Now. This hour. This day. Tonight." He moved his fingertip to trace the scar from her ear to the center of her collarbone and had to see the pulse jump in her neck.

"Come home with me," he urged again.

She sighed and said, "Yes."

Chapter 15

Memories are made of this . . .

*E*than was wound tighter than a two-dollar watch. In fact, it was an indication of how tense he was that he would even think such a cliché. His biggest fear was that he would touch Wendy, or she would touch him, and he would uncoil with shocking speed, Slinky-style, resulting in his jumping her bones on the spot . . . inside his Lexus, against the passenger door, over the trunk, against the mailbox at the end of his lane, against the back door of the house, on the porch swing, straddling a kitchen chair, on the floor.

Pathetic, pathetic, pathetic! She'll think I'm as needy as a teenager with raging testosterone.

More clichés!

His game plan, if you could call it that, was to *not* think, to tune out any niggling thoughts about what an insane, bound-to-fail, fucked-up idea it was to imagine that they could have sex and then just walk away, no feelings hurt, no hearts broken. *Teflon sex, some people called it. In and out. Nothing sticks. Yeah, right!*

As a result, Ethan didn't speak at all on the ride back to his house, but he did hold Wendy's hand on the seat between them. She didn't speak, either. He hoped it wasn't because she was having regrets already.

"Everything looks the same," she remarked when they walked toward the house. He'd left the kitchen light on, which shone out over the back porch.

"It pretty much is, except for a second bathroom and a few odd renovations. Nana likes it to stay the same as it was a hundred years ago when it was a small farm, the only one at this end of the Outer Banks."

Harvey was barking up a storm, welcoming him home and somehow sensing a new person to sniff up. As soon as Ethan opened the door, the dog was on his hind legs, paws on Wendy's shoulders, trying to lick her face.

Wendy was laughing and trying to avert her face. "And who is this handsome fellow?"

He grabbed Harvey by his collar and yanked him away. "This 'handsome fellow' is Harvey the Bad Boy who knows better than to slobber and shed dog fur all over our guests."

She continued to laugh as he settled a woeful-looking Harvey on his dog blanket near the door, wagging his forefinger in warning. As a second thought, he tossed him a rawhide bone to keep him in place.

"Where are Bonnie and Clyde?"

"Long gone over the Rainbow Bridge," he replied. "We just have Harv now, and two cats." He pointed to the two felines who were sprawled out on an old-fashioned cupboard on the other side of the kitchen, not interested enough to come down to greet him, or any newcomer, to the house. "And a bunch of rabbits out back that can't stop multiplying. Don't suppose you want a pet rabbit . . . or five?"

He took off his jacket and hung it over a chair, followed by his tie.

Are her lips parted because she's as breathless as I am?

She watched closely as he unbuttoned one, then two buttons on his shirt.

Yes, she's definitely breathing hard, and her eyes are kind of glazed. Too much wine at the party? No, she's high on me. He smiled at his wishful thinking.

But then, she smiled back.

Ethan did a mental fist pump in the air.

No words. By unspoken agreement, they would not speak. Not yet. If they did, the spell might be broken.

But it was time they got this show on the road if they wanted the main event to take place on a bed and not here on the kitchen table. He held out a hand for her to come with him.

They made it only as far as the hall before he had to kiss her.

Just once, he told himself.

Okay, twice.

Maybe up against the wall.

Oh, hell! Oh, damn! Oh, heaven and hell! He succumbed to an unending kiss, with teeth and tongue and wetness, and memories, memories, memories. Her lips became pliant and equally demanding.

Oh, I remember this.
And this.
But this is new.

Somehow the rest of his shirt had gotten unbuttoned and pulled out of his waistband, and her hands were on his bare chest and around his back. Caressing. Relearning old parts. Discovering new ones.

Yes! Touch me there.
Harder.
You remember that spot? You do! Oh, perfect!

He unzipped the back of her jumpsuit down to her butt and had it off and puddled at her feet. Like magic.

Leaning back, he looked at her. A nude-colored lace bra and bikini panties.

"Beautiful. Still beautiful after all these years," he murmured, admiring her slim, well-toned body. The same, but fuller in some places, tighter and more muscled in others.

But it could only be a quick scrutiny because her hands were busy, unbuckling his belt, unzipping his slacks, and pushing both his pants and briefs down to his knees in one sweep.

She stepped out of her garment and spread her legs, still in high heels. "Now!" she demanded, leaning against the wall, eyes closed, neck arched, exposing the long scar, which was somehow erotic, against all that creamy skin.

"Condom," he cautioned, about to lean down and take one out of his wallet.

She pulled him back up and said, "Implant. I'm safe."

He was ready, more than ready, obviously, but how about her? She was still in her underwear. No matter! Slipping his fingers under the crotch of her panties, he almost passed out at the sheer pleasure of the wetness he found.

Then, he shoved the fabric aside, and:

I'm in!

Warm.

Slick.

Clutching me.

So good!

Don't come. Just don't hot damn come this soon. Dammit!

And so it was that he took her for the first time in twelve years, or she took him, against the wall, then halfway up the stairs, him on bottom, then her reversing roles, as they staggered and crawled up to the second-floor hallway in one unending fuck unlike anything he'd ever experienced in his life. It was love remembered and lost, new and old sexual triggers, lovemaking and payback at the same time.

"You bastard!" she said, but so softly he couldn't be insulted.

"You left me," he retorted.

"I had to. I hurt so bad."

"I'm sorry."

"Oh, yes, touch me there," she said on a moan.

He chuckled. "You always liked that. Remember the first time we discovered this spot."

"The first time and the second, and the fiftieth."
She tried to laugh but it came out as a choke. "How
about this, though?"

He saw stars, practically, as she held his favorite body part between both hands and moved it
just so, while he was still in her, the short span of
cock just outside her body. "Yes, I remember," he
gasped out.

"It's never been like this with anyone else," she
confessed, and there were tears in her eyes.

"I know," he agreed, and he might have had tears,
too. *You have ruined me for anyone else, Wendy.*

"I don't want this to ever end. Don't stop."

As if I could! "We're going to be black and blue,"
he pointed out. "Or else I'm going to have splinters
in my ass."

"War wounds," she said, sitting atop him now as
he lay splayed out on the hallway floor outside his
bedroom. She still had on a bra, but her panties had
vanished somewhere along the stairway. She began to ride him then, first slow, then fast, and faster.

Caught in a whirlwind.

Hang on.

Spinning.

Out of control.

Faster. Fasterfasterfaster!

Oh! Ohhhhhhhhh!

Blast off!

When he finally came to his senses, they had
moved several more feet toward the open doorway
of his bedroom, and he was on top now, still imbed-
ded in the aftershocks of her climaxing muscles.

He stared at her in wonder, disarmed, yet pleased by her uninhibited sensuality. *Was she always that way? I can't remember. Hell, I can't remember my own name at the moment.*

She was staring back at him through caramel-colored eyes glazed with passion, only temporarily sated. *I hope.* Her lips were kiss-bruised and parted. *Like Botox, but better.*

What was she thinking?

That I'm a good lay?

That I'm not as good as I used to be, or better?

That I'm nothing compared to those notoriously virile SEALs?

That now she finally has closure?

He knew what he was thinking.

I love you.

But he couldn't say those words aloud. Not now. Not ever again.

Tonight was for memories. Not forever.

Love sucks . . . sometimes . . .

I love you, Wendy thought. And she was shocked. Oh, she'd known she was still attracted to Ethan. That had been apparent on their first encounter back on the ferry. But love? That had died a sudden death twelve years ago, or surely faded over time.

Or so she had believed.

Until tonight.

They'd engaged in hot, frantic, almost-embarrassing

sex in the hall and on the stairs, unlike anything she'd ever experienced before. And then they'd made slow love in Ethan's bed. Both events should have been alarming to Wendy, and the intensity of her response to Ethan was shocking, but, at the same time, surprisingly satisfying. Almost fated. Inevitable. Something she wasn't fighting anymore.

Not that she was going to tell Ethan about her suddenly realized feelings! Oh, no! That was a road she had no intention of going down. Commitment and an impossible future together lay in that direction, both of which had no place in the new and reinvented Ethan and Wendy scenario.

Still, *I love you*, she continued to muse as she lay on her side, propped on one elbow, staring down at his body, relaxed in sex-satiated slumber. A crisp white sheet covered him from the navel downward, but the rest of him was exposed for her private appreciation. There was a dim bedside lamp that gave the room a warm glow.

Despite being a businessman now, Ethan must still work outdoors a bit because his arms and neck and face were "farmer tanned." She didn't see him as the exercise club kind of grunt, but his body was well-muscled in the biceps and in the planes of his abdomen. Perhaps not the hulking muscles that some of her SEAL buddies displayed from continual grueling exercise, but a modest six-pack to be sure.

She liked that he had some dark hair on his chest, leading down a "happy trail" below the sheet. And she also liked the "five o'clock shadow" that feathered his face. But she love, love, loved those thick black lashes that lay like fans against his cheeks.

"Do you like what you see?" he murmured, opening his eyes slowly, the blueness dazzling in its intensity. His lips twitched with humor.

"Maybe," she said, slapping at him playfully. "How long have you been awake?"

He grabbed her hand and kissed the fingertips. "I haven't been asleep at all. Do you think I'd waste the little time I have with you by sleeping?" He tucked her to his side with an arm around her shoulders and her face resting on his chest.

The "little time." Yes, he was right about that. So little time! Not to be wasted! "Hmmm. I guess not," she murmured. "And, yes, I like what I see."

"Vice versa, baby. Very vice versa!" he said, making a growling noise against her neck. Then, "Tell me about your work in California. What is a typical day like?"

She was the one lying on her back now, and he was propped over her.

"I'm not sure there is a typical day, but, even when we're not out on a live op, or preparing for a mission, we always, always have to be in shape. That means exercise every day, and not just five-mile runs before breakfast. It's carrying a log, climbing the cargo net, sugar cookies on the beach, drownproofing, surf penetrations, every kind of body torture imaginable, all to make us be in the best physical condition at any one time. You never know when your body's ability to survive in the wild will be tested."

"What's the most dangerous thing you've ever done?" he asked, a fingertip idly tracing the scar on her neck. He was fascinated by that scar, or perhaps repulsed, she wasn't sure.

Snuck into a Syrian compound, dressed in full burka, to help rescue three Marines who'd been imprisoned for a year. HALOed into hostile territory in Afghanistan. Took enemy fire in Nigeria. "I can't really tell you."

"Or you'd have to kill me?" he quipped.

"Something like that."

"You ever shoot anyone? No, forget I asked that. Do you have any trouble killing someone?"

"Not at all. The tangos we go after—that's a SEAL name for bad guys—these are the dregs of the world. Evil-to-the-core terrorists."

Ethan cringed at her words. "I don't like that you have to do these things."

"Someone has to. Besides, I choose to. In fact, I'll probably re-up in June."

He shrugged. "I just wish—"

She interrupted him. "Tell me about your work."

He seemed reluctant to give up his questioning, at first, but then he acquiesced. "The first couple years after you left, I worked with my dad on tree farming, until his death. I soon learned that he loved the farming aspect, but was an incompetent businessperson. He didn't go out and seek customers or new markets, just waited for people to come to him."

"Where did you learn to do those things?"

"A few nighttime college courses, some online, but mostly instinct, and I guess an aptitude for business. We sell trees to some of the largest wholesalers and department store chains, and I just bought additional land to expand the business. The key to the future is hiring aggressive salesmen and some young people with innovative ideas for what the future holds. The world is changing fast, even for something as simple as Christmas trees."

"I can see that you love what you're doing."

"I don't know about love, but I'm content with it now."

"Tell me about your daughter."

"Ah, Cassie is what makes it all worthwhile."

"So, no regrets?"

"Oh, I have regrets, all right, but Cassie makes up for everything."

Wendy felt oddly hurt at his words. By regrets, she knew he referred to her.

"Will you come with me and Cassie to the pool tomorrow?"

She hesitated. *It's best to make tonight be a one-off. Best not to establish any connections with his daughter. Best if I leave right now and don't look back.* "Sure," she said.

"In the meantime, I think I need a few swimming lessons of my own." He stood suddenly, unconscious of his nudity, although she was very aware of it if the sudden lurch in between her legs and the ache in her breasts were any indication. Extending a hand, he pretended to leer at her as he said, "Come see my pool, Flipper."

His pool was the claw-foot tub in the bathroom, one she was more than familiar with from days gone by. In the soapy water (courtesy of his daughter's bubblegum-scented bubble bath), he showed her a few moves he'd learned over the years. Then he had to check out every inch of her body to make sure she was in as good a shape as she'd proclaimed all the special forces men and women had to be.

He licked the bubbles off her breasts and sucked the nipples into hard points of almost painful arousal. He cupped her buttocks and coaxed her to take him into her as he watched. He kissed the dimples in her lower back, which she informed him were called "Venus dimples" these days, an indicator of a woman's sexuality. He seconded that opinion with more kisses in that region.

Telling her, explicitly, what he liked, he also encouraged her to speak of her own desires, the things that excited her most.

"Do you still like me to stick my tongue in your belly button?" she asked.

"Only if you're holding my cock at the same time."

"Will you flutter your eyelashes over my nipples, like you did before? Oh, my God! That is so hot!"

"Remember the time I finger-fucked you behind the pool house at Jennifer Wilson's birthday party?"

"And you had a bit of premature ejaculation into your swimming trunks when you thought Jennifer's dad was about to walk in on us? The SEALs have a slang term for it: dishonorable discharge."

"I don't recall that," he lied.

So, they played with each other's bodies and

laughed and moaned until Ethan stood and took her against the tiled wall behind the tub, with her legs wrapped around his hips. A couple times he almost slipped and dumped them into the tub. When they were done, they were both laughing and the floor was covered with water.

Once they were toweled off and heading back toward the bed, Wendy remarked, "Those are the nicest sheets! Do you hire someone to press them?"

He looked at her, shook his head ruefully, and said, "Don't ask."

It was three a.m. by then and Wendy said, "You need to take me home."

"What? Why?"

"I am not going to do the Walk of Shame this morning among a gauntlet of senior citizens and military types. Believe me, Navy SEALs do not engage in political correctness. Hoochie Mama comes to mind. And those seniors of Aunt Mil's aren't any better. They have no filters whatsoever. I wouldn't be surprised if they asked me how many orgasms I had."

He grinned and asked, "How many *did* you have?"

"Four if you don't count . . . well, you know what."

"I definitely count *that*," he said, then suggested, "How about you take my car and come back here for breakfast? We can go pick up Cassie and drive to the pool from there?"

She nodded, reluctantly.

Once she'd gathered her clothes, from their path through the house, she dressed and was about to leave. Ethan, wearing a pair of boxers and nothing else, kissed her and said, "Thank you." That's all.

She shouldn't have been disappointed. She didn't want him to say that he loved her. She really didn't. But still . . .

He looked a little bit sad, too.

"What might have beens" sucked the big one.

Chapter 16

Feeding the hungry . . .

*E*than couldn't go back to sleep after Wendy left. His mind churned with too many questions, foremost of which was: *Will she return?*

I love her, he thought. *I never stopped. How did I not know that before? Have I really been that clueless?*

He put a load of towels that had been used to mop up the bathroom floor into the washing machine, and replaced the sheets on his bed. *No, the new ones are not ironed, thank you very much.* He didn't want his grandmother sniffing around and giving him "the look." Not that she hadn't planned it all, anyhow, or at least set it up.

I can't tell Wendy that I love her. Whatever I do, I have to keep my mouth shut. She doesn't want forever from me. Not now. Maybe she never did. But that's okay. I'll take today, and maybe the next few days.

Besides, I doubt whether Nana will be leaving the house like this again. No privacy in a small town. This is a one-shot deal.

Once he took a shower and dressed, he put together a bag with his and Cassie's bathing suits, beach towels, her flippers and goggles, a change of clothes, and some toiletries. By then, he was able to toss the towels in the dryer and put the sheets in the washer. He couldn't recall the last time he'd used either machine.

After starting a pot of coffee, he put some bacon on to fry and whipped some eggs and cream but set the bowl aside. He took out a loaf of whole wheat bread, and set it by the toaster, along with a dish of butter. Orange juice could stay in the fridge for now.

What if she doesn't come back? Should I call? No, that would be pushing it. And it would be no big deal as far as Cassie is concerned. She doesn't even know about today's trip to the pool. But, yeah, it would be a big deal to me.

Aaarrgh! She's driving me crazy, already. I'm driving myself crazy, already. This whole damn situation is crazy, already.

Just then, he heard the sound of a vehicle pulling around back, and he breathed a sigh of relief. Harvey started up barking, and the cats hissed at the dog for waking them from their slumber. By the time she opened the door, without knocking, there was a whole lot of howling and meowing going on.

She smiled.

And his heart grew several sizes larger, he could swear it did. How was that for a grinch comparison?

He smiled, too, and said, "You came back."

"Didn't you expect me to?"

"I wasn't sure."

She reached down to ruffle Harvey's ears and

petted the two cats who'd deigned to notice her existence this morning by rubbing up against her legs. She was wearing tight green, calf-length yoga pants with an oversized white U.S. Navy sweatshirt and white athletic shoes. Her reddish-brown hair was damp from a recent shower. Her face was free of makeup and showed signs of their recent lovemaking . . . bruised lips, brush burns from his whiskers on her face and neck, a kind of sated, relaxed expression.

He loved that he'd marked her in this way. *How immature is that? Next I'll be planting hickeys all over her so my buddies, and everyone else, will know she's mine.*

She sniffed the air. "Something smells good. I'm hungry. What can I do?"

"Well, first things first." He stepped forward to take her into his arms. "Hi!" he said and leaned down to kiss her.

She put her arms around his neck and kissed him back. "Mmm. You taste like bacon."

He'd sampled some while frying. "And you taste like peppermint toothpaste."

"Do you like peppermint?" she teased, nipping at his chin.

"My new favorite mint," he replied.

Somehow, he was sitting on a kitchen chair. *Did Wendy really push me down?* And she was sitting, straddled on his lap.

"I kept thinking about this on my way back," she murmured.

And I was doing frickin' laundry! What a waste of

time when I could have been fantasizing this! Apparently my expectations are too low.

He had no time for thinking then as she did the most amazing thing to his ear, alternately tonguing it, then blowing it dry. He felt the zing of pleasure all the way to male central and beyond.

Which caused him to reciprocate.

She moaned and shifted her butt closer to said male central which was long and hard and wanting more. Like skin to skin. Like reddish brown curls blending with black curls. Like long-and-hard inside tight-and-slick.

He reached under her sweatshirt and caressed her back, undoing her bra. Then he took her breasts in both hands, palming them from underneath, flicking the nipples with his thumbs. She must be sore from all his fondling of the past night, but he couldn't think about that now.

She gasped and opened her mouth wider against his invading tongue which was engaged in a never-ending kiss, which was wet, and hot, and demanding, from both of them.

He'd thought sex with Wendy twelve years ago was spectacular, but it was nothing compared to this. What was she doing to him *there*? Where had she learned *that*? He couldn't let his imagination go in that direction. If she'd been with other men in the interim, and she surely had, he had no one to blame but himself. But, oddly, though he felt a twinge of disquiet, of jealousy, he was okay with it, too, even happy that Wendy had found some measure of happiness over the years.

But all of this speculation was not for now, not when she was doing *that*.

When he slid his hands inside the back of both her pants and panties, cupping her buttocks, she raised herself up so that he could shove the fabrics down to her knees. At the same time, she was undoing the tie on his sweats, shoving his boxers down to his knees, and taking him in her hand, then guiding him into her where he was welcomed with convulsing muscles.

She's climuxing? Already? Oh, man! Oh, shit! Not yet. Wait a minute. No! Yes!

With his hands on her hips, he held her in place, in to the hilt, until her spasms slowed down, coming to a stop. Only then did he guide her in the rhythm he wanted. Long strokes, drawn out, not short and hard thrusts like she seemed to want.

The whole time they were still kissing, or he might have told her to slow down. Or maybe not.

It was a combat of wills as she tried to ride him in a frenzy of bucking, while he held firm, putting on the brakes. As long as he could. When he finally surrendered . . . *What else could he do?* . . . she was making those little squeaking sounds he remembered as she climbed to a second orgasm, and he was arching his neck and letting loose with a guttural roar of torturous pleasure.

For a long moment, she sat on his lap, with his no longer rigid cock still inside her. Her head was sagging against his shoulder, and she seemed to be shaking. Was she crying?

Had he taken advantage of her? No, he was pretty

sure that she was the one who initiated the sex. But maybe he should have been the sensible one knowing she would have regrets. *Oh, God! Don't let her be regretting already.*

"Wendy?" he said, raising her face in his cupped hands so he could look at her.

She wasn't crying. She was laughing.

"I told you I was hungry," she said.

He laughed then, too.

Like sand through the hourglass, their time together was sifting away . . .

Wendy was looking forward to her time at the pool. She couldn't remember the last time she'd swum and dived, just for pleasure. Added to the fun was Cassie's excitement over something that had meant so much to Wendy.

From the time they'd picked Cassie up at her friend's house, the girl didn't stop talking. Which, in a way, was a good thing because it kept Wendy from thinking about last night and this morning and her outrageous, out-of-character, mind-blowing (*and other kinds of blowing, forgive my crudity*) sexual romp. That's how she had to refer to it in her mind . . . a romp, insinuating a casual encounter, nothing permanent or even long-term. The idea of "*love*-making" was more than she could handle at this point.

So, she leaned back in the comfortable leather of the Lexus passenger seat and listened with amusement to Ethan's daughter.

"Miss Wendy . . . I mean, *Wen-dy*!" she squealed. "What are you doing here? The pool? Today? Oh, Dad, that is the best Christmas surprise. You don't even have to buy me a Christmas present now. Except for an iPad Mini, hair chalk, a bracelet bead kit, a mermaid blanket, a cat purse, cupcake-scented bath bombs, a karaoke machine, and a ukulele, but Santa can bring those." She batted her eyelashes at her father.

Ethan just rolled his eyes at Wendy, while Cassie buckled herself into the backseat of the sedan, and said, "That's the first I've heard of a ukulele."

"I just added it to my list. Maggie Olson brought one to the sleepover last night, and it was so cool!"

Ethan explained to Wendy, "Her Christmas list changes by the day—by the hour, even."

But Cassie was already off on other tangents.

"Did you get my choir gown from the dry cleaners? I have dress rehearsal for the children's bell choir tomorrow morning."

"How long till we get to the pool?"

"Did you bring my pink sparkly bathing suit, or the pink unicorn one? Oh, good! Maybe I'll buy a blue one next time. Blue to match my eyes." Wendy turned and smiled at her for that latter remark.

"Nana said I could stay up as long as I want on Christmas Eve. Well, maybe she didn't say that exactly, but I bet she would let me wait up till I hear Santa's sleigh bells." She gave a mischievous grin to show she probably didn't believe in Santa anymore.

That was proved when she added with an almost-adult cynicism, "Do you think Santa gets his sleigh bells from Bell Forge?"

"Why is your mouth all kinda red, Dad? Do you have chapped lips? You can use my Chapstick if you want."

Definitely an almost-adult cynicism.

"Your lips are chapped, too, Wendy. Were you out in the wind? My lips get chapped in the summer when I'm on the beach too long."

"You're pushing it, kiddo," Ethan said.

"Guess what, Dad? Melanie's mother said you're a hottie. She was talking to Maggie's mom in the kitchen."

"I'm hungry."

"My sweater itches."

"Is Mrs. Santa Claus the mommy to all those elves?" she inquired, back on the Santa joking issue.

"Will it snow for Christmas? I wish it would. Nana says snow for Christmas is good luck."

By the time they got to the Sunset Dunes Health Club, Wendy's head was beginning to ache, but she had to admire Ethan's patience with his daughter. Even as he rolled his eyes, or arched his brows, or laughed out loud at the absurdity of some things Cassie said, he still took the time to respond. Not always in the affirmative, but in such an understanding way that she realized, not only had the boy Ethan grown into a successful businessman but he was also a really good father.

Oh, and, by the way, a super lover, too.

Even though it was a Saturday, there wasn't a big crowd at the club due to the holiday weekend. About a dozen men and women worked out in the weight and apparatus areas, and another half dozen were in the pool.

Wendy went into the ladies' locker room with Cassie who donned a pretty pink sparkly two-piece, and Wendy put on her old high school, faded black tank suit. Cassie seemed self-conscious about the scars on her upper leg leading to her hip until Wendy pointed out that she had scars, too.

Cassie's eyes went wide with wonder and she reached over to trace the line on her neck when Wendy bent down to give her a better view.

"If anyone ever makes fun of your scar, you just tell them that it's a sign of valor. That means bravery. You and I know what it's like to have pain for a little while, and then God gives us these scars like a badge of honor."

"Really?" Cassie beamed and ran out to give her father the news.

"Slow down, honey," Wendy called after her. "You don't want to slip and fall."

They met Ethan poolside, where the air was warm with humidity and the pungent scent of chlorine, and he was testing the water with a big toe. He wore a pair of navy trunks that hung low on his hips. He arched his brows at Cassie's chatter about scars and badges and bravery, then mouthed "Thank you!" to Wendy.

Wendy decided to loosen up first with a few laps.

Diving off the side, she swam a number of different styles, nothing strenuous. A front crawl for one lap, followed by the backstroke, then breaststroke, a butterfly, then another front crawl. Swimming over to where Ethan was in the water with Cassie at the lower end, she finger-combed the wet hair off her face and smiled at the little girl who was floating on her back, with her father's help.

"Take a few laps while I check out your daughter's swimming skills," she advised Ethan.

He hesitated, and Wendy knew he was worried that she would have Cassie do something that might harm her hip.

"I'll be careful," she promised.

He did a shallow dive from a standing position and swam the length of the pool, underwater, before coming up with a dolphin splash, then twisting into a slow crawl.

"Can you swim at all, Cassie?" she asked.

"Sure!"

For the next fifteen minutes, Cassie demonstrated her rudimentary skills, and Wendy showed her how to improve her breathing underwater and perfect her speed by tucking in her legs and using her overhead strokes in a straight path. The little girl was a fast learner. Within a half hour, by the time her father returned to them and made them both yelp when he shook his hair at them like a shaggy dog, Cassie was able to demonstrate improvement. Wendy was pleased to see the surprise on Ethan's face that she'd accomplished so much in such a short time.

"Can you dive at all, Cassie?" Wendy asked.

The girl shook her head, sadly.

"Um, I don't think . . ." Ethan started to say.

"Trust me, Ethan. I won't let her get hurt."

He nodded.

Then she suggested to Cassie, "How about we try just a few low dives off the side of the pool, first from a sitting position, then kneeling, then standing on the edge." To Ethan, she added, "You could stay in the water to spot Cassie, if need be, but I don't think it'll be necessary. Are you game, Cass?"

The little girl nodded.

Somehow, all the lessons that Wendy had been given over the years came back to her:

"Remember, always keep your arms straight overhead, with your elbows touching your ears. That's right. Just like that."

"Enter the water fingers first and make sure you bend to avoid a belly flopper."

"Toes curled over the edge!"

"Relax. Loosey-goosey saves the day."

"No, I don't think you're ready for a running dive yet, honey."

A short time later, with Wendy guiding her slim body into the various positions, Cassie was giggling with delight. "I can do it, Dad. I can do it!" And she did, many times.

Finally, Ethan got out of the pool and held out a towel for Cassie. "Time to take a break, princess. Your body is starting to protest."

Wendy could see that the girl was overdoing it, the exhaustion showing in her heavy breathing and the trembling of her muscles, not to mention her bluish lips. She hadn't noticed until Ethan had called it to her attention. She supposed it was the kind of thing a parent would notice, but not an outsider. Which she was, she had to remind herself.

Ethan sat down on a bench and pulled Cassie down beside him. "Maybe Wendy can give us a demonstration of how the big girls dive."

"Oooh, yes! A swan dive!"

"Okay. I'm a bit rusty, so, don't expect too much."

She climbed to the high dive and prepared herself mentally with a few deep breaths, reminding herself of all the aspects of the dive, just as she had in her old competition days. Starting stance. The approach, using no more than three steps . . . the clank, clank, clank of the springboard like music to a diver's ears. The forward hurdle from the last step. The take-off, making sure to be a safe distance from the board. The flight—the best part, in her opinion—which should be smooth and graceful with arms outspread, easing into one of the four positions: tuck, pike, straight, free. Then, arms overhead, and a clean entry into the water, as close to vertical as possible.

When she came up to the surface, she heard applause. Not just from Ethan who was whistling and clapping at the same time, but from Cassie, and all the others in the pool at that time.

It hadn't been a perfect dive, but not bad after all this time. She did six more, one after the other, enjoying herself immensely. When she came out of the water for the last time, a guy wearing a shirt with a Sunset Dunes Health Club logo came up to her and introduced himself as Mike Sullivan, the manager. "I saw you teaching that little girl to swim and dive earlier. Any chance you'd be interested in giving lessons?"

She laughed and informed him that she was only visiting the island.

They chatted a bit about the club and about her history of competitive swimming on the island. He asked her to give him a call if she ever changed her mind.

When she got back to Ethan—Cassie was in the water again, dog paddling around with another little girl she'd become friendly with—he said, "What was that all about?" He motioned toward Mike who was talking to an elderly woman who was about to enter the pool.

"Job offer. Swimming instructor."

"Really?"

"What? You thought he was hitting on me?"

"Why not? I'd like to."

"Don't you think you've done enough hitting on me already?" she teased, casting him a flirtatious sideways glance as she towel-dried her hair.

"Not nearly enough," he whispered, leaning forward to nip at her ear.

They left soon after that, Ethan saying that Cassie had had enough exercise for one day. In fact, after a quick late lunch—at McDonald's, at Cassie's urging—the little girl fell into an exhausted sleep in the backseat, her head nestled on a small pillow and burrowed under a fleece blanket, both of which Ethan carried in his trunk for just that purpose.

"She'll probably have to use her crutches this evening and maybe tomorrow at her bell choir practice," Ethan said. "Rehab and too much exercise has that effect on her."

"Oh, I'm sorry. I didn't mean to make her overdo."

"It's not your fault. She loved it." He reached across the seat and took her hand in his, squeezing. "Thank you for taking your time with her."

"It was my pleasure."

"I only wish . . ." He stopped himself from saying more.

But she knew what he'd been about to say. He wished she would be around to help her more. "I've told my aunt that I'll come back more often. If . . . when I do . . . I'm willing to work with her again."

He nodded, but she could tell that wasn't enough, both for his daughter and for him.

"I know you want to spend some time with your aunt and your friends from California, but would you go to the dance they're holding at Gabe's house with me tomorrow night?"

"You mean, like a date?" She turned in her seat to look at him directly.

"Don't look so worried." He chucked her under the chin, playfully. "We probably won't have another chance to be together, like we were last night. But I'd like to spend some time with you before you go back to California."

That sounded harmless enough.

She should have known better.

Chapter 17

Christmas magic or Christmas madness? . . .

*I*t was a hectic Sunday for Ethan and his family, from the moment they woke up, starting with Harvey having chewed up his reindeer headgear and barfing all over the kitchen floor. Yes, Ethan had agreed to let the dog be part of the festivities and would no doubt regret it. He already did. He made a quick run to the general store for Gorilla Glue to repair the damage.

A rushed breakfast followed, in which Nana did nothing but complain. Foremost was: "Two days before Christmas! It's practically a sacrilege that a Christmas tree farmer has no tree up yet in his own home. Deck the halls with boughs of . . . nothing."

"I'll bring one home today."

"And we can decorate it tonight?" Cassie said, hopping excitedly in her chair. The girl was all hyped up, from sugar in the massive amount of syrup on her waffle, or the season itself, or a combination of both. She'd be dead on her feet by noon, or limping like crazy.

"I'm going to a dance tonight. We'll do the tree later this afternoon," he promised.

"What dance? The annual Bell Ball? Who are you going with?" his grandmother wanted to know.

He declined to answer, which was an answer in itself.

His grandmother didn't even bother to hide her smirk.

After that, it was a full dress rehearsal for Cassie in the children's bell choir at nine (which involved full-out panic when her black patent leather shoes couldn't be found), opening the Christmas shop and tree lot for the day (many people didn't buy their trees until the last minute, himself included, mea culpa), preparations for the first annual Christmas Grinchy Parade (Don't ask!), making sure they had enough employees on hand while he, Nana, and Cassie attended eleven o'clock Sunday church services at St. Andrew's (looking for Wendy in the congregation, even though he knew she'd be over at Our Lady by the Sea, if she attended at all), then lunch at the Cracked Crab (where the special of the day was Crab Who-Hash, which was amazingly delicious. Cassie had the Cindy Lou bread pudding. More sugar!).

Cassie wasn't the only one amped up on holiday madness. Excitement was in the air in all of Bell Cove, more than usual, and the bells seemed to be ringing almost incessantly. Everywhere he looked there was something related to grinches, either the book or its characters or the contest. A sign in The Book Den window announced that *How the Grinch*

Stole Christmas was sold out until January 12th. He noticed at least a half-dozen men in grinch costumes, including Baxter who'd also managed to dye his skin green, thanks to Francine, no doubt, and a lot of Cindy Lous and other Whoville kids. A perfectly shaped Douglas fir tree from his lot had been placed in the middle of the town square gazebo, right next to the newly installed Nativity scene.

News media vans were double parked all over the place, giving Bill Henderson a fit as he wrote out one ticket after another, which prompted a ton of grinch votes for him. From now until tonight when the grinch would be crowned at the dance, the final tabulations were being kept under wraps. The lucky so-and-so would be totally surprised.

It better not be me!

Meanwhile, all the town people were being sickeningly sweet in an obvious attempt to avoid grinch votes. Or, in their defense (but not much), maybe they were just happy to have this influx of business. A holiday cash bonanza!

Ethan fielded five cell phone calls from the mayor, three from Laura, and two from Gabe. Everyone was anxious over last-minute details related to the parade, the dance, the contest, tomorrow evening's traditional bell walk, etc., etc., etc.

At least all this frenzy was keeping him from obsessing over Wendy too much, and how her time in Bell Cove was winding down. Soon she would be gone. Again.

He couldn't think about that now.

Hometown hokey . . .

Wendy spent Saturday evening with her aunt Mildred and all the guests at the Patterson house. That didn't mean that her thoughts weren't with and about Ethan after last night at his house, then today with him and Cassie at the pool. Oh, no! It was like she had an Ethan chip embedded in her brain now, and it went off regularly, like the bells of Bell Cove.

While they played cards Saturday night, and Elmer raked in a huge $137 pot at poker, Wendy mused:

I love the man. I really do. More than I did twelve years ago, if that's possible.

But it hurts to know there's no longer any future for us . . . Christmas tree farmer on the Outer Banks, Navy WEALS soldier on the West Coast. A relationship doomed to failure.

Later, while some of them watched *It's a Wonderful Life* on TV, Wendy's mind wandered again:

Men have it all wrong, those men who glorify sex without commitment. Well, some women do today, as well, I suppose. But not me. Every act, every touch, not just the most intimate, has to have meaning in lovemaking, or it's sordid. Okay, maybe not sordid, but empty. Why do I feel so empty?

In her bedroom that evening, she stared at her phone, willing it to ring. Ethan had her cell number now, or at least Cassie did. The little girl had asked Wendy to input the number into her iPhone in case she ever had a question about swimming or diving. But Ethan never called. Nor did Cassie.

I loved being with Cassie. That's a surprise. I didn't realize I enjoyed being around children. I haven't been for years, not since I was a counselor at summer camps. Is it because Cassie could have been mine, or a child just like her, if I'd stuck around? No, no, no! I am not going there.

When she went for an early run on Sunday morning, she let her surroundings seep in, enveloping her in the comfort of familiar things—the turbulent waves of the Atlantic Ocean on one side, the calmer lapping of Bell Sound on the other, the bells of the churches and town hall tolling, the neighborhoods that remained almost the same, the scent of salt air, the swoop of sea birds.

This is home. Whether I sell the house and never come back, this will always be home.

When she returned, Geek and K-4 were preparing to go for a breakfast meeting with Gabe Conti. They were taking Harry Carder with them, for his financial expertise.

"So, you're really considering the treasure-hunting company? And bringing it here?" she said to Geek.

What few single women there were in Bell Cove would love having him around. With light brown hair, a young, unlined face, and a lean but very fit body, despite his being well into his thirties, he was a good-looking man. Not to mention being super intelligent and wealthy, to boot.

I wonder why I was never attracted to him. Probably because SEALs and WEALS feel more like brothers and sisters.

Geek nodded. "More than considering. I love your hometown. The remoteness and isolation appeal to me. It seems so far removed from . . . the rest of the world."

Wendy knew what he meant. Terrorism. In special forces, they encountered so many bad things . . . genuinely evil people bent on mayhem and murder. It was hard to believe that such malevolence could exist here. Maybe it was a false reality. The tangos could be anywhere, of course, but for now, at least, it seemed that they hadn't discovered the Outer Banks.

"Could you give up the SEALs?" she asked Geek.

"Maybe. I've been in the teams for a long time."

She turned to K-4. "And you?"

Kevin would be a great addition to the single-bachelor pool of Bell Cove, too. Almost the opposite of Geek in appearance, he had black hair, an olive complexion, and a more bulked-up body. Plus, he appealed to women who liked to think they could heal a sad-eyed widower.

"Still thinking about it," K-4 answered. "Unlike Geek, I'm not sure I'd like being this cut off. But the treasure hunting could be fun."

The military would not be happy to lose any of them, but especially not a bunch at one time, and not just because of their skills. It cost anywhere from $350,000 to $500,000 to train any one of them. But, once they'd fulfilled their commitments, it was an individual's choice.

Anyhow, JAM had already indicated that he wasn't ready to leave the teams.

"And Gabe . . . is he interested in joining your venture?" she asked Geek.

"Maybe. An in-kind investor, as in his property, or part of it."

She shook her head in wonder. "He seems like such a conservative guy."

"Hey, there's a gambler in all of us if you dig deep enough," Geek contended.

Am I a gambler? Do I take risks? Hmmm. An interesting question.

"I'm even thinking about investing," Harry said, rolling up to them in his wheelchair. "My son would shit a brick if he thought I was gambling away his inheritance. The best reason of all to do it."

They laughed then, all of them aware of the selfish son who went skiing with his family instead of having his father with them for the holidays.

Geek named several other people that might be willing to join the project. He said he was going to be careful about who he invited, though. Maybe he would just throw another invention out on the Internet and take sole ownership. Nothing was final yet.

What about me? Would I like to be a treasure hunter? Could I excel in those skills, like I have in WEALS? More important, could I move back to Bell Cove, knowing such a decision would have implications for me and Ethan?

No, no, no! I gave up my dreams for Ethan once before. Do I want to give up my life . . . a life I love, work I'm darn good at . . . for him, again?

No, I decided long ago, that path is closed to me. The best lovemaking in the world isn't going to change that.

Then why don't I avoid Ethan like a bad rash? Why am I going to the dance with him tonight?

*A last hurrah? Or would that be a "Hoo-yah!" in
SEAL lingo?*

Hah!

After the three men left, Wendy went to early
Sunday mass with JAM, Aunt Mildred, and Raul.
The church was beautiful in all its Christmas garb,
even more so than when she and JAM had stopped
in a few days ago. The scent of evergreens filled the
air, and the bright red of the dozens of poinsettias
against the white marble of the altar was a spectacular sight. All was in preparation for tomorrow
night's bell choir concert and then Midnight Mass.

She couldn't help but say a prayer about her current issues. *Please, God, help me decide what is the right
thing to do. For me. Aunt Mildred. Ethan. And Cassie.*

After a quick lunch back at the house, they all
prepared to walk downtown to watch the grinch
parade and to do a little last-minute shopping.
Gaily-wrapped presents already abounded under
the Christmas tree. She and her four friends had
agreed not to exchange gifts, but she knew that
they bought a little something for each of the six
seniors, in thanks for the hospitality. The seniors
bought presents for one another. Then Wendy and
her aunt always bought something special for each
other, even when they had to be mailed. Which
meant, exponentially, the number of gifts would be
huge. Well over fifty, for sure. They'd be unwrapping presents all day on Christmas, but, no, they
couldn't do that because of the open house. Oh,
boy! Maybe they should postpone some of the gift
exchanges for the day after Christmas.

Everyone was leaving now, except for Harry, and Gloria, who had suffered one of her bouts of dementia during the night in which she'd apparently removed all her clothes, put on a coat and shoes and was about to walk to her job at the library. At three a.m.! And her not having been a librarian for at least a decade now! The whole house had been alerted to Gloria's intentions by the barking of Elmer's pain-in-the-neck dogs, who were now being lauded as heroes. Claudette, fast asleep on the sofa bed in the same room as Gloria, hadn't heard a thing because she wore earbuds playing soft music to help her with intermittent insomnia.

Even though Gloria didn't remember anything about her nighttime episode, Aunt Mildred was fearful that there might be a recurrence and therefore didn't want to leave Gloria alone. Harry offered to stay with Gloria today, being tired from his morning meeting. In private, Wendy was informed by her aunt that a room would be available at a nice nursing home on Long Island, where her daughter lived, on January fifth; she had progressed beyond the capabilities of an assisted-living facility in a few short weeks and certainly beyond her aunt's expertise.

Isn't it interesting that Aunt Mil, even at her advanced age, has found a new way to have a meaningful life? Yes, to curb her own loneliness, but also to help others. I thought I was doing meaningful work in WEALS. I am doing meaningful work. But is it time for a change?

The parade wasn't supposed to start until two p.m. and by the time they arrived on the square in front of the newspaper office, the streets were crowded three deep with townspeople and tourists. Parking had been banned from the main streets for the day, thus all the side streets were bumper to bumper with vehicles, including a number of news vans.

"Over here!" Laura yelled, waving them toward a small section which she had cordoned off for them. Four folding lawn chairs were arranged for the seniors, while Wendy and her friends stood behind them. Across the street in the center of the square was the gazebo with a recently installed Nativity scene next to the usual fir tree bedecked with fairy lights. This was a new addition to Bell Cove since the days when Wendy was growing up here.

Laura was dressed all in red today. A red tunic over red-and-white candy-stripe tights with a red Santa cap on her blonde hair, but her skin had been painted a puke-green color.

Wendy laughed. "Who are you supposed to be?"

Laura put her hands on her hips in mock consternation. "Mrs. Grinch, of course! Can't you tell?"

"Well, now that you mention it . . ."

Laura struck a pose for a passerby who had raised a cell phone to take her picture. "If you're posting that on the Internet, make sure you identify me as Laura Atler, A-T-L-E-R, editor of the Bell Cove newspaper, *The Bell*."

"You're really into all this stuff, huh?" Wendy remarked.

"Why not? It's all for the good of Bell Cove. And it's fun, too. Loosen up, girl." And she was off to talk to one of her employees who was updating the grinch contest tally on the newspaper window. Ethan was still up there in the top five, along with Gabe Conti, Frank Baxter, Sheriff Bill Henderson, and some woman named Miriam Hostetler, who'd apparently opened the large driveway of her house for off-street parking for this weekend and was charging a grinchy fifty dollars a day.

This latter news was imparted by Aunt Mildred, who giggled and said she probably would have done the same if her house had been closer to town. But then she quickly added to Wendy, "Just kidding, darling," figuring that once her niece was back in California she would be imagining all kinds of schemes added to her aunt's list of crimes, aside from opening her home to swinging seniors.

Laura wasn't the only one into the grinch costume idea. There were lots of grinches, mayors, Cindy Lous, and various other Whoville residents. And the storefronts as far as Wendy could see were into the whole Dr. Seuss theme, offering items related to the famous story.

It was fun. Laura was right about that. And everyone was being so nice. Probably because they didn't want to get any grinch votes, but still the atmosphere was welcoming. She could see why Geek was attracted to the place.

Our Lady by the Sea church bells tolled the hour then. One, two distinctive chimes. Followed by St. Andrew's. Bong, bong, different but equally pleasant. And then the town hall clock, clang, clang. It was the signal for the parade to begin.

The Blue Harbor High School band led off the

parade with a whomping loud rendition of "Jingle Bell Rock." Fred's Fresh Fish Market followed in a pickup truck decorated with cardboard waves along its sides. In the back was Fred's son holding a fishing rod bigger than he was with an enormous stuffed blue marlin on the end of the line. Said fish had no doubt been mounted on someone's wall a short time ago, maybe even Gabe Conti's. Supposedly one of Gabe's ancestors was into taxidermy-chic décor.

Several spiffy boats were towed by an Outer Banks marina which sold oceangoing vessels of the luxury type. Mini-yachts. More suited to Corolla or other mansion-heavy communities. But interesting, nonetheless.

Which called to Wendy's mind the time she and Ethan had made love on a friend's boat. Not a mini-yacht by any definition. More like a small fishing boat, so small that Ethan couldn't fit his six-foot-two frame onto the cot.

We were so happy then. Had no clue what we were doing sex-wise, other than making use of condoms by the dozen. Just joyful to be together, innocently inventive, and enthusiastic in learning how to do this or that, often with funny results. Like the time Ethan heard that the 69 position was especially hot, and we thought it meant spoon-style.

"Our dance club was invited to do a float in the parade," Aunt Mildred noted idly as they watched the parade.

"Really?" This was the first Wendy had heard about that.

"Yep, and we could have put on a good show if

we'd had time. Dancing demonstrations to Christmas music. Maybe some hot cha-cha outfits like you see on *Dancing with the Stars*. We could even have Elmer play his accordion. Did I mention Elmer is an accomplished accordionist?"

Wendy just gaped at her aunt. "So, why didn't you?"

"No time with you and your friends coming home for the holidays and all the preparations. Not that I'm complaining, sweetheart. Maybe next year."

Oh, boy! Wendy smiled at the image that came to mind and almost missed the St. Andrew's Bell Choir parading in their red choral gowns as they rang a pretty version of "Silent Night." When Wendy had been in high school, there was a waiting list to join the group which traveled throughout the state to perform. They even appeared on EWTN-TV occasionally, and made an appearance before Pope Francis when he came to the United States. They were that good.

A Rutledge Tree Farm truck driven by a young high-school-age kid came next with Cassie a.k.a. Cindy Lou standing on crutches tossing candy to the crowd. Sitting in a chair next to her was Eliza Rutledge wearing a Santa hat, her only concession to the holiday; she was holding the leash to a dog with lopsided reindeer horns, Harvey a.k.a. Max, who looked as if he'd like to bolt over the side.

Wendy was a little concerned about the crutches, wondering if she had overdone the exercise with the girl yesterday.

When Cassie saw Wendy, the girl waved madly,

and Harvey barked hello, too. Eliza Rutledge just grinned.

The mayor came by, sitting on the backseat of a convertible. She was still a little orange from her daughter's tanning efforts. Undaunted, Doreen Ferguson smiled as if she were queen of the world in a deep green sweater with sparkling snowflakes.

A dozen motorcycles driven by an Outer Banks Harley club followed, revving their engines. Some of the tattoos that adorned these bad boys, the men, not the bikes, would make the Grinch blush.

Another high school band, accompanied by their twirling unit, all in elf outfits, performed "Let It Snow." Next came the Bell Cove Boy Scout and Girl Scout troops. Our Lady by the Sea's combined vocal and bell choirs provided more music.

Then, there was a flatbed truck with a banner reading "Bell Cove First Annual Grinch Contest," featuring an empty throne (one of the altar chairs from Our Lady by the Sea) with a garish gold crown on its seat, a dismal Rutledge Tree (or perhaps it was supposed to be a Charlie Brown–type evergreen) with a lone star and a few scraps of tinsel, and standing on either side of the truck were some of the top contenders for the prize, wearing poster boards about their necks. At their feet were large kettles for folks to toss coins as votes as they passed by. Everyone was laughing and shouting out comments, including the contestants, who were being good sports about the whole thing.

Frank Baxter's sign read, "What? Me? Grinchy? Only Smiles at Hard Knocks Hardware Store." He was dressed like a grinch, right down to his green skin, a la Francine, like Laura, Wendy surmised.

Gabe Conti, whose face was flushed with embarrassment, not green face paint, wore a sign that said, "I love bells! Honest!"

There were several others as well, including Ethan, to Wendy's surprise. His message was: "I'm Not Moving!"

Everyone was laughing.

When Ethan saw her, he winked, and shrugged as if to say, "How could I refuse?"

She loved that he would do this for his town, and probably his daughter, and have enough self-confidence to take the ribbing from the crowd.

Would I be in this parade if I lived here? Probably. On a Rutledge Tree Farm entry, or a grinch contestant float, or a Patterson Dance Club demonstration? That is the question. Where do I fit in anymore?

Another band went by and then the grand finale float with Santa on his sleigh with two life-size fake reindeer. *Another contribution from Gabe's ancestor?* she wondered. Red-and-green cellophane-covered popcorn balls were tossed to children along the way. JAM caught one and handed it to her.

The crowds thinned out then, some going off for last-minute shopping, some to late lunches or early dinner, some to go home and rest before tonight's Grinch Ball, the dance to be held at the Conti mansion.

Tomorrow night was Christmas Eve with Midnight Mass. Then Christmas Day with the open house. Time was moving so fast. Wendy felt a bit of panic realizing her trip back home was already winding down.

What would happen with this rediscovered love for Ethan when she was back in California? Would it fade away like some vacation romance . . . great while it lasted, but soon forgotten? Or was this the forever kind of love she'd once thought it to be? If that was the case, how would she survive this time?

When she got back to the house, Wendy made a trip up to the cedar closet in the attic to see if she could find something to wear to the dance that night. The Pattersons were Scottish and therefore thrifty. In other words, they saved everything. What modern people called hoarders, but she preferred to identify as selective savers.

She found what she was looking for almost immediately. Her mother's 1980s prom gown. It was a cocktail-length concoction of rose-colored, silk organza. Strapless, except for thin spaghetti straps if she chose to use them. An empire waistline under the pleated bodice with a rhinestone belt accent. And layers upon layers of the sheer rose fabric in a petal fashion. She could wear her strappy silver high heels with the dress. And maybe Grandma Patterson's silver cameo necklace. That's all. Any more accessorizing would be too much for the fancy outfit.

Was it too high-schoolish?

Maybe.

She didn't care.

Diane had followed Wendy upstairs and she oohed and aahed over what she called a vintage paradise. Wendy lent Diane a 1950s era, green lamé sheath, with a conservative knee length and a modest cowl neckline, but with a plunging back down to the waist. Wendy had no idea who this dress had belonged to. She would have to ask Aunt Mildred. The color was certainly appropriate for the holiday.

The guys—JAM, and Geek, and K-4—even borrowed some of her father's old sport coats. Her father had been a big man, and some jackets never went out of style, or else they came back periodically. Even if they were worn over jeans or casual pants.

When Wendy was dressed for her date, she modeled her attire for her aunt, as well as for Gloria and Claudette.

"It's chilly tonight, honey. I swear, the temperature dropped ten points in the last hour alone," her aunt pointed out. "You'll need to wear a coat, which is a shame, covering up such a pretty dress."

"Wait. Ah have just the thing," Claudette said, rushing away. She came back with a spider-fine, knitted shawl of cream cashmere, which was light but warm at the same time. "Ah wore this at mah debutante ball many years ago. It used to be pure white, but has aged into a nice color, don't you think?"

"It's beautiful. Thank you so much," Wendy said, hugging the Southern lady who was so secretive about her past. A debutante, huh?

Claudette's eyes misted over with emotion after Wendy's hug, and she turned away.

Not to be outdone, Gloria lent her a pair of platinum bangle bracelets in a blue Tiffany box. "They were a gift from my husband on our fiftieth anniversary, just before he died."

"Oh, I couldn't . . ." Wendy tried to hand the bracelets back.

"No, dear, I want you to wear them. It will be almost like I'm there."

Gloria also had weepy eyes after Wendy hugged her.

"I feel like Cinderella," Wendy said with a laugh, "and you're all my fairy godmothers."

"You couldn't have said anything nicer," her aunt whispered.

"Make sure you don't lose your shoe," Elmer quipped.

"Or anything else," JAM muttered under his breath.

Claudette also managed to find a pretty, white, fake-fur jacket for Diane. Everyone teased Diane that folks would think she'd shot not just a grizzly, but a bunny rabbit, as well.

Soon after that, "Prince Charming" rang the doorbell, which reverberated through the house, echoed by the ruff-ruff-ruffing of Elmer's dogs. Ethan wore a black suit, a pale blue, crisply starched shirt, and a thin black tie, with gold knot cuff links peeping out of the sleeves. He didn't say a word—at first—about how she looked, but his blue, blue eyes said it all.

Then they were off to the ball.

Chapter 18

*Walking (Dancing) in a
Winter Wonderland . . .*

*I*t was a magical night, in Ethan's opinion, and he
didn't care if that made him seem less than manly.
It was what it was. Perfect.

The moon was full. (*There is nothing like the sky
over the Outer Banks when fully lit.*) The air was crisp
with the promise of snow. (*Perennial Bell Cove wishful thinking, no doubt.*) Wendy looked heavenly in a
pink (*Rose, pink, same thing!*) cotton candy fluff of a
dress with silver shoes, the bare skin of her shoulders and arms like sweet cream (*or foam on a Bud
Light, take your pick*), the twinkle of promise in her
caramel-colored eyes (*Good enough to eat!*).

From the moment Wendy got in his car and
leaned in for a kiss to the moment she sighed at the
transformation of Gabe Conti's mansion ballroom
into a winter wonderland, Ethan was entranced.
Cassie had asked him to take some pictures of the
evening's events with his cell phone, but more than
that, he wanted to imprint every part of this night
with Wendy on his memory to savor for years to

come. It might be the last night they could be together, alone, or as alone as they could be as a couple in the middle of a dance party, and he didn't
want to waste a second of it.

If he couldn't have a forever kind of love, he
wanted this night to last forever. What better place
for that than Gabe's converted mansion!

Under a canopy of thousands of hanging snowflakes, fake trees—dozens of them with frosted
limbs—were arranged around the perimeter of the
room into a Christmas forest. Peeking out from behind some of the trunks were deer (not reindeer, but
regular deer) and other wild game—foxes, squir-
rels, even a bear.

"Can you believe this?" Wendy said, gazing
around. "Where do you suppose they got all this
forest stuff? The trees alone must have cost a mint,
even if they're rented."

"At a hundred bucks a ticket, they had a good
amount of cash to work with," Ethan pointed out.

"Still . . ."

"Laura probably made a deal with some theatri-
cal company," Ethan guessed. "They could have
had all the cut trees they wanted, for nothing, day
after Christmas. That's when all my unsold trees
become mulch." Ethan realized, belatedly, how
unromantic that sounded.

But then, Wendy's friend Geek's mind ran in a
similar practical direction. "I bet the animals are
from Gabe's inherited collection," Geek said. He
and Wendy's other California friends had followed
them here in a rented SUV, and they'd just walked

into the hall, equally stunned by the transformation of the house.

Ethan nodded. "Could be, although I don't see the infamous ten-foot gorilla anywhere."

"He better do something soon, or the Fish and Wildlife Service will be driving up with a U-Haul and an arrest warrant. We laugh about it, but it *is* against the law," Wendy noted.

"When did you become Miss Law and Order?" K-4 teased.

"Ignorance being no excuse for Gabe?" Ethan asked.

"Nope," Wendy replied to Ethan, giving K-4 a cross-eyed look of disdain for his teasing.

After Diane's fake rabbit coat (Cassie would be so upset!) and Wendy's wrap (or whatever you call those shawl things) were taken to a makeshift coatroom, they all scattered, for drinks, dancing, or just mingling. There were already about fifty couples in the ballroom, some of them dancing to the music of Nostalgia, a Cape Hatteras classic rock group of local fame, who were situated up on a portable stage. People also stood about in the hallways and off in the one addition where beverages were being served and furniture was arranged into conversation areas.

Coming up to greet them was Laura, no longer painted green like she had been that afternoon, but wearing a tight black gown that would do Beyoncé proud. Not that Ethan knew much about popular singers, except what he saw on his daughter's TV when passing through a room. *Oh, no! Does that make me an old fogey? I hope not!*

Laura hugged Wendy, but just gave Ethan a curt
nod. He was still on her twelve-year-old shit list.
"Isn't this wonderful?" she cooed.

"Spectacular! Is this your work?" Wendy asked.

"Mine and about twenty volunteers. I would've
called you to come help, but I know you want to
spend as much time as possible with your aunt before you have to leave."

Another reminder of time going by at the speed of light.
He sighed over the tightness in his chest.

"I love your dress," Laura said, forcing Wendy to
spin and show her all sides. "Where did you find
it? Don't tell me. That hoarders' fashion mecca up
in your attic?"

"Uh-huh. This was my mother's prom dress."

"You're kidding!" Laura exclaimed.

You're kidding! he thought, giving the dress a second look. Her mother must have been a hottie in
her day. Not that Wendy's outfit was overly sexy,
like Laura's. More like subtly sexy. *What? Where did
I come up with that term? Is there even such a word?
Like I'm an expert on fashion! Not! My brain must be
melting with Christmas cheer . . . or something else.
Maybe subtle horniness. Yep, brain meltdown!*

"And how about you, Miss Sexy! I would never
have the nerve to wear a frock like that," Wendy
said, as she gave Laura's gown an approving nod.

*That's a good one. Frock. A fuck frock. Or a frock for
fucking. Oh, please, God, don't let me have said that out
loud.*

"Is it too much? Does it make my butt look too
big?" Laura asked, giving her rump a little slap.

Yes.

"Sweetie, butts are in, dontcha know?" Wendy replied.

Ethan coughed to remind them of his presence, and said, "I think I'll go get a drink. White wine for you, Wendy? And how about you, Laura? Whiskey straight up, or will you chug it from the bottle?"

Wendy and Laura both laughed.

"I'll go with you." Wendy, still laughing, grabbed for his hand.

"See you later," Laura called out to Wendy, then added for Ethan's benefit, with ominous intent, "Make sure you stick around for the grinch winner announcement."

He thought about flicking the bird at Laura's back, but restrained himself because of Wendy's presence. But then he noticed the twinkle of amusement in her eyes. She knew just what he'd been thinking.

After that, it was almost like they'd wiped out all the years and were back in time, to when they'd been teenagers. They slow danced in an endless agony of what could pass for foreplay, they fast danced—well, shagged—till they almost dropped, they drank (not too much for him), and they talked and laughed with friends. All the time, they were aware of each other in a way only lovers could be. Their gazes kept returning to each other, even across the room, their eyes sending secret messages.

Finally, Doreen, whose orange complexion had faded to a deep tan, stepped up onto the stage and took the microphone. "Listen up, everyone, we have a winner in the grinch contest."

Several of the news media representatives moved up closer to the dais to get the best pictures. A number of the contenders moved farther away, not wanting to be noticed.

"First of all, we raised thirty-three thousand, five hundred and twenty dollars."

There were gasps of surprise, followed by applause.

"As for the contest, it was a close race, until the last minute," Doreen said, "but then a dark horse came up out of nowhere."

Ethan, and a bunch of other reluctant nominees, relaxed at those words.

Wendy grinned at his obvious pleasure in not earning the dubious honor.

"The winner of the first annual Bell Cove Grinch Contest is . . ." The band did a drum roll as Doreen paused. ". . . Jeremy Mateer."

No one was more shocked than Jeremy who exclaimed, "What? Me? What did I do?" He hadn't even been on the list, as far as Ethan recalled.

"It seems that Jeremy pulled an all-time male Christmas blooper that caused his wife, Darlene, to plunk five thousand dollars into the grinch kitty."

"What?" Jeremy yelled, turning to glare at his wife.

"Jeremy, my friend," Doreen continued, "did you really buy your wife a synthetic diamond ring for Christmas, which also happens to be your twentieth wedding anniversary?"

Jeremy's face turned a bright red and he mouthed to his wife, "Oops!" To his apparent relief, Darlene was laughing.

Once Jeremy was on the stage, having been crowned "Grinch of the Year," the crowd began to sing a new version of "For He's a Jolly Good Fellow," which was "For He's a Jolly Grinch Fellow." Hokey as hell. Probably another of Laura's half-brained ideas.

Speaking of . . .

While the band took a break, Laura called Wendy off to the side. Ethan didn't know what was being said by Laura (probably something snarky about him). Wendy at first looked stunned.

I don't recall doing anything that snark-worthy.

But then, Wendy was laughing, hilariously.

I don't recall anything particularly funny, either. But then, Laura's idea of funny and mine would be totally different. She would consider it hilarious if I tripped and fell and broke my nose.

In the end, Laura handed Wendy something which she slipped into the side pocket of her dress.

A dagger, maybe?

"What was that about?" he asked when Wendy returned.

Wendy rolled her eyes and said, "You don't want to know!"

Yes, I do. I think.

After that, they were talking to Gabe and Matt about Bell Forge for a few moments when the band took the stage again. The female singer/guitarist spoke into the mic. "This next song is a special request." And then her clear, surprisingly beautiful voice rang out with that old Whitney Houston song, "I Will Always Love You," before the band joined in.

"She didn't!" he and Wendy said at the same time and turned to glare at Laura who was standing by the stage.

Is that what the laughter was about? No, Wendy wouldn't have allowed her to do this, nor would she find it funny.

The unapologetic meddler just grinned and gave them a little wave.

It had been their song in high school. Corny as that was. He and Wendy had been driving to the lighthouse, that first time they'd made love, when they were only sixteen years old. The song had been playing on his car radio.

With a sigh of resignation, Ethan stepped forward onto the dance floor and opened his arms.

Wendy didn't hesitate, either. She put her hands behind his neck.

He looped his arms around her waist and tugged her closer.

With her face resting on his shoulder and his lips touching her hair, they swayed to the music. Young love/mature love melded. Forever became a hopeful possibility, at least while the song lasted.

Those who'd known Ethan and Wendy "back then" were touched. Those who hadn't could tell that something special was happening.

Soon the dance floor was crowded with couples, but Wendy and Ethan felt like they were alone, sixteen, and deeply in love.

When the song was over, Wendy leaned back and said, "When Laura called me over to talk before, she mentioned that you're still a bastard."

"Nothing new there." *Why else would she pull the prank of this song? To punish me.*

"She definitely doesn't like you very much," Wendy continued, "but—"

"I'm not too fond of her, either, by the way," he interrupted.

"—then she gave me something." Wendy reached into her pocket and pulled out a key, waving it in front of his face.

He frowned in puzzlement.

"It seems that Laura is going to stay here tonight and help Gabe clean up. She probably won't be home until six a.m. when she needs to work on a special edition of her newspaper."

Ethan was still confused. The key looked like a door key. Oh, good Lord! Was Laura offering them the use of her apartment for the night?

He arched his brows at Wendy.

She arched her brows back at him.

"I'm starting to like Laura a little bit more," he said with a smile.

"You should."

Deep inside, he knew this was a mistake. Continuing this relationship, which wasn't really a relationship, was a sure road to disappointment and worse. If he had a lick of sense, he'd end things now with a kiss good-bye. *It's been fun. Sayonara.*

But his desire for Wendy overrode everything, especially something as boring as common sense.

With a sudden burst of joyous laughter, he twirled her around to whatever song the band was playing.

He couldn't tell for the buzzing in his ears. She was laughing joyously, too.

"Merry Christmas to me!" he said, taking the key in hand. Then he put a fake doleful expression on his face, just like Harvey when he was up to no good. "But I don't have a present for you. Well, actually, I do, but it's not wrapped."

"Maybe I could grab a hank of red ribbon off one of those wreaths on the way out, and I could tie a bow on *it* for you."

He winked at her. "That's a promise I'll hold you to, sweetheart."

Getting to know you, all over again . . .

Never, back in Coronado, when she'd been contemplating this visit back to Bell Cove, had Wendy imagined anything like this happening.

Oh . . . My . . . Goodness! Be . . . Still . . . My . . . Hormone-hammering. . . . Heart!

Can a person faint from lust overload?

She was standing in Laura's bedroom being undressed, piece by agonizing piece of clothing, by Ethan, who whispered praise at each bit of skin he uncovered. When he was down on one knee, tugging off her silky scrap of bikini panties, he looked up at her, lazily, through half-lidded eyes, with those wonderfully long lashes, and groaned. "You make my balls sweat."

"You romantic, you!" she countered. "But that's

good because you make my bones melt." *And a certain part of my body might be sweating, too.*

Grinning, he gave a brief butterfly kiss to the crisp curls of her mons, then stood, still fully clothed, and surveyed her, head to toe, in her strappy silver high heels and nothing else. He nodded his approval, then ordered, "Don't move."

Stepping back, he began a slow striptease of his own for her. Oh, not the Magic Mike or Chippendale type. Just a removal of one item of clothing after another, with teasing slowness.

Is there anything sexier than a man taking off his cuff links and placing them carefully on a dresser, holding my eyes the whole time, alerting me to his carnal intentions?

Once totally nude, he walked up to her, so close she could feel the heat coming off his skin. His expression was serious, but he seemed to be happy. At least, his penis was happy.

He placed his fingertips on the pulse in her neck, or maybe he was touching her scar. He had a fascination for that war wound of hers. There were others, less conspicuous. Would he notice them?

Then, he trailed his fingers upward, running the pad of his thumb over her bottom lip, then tracing the seam of her mouth, parting her for a kiss. She was more than ready to comply and reached out to put her hands on his shoulders.

"No," he said, placing her arms at her sides. "My game. My rules."

Okaay.

With his fingers tunneling her hair, he bit her bottom lip gently, then not so gently, as his tongue invaded her mouth. At the same time, his hands began to search for all the pleasure points on her body, old and new. When he found them, he made a rough sound of triumph deep in his throat, then moved on in his agonizing exploration.

Each caress of his hands, each lick or suckle of his mouth inflamed her, moving her further and further up the scale of arousal. When his thumbs flicked her nipples, then he took them into his mouth, one after the other, her mewling sounds turned to incoherent pleas.

"If you don't end this soon," she gasped out, "I just might scream."

"I feel like screaming, too," he said and lifted her off the floor by the waist and walked them to the bed where she landed on her back with her shoes on the floor. Before she had a chance to blink, or question what he was up to, Ethan parted her legs with his knees and knelt, exposing her to his close scrutiny.

"Oh, no! Oh, wait! Ooooh!" She tried to sit up, to no avail.

He gripped her ankles and raised them to rest on the edge of the bed, still in those silver high heels. Then he spread her even wider and made love to her *there* where liquid pleasure pooled, just for him.

His ragged breath against her was the only indication that he was as aroused as she was.

Her inner walls fluttered, then morphed into soft spasms that had her tensing her legs and undulating reflexively against his mouth which was wet with her. She was too far gone to be embarrassed. The sweet burn became a flickering flame as he cupped her bottom tipping her up, and his tongue found and lightly worked her clitoris.

Her climax came in a burst of wildfire that spread in ripples and rushes throughout her body. Even her fingertips and toes tingled.

She must have passed out for a moment because when she opened her eyes she was up on the bed, the high heels gone, and Ethan poised above her body, gazing down at her, expectantly. Why? She wasn't sure. It was as if he was waiting for some cue from her. A condom had already been rolled over his erection. What was he waiting for?

She wanted to remind him that she was safe, but her tongue wouldn't work. She wanted to say there was no reason for him to hesitate, she was willing. She wanted to ask why he always looked so sad, even when he was smiling. She wanted to say so many things. Like:

"I have missed you so much. It was dumb to leave."

"Will it always be this way?"

"I left a piece of my dumb heart in Bell Cove."

"Will my already broken heart be broken more when I leave this time?"

"I want you."

"I love you madly, I love you gladly. I love you dumbly, I love you smartly. I love you, love you, love you."

But the only thing that came out when he continued to stare at her inquiringly, waiting for something . . . maybe a commentary on his performance, was, "Hoo-yah!"

How dumb was that?

Chapter 19

Smile while your heart is breaking? . . .

*H*oo-yah? *What the hell does that mean?* Ethan wondered as he stared down at Wendy, offended at her lack of sentiment.

A simple "I love you" would be nice. Or thanks for the Big O. But, no, Wendy has to remind me that she's in the military now, and old times are long forgotten.

This was sex, and nothing more.

At least from her side.

From his side, it was love, always had been, always would be. And he'd told her so a few moments ago before she'd swooned off to La-La Land. Either she hadn't heard him, or she'd chosen to ignore his declaration with that casual "Hoo-yah!"

"I love you, Wendy," he'd said.

"Hoo-yah!" she'd replied.

I'll be damned if I say those three words out loud again.

When will I stop hoping that we still have a chance? They say hope is eternal. Hah! Hope is a big fat kick in the gut.

He probably would have gone flaccid then, except Wendy had him by the base of his shaft now . . .

UN-BE-LIEV-ABLE! . . . and was guiding him . . . *AY-YI-YI!* . . . into her rippling folds. He was panting like a race horse, trying to avoid going over the finish line waytoofast.

She must have sensed his negative—*or shocked, take your pick*—emotions because her voice was quivery as she said, "Make love to me, Ethan. Please."

Not "Fuck me."

Or "screw me silly" for closure.

Not even, "Do it!"

She'd used the word "love," even if inadvertently.

So, sucker that he was, that's just what he did. Made love to Wendy.

And he was good.

She was good, too.

It was good.

Face it, they were good together.

He took her hands, encouraging her to caress him as he rocked inside her. Skin to skin, heart to heart, they moved as one. They *were* one.

His blood thickened and heat curled in his belly and shot out to all his extremities. His heart rate rocketed through the roof.

Softly spoken words were exchanged:

"Your heat is scorching me," he murmured.

"Sweet burns are the best," she countered.

"You taste like heaven."

"Your eyelashes should be outlawed."

"I'm addicted to your kisses."

"Don't stop."

"I can't stop."

"Oh, Ethan!"

"Wendy!"

"You're trembling."

"For you."

"Make it last, Ethan."

"Forever," he promised.

That last was a lie. There was no forever, not in lovemaking and not among lovers, Ethan reminded himself.

But then, he rolled to his back, and she was sitting astride him, smiling like a cat who'd just lapped up a bowl of cream. After she shifted her butt on him, which caused her inner muscles to give his cock another "Yo, howdy!" welcome, which caused his eyes to practically roll back in his head, she looked down at him and smiled some more. Not a self-satisfied, teasing gesture now, just a sweet, I'm-glad-to-be-here smile.

That made everything all right with him. If this was all they had, it was enough, and, yes, he'd told himself that before, but this time he meant it. So, he inhaled and exhaled to slow himself down, then gave his full attention to the present and making love to Wendy.

And what a result!

Forget Navy SEALs and their legendary staying power. Ethan outlasted the best of them. And Wendy . . . *oh, Lord!* . . . he didn't want to think about where she learned how to do *that*!

She rode him like a rodeo cowgirl.

Not to be undone, he flipped her and drove her across the mattress, like . . . what? A NASCAR driver? A bulldozer? An Olympic curling contender? A raving maniac?

They were laughing.

They were gasping.

They were loving.

This was lovemaking the way it should be. A mix of skill and uninhibitedness with a dash of humor.

Of course, they weren't laughing when they came to a mutual roaring climax. She arched her body up off the bed, taking him with her . . . *There is something to be said for special forces exercise!* . . . as he thrust in one last time, to the hilt, threw his head back, and gasped out, "Yeeesss!" Even when he shot his wad, her vaginal muscles continued to clasp and unclasp him with diminishing strength until he could barely breathe, *in a good way*.

When they lay sated beside each other, she turned on her side and kissed one of his nipples. Glancing up at him, she whispered, "Thank you."

Well, it wasn't "I love you," but it was nice just the same.

"No, thank *you*."

Talking Heads (or "Why Do Fools Fall in Love? Wah, wah, wah!") . . .

Wendy lay in Ethan's arms and thought, *Say it, you fool! Tell me you love me. Ask me to stay.*

Ethan kept his eyes closed, just relishing the afterglow of lovemaking and the simple pleasure of holding Wendy in his arms. *Tell me you love me. Stay with me, Wendy. Don't go away, again.*

No, no, no! I don't wish that. Yes, I want him to love me, but I can't stay. What am I thinking? I'm not thinking, that's what.

What am I thinking? I am such a fool! She can't stay. Even if she wanted to, she has a commitment to Uncle Sam. But I wish . . .

I should tell him how I feel.

I should tell her how I feel.

Neither of them said anything.

Forget about sugarplums dancing in their heads that night. It was Frankie Lymon crooning, "Why do fools fall in love? Wah, wah, wah!"

Peace comes, and peace goes . . .

*I*t was Christmas Eve. Already. Time was passing so fast for Wendy, and there was still so much to do. And that didn't include Ethan. Because she didn't have a clue what to do about him.

That morning, following her wonderful night with Ethan, events moved from one crisis to another. Which at least kept her from obsessing over Ethan.

First crisis: Gloria was in full-blown dementia mode. When Wendy tried to return the Tiffany bracelets, Gloria accused her of theft and wanted to call the police. When Wendy tried to calm Gloria down, she attacked her by clawing at her face and had to be pulled away by JAM and K-4.

Luckily, Jefferson Hale, the new doctor who was opening a clinic in Bell Cove, had come by with a U-Haul to pick up more of the medical equipment and furniture from the offices of Wendy's late father. He examined Gloria and gave her a sedative which put her to sleep, and he prescribed some pills that should calm her down on a temporary basis. "She needs to be in a skilled nursing facility ASAP, though," he cautioned them. Gloria's daughter was coming tomorrow to take her back with her to Long Island where a different facility had been found for her, one that could take her immediately, unlike the previously planned one which didn't have a room vacant until January 5th.

Wendy liked the new doctor, who asked her to call him Jeff, and she could tell that he liked her, too. Oh, not "like" in her case, as in sexually attracted, as she was to Ethan. Jeff felt a little different, as evidenced by how eagerly he accepted Aunt Mildred's invitation to tomorrow's open house and gave her a little wink.

About thirty-five years old, Jeff had recently completed his residency in family practice. He was part of that government program that paid a med student's school expenses as long as they promised to serve for a number of years in remote regions where medical care was not readily available. Which described Bell Cove to a tee with an hour traveling time for an ambulance to the nearest hospital, including the ferry ride. Her father's practice had been sorely missed these past five years since he'd died.

Second crisis: The U-Haul wouldn't start once it was loaded, and the guys had to jumpstart it from their rented SUV.

Third crisis: Elmer insisted on their having goose for their feast on Christmas evening, after the open house. But no one, least of all Wendy and Aunt Mildred, had realized that it would start with a live goose, which everyone was chasing across the dunes as it escaped its doom.

"If I had my rifle with me, I could shoot that bugger in no time," Diane said. "Maybe Gabe has one we can borrow from that ancestor of his." Which Elmer and the guys thought was a great idea, but Aunt Mildred put the kibosh on that suggestion immediately. "There will be no guns fired in Bell Cove."

In the end, they let the stupid bird go. It was probably hiding in a flock of sea birds on the rocky shore.

A grumbling Elmer went to the Shop-a-Lot where he had to settle for two fifteen-pound frozen turkeys since they were sold out of the big ones. "My dogs could have tracked the damn goose down if you'd let them loose."

Fourth crisis: Diane sampled too much of Aunt Mildred's punch, which was heavy on Scotch whiskey, and fell into a drunken doze on the sofa before the fire. Even the dogs took one sniff of her breath and chose to lie on the other side of the room.

Fifth crisis: Aunt Mildred ran out of Glenlivet 12 and insisted that Geek drive to Nags Head where they had the best prices on that particular year. Since she needed ten bottles, it was worth the trip, in her aunt's opinion.

All Wendy could think was: *Ten bottles of whiskey? Holy hangover!*

Laura dropped by for a little "girl time" with Wendy. That wasn't a crisis, but a welcome respite from the constant ups and downs.

"What did you think of the dance?" Laura asked when they sat in the kitchen alcove sipping cups of ginger chai tea and munching on raspberry short-bread cookies.

"It was wonderful. I can't believe how you transformed that ballroom in less than a day."

"Gabe couldn't believe it, either." Laura rolled her eyes with mischief.

"So, is it something serious with you and Gabe?"

"I don't know. He went back to Durham today, and I'm not sure when he'll be back. I think I scare him."

Wendy laughed. "Sometimes you scare me with your wild enthusiasms."

"Hey, without wild enthusiasms, life would be boring. Speaking of boring, how is Ethan?" She waggled her eyebrows, knowing that they had spent the night together in her apartment. "Are you two a thing again?"

"Hardly. Oh, Laura, I still love him, after all these years. But I don't know how he feels about me. And what's the point anyhow?"

"Are you kidding? The jerk is crazy in love with you like he always has been. Disgusting, really! And the point? Does love have a point?"

Wendy's traitorous heart lifted at those words. "How do you know that Ethan still loves me? He hasn't said so."

"Have you said it to him?"

"Well, no. He should say it first."

Laura sighed and said, "You two remind me of a bad romance novel. No, I'm not saying all romance novels are bad. I devour them, just like you do. I'm talking about the ones where the hero and heroine just can't get together because of all these miscommunications, and the reader wants to yell at them, 'Just talk to each other, you idiots!' Know what I mean?"

That was easier said than done.

"By the way, you people planning on opening a Christmas store?" Laura asked.

She was referring to the huge mountain of wrapped presents that were under the tree, around the tree, and spilling out into the hall.

"The gift exchanging got a little out of hand. We're going to start unwrapping this evening, after the Bell Walk but before Midnight Mass. You going?"

"I wouldn't miss either of them. Or tomorrow's service at St. Andrew's. This is what Bell Cove is all about, honey."

"And the open house here, too. Don't forget. If Gabe is still out of town, you might want to meet the new doctor."

"Jefferson Hale? You've met him? Is he hot?"

"Fickle much, girlfriend?" Wendy remarked with a smile. "I don't know about hot, but I think you'll like him."

"Wow! Sex and the Single Bell Cove Girl is suddenly getting a boost with an influx of males." She glanced pointedly toward the dining room where Geek and JAM and K-4 were looking over some maps with Frank.

About seven p.m. the Bell Walk began. With the town and its environs sectioned off into quarters, members of the two church choirs split into four groups and began singing carols as they moved from the farthest points toward the center of town. Some of them were dressed in Edwardian era attire (men in top hats and waistcoats, women in long gowns) while others just dressed in normal attire, and still others wore choral robes. Because there was a chill in the air, Wendy wore her mother's red coat.

As they sang, and rang their bells, people emerged from their homes and joined the walk. All of them carried candles in paper cones and bells of all sizes, everything from tiny dinner-type bells to school bells to cowbells. They sang and rang their bells at the end of each lyric. It should have been discordant, but it wasn't. There was an odd harmony to it all.

Adding to the aura, snowflakes began to come down, lightly at first, then heavier. Everyone smiled. Snow at Christmas on Bell Cove was considered a gift.

Starting with "Do You Hear What I Hear?" leading to "O Come, All Ye Faithful," "Silver Bells," "O Holy Night," and all the old traditional songs, the line of carolers got longer and longer until they reached the town square where there was already a crowd of business people and tourists. By now, a half inch of snow lay on the ground, and it was still coming down. It was beginning to look a lot like Christmas, Wendy and many others remarked.

All the bells began to ring at once. Circling around the town square, the marchers stopped, went silent for a moment, then everyone yelled, "Merry Christmas." And rang their bells some more.

JAM and Geek and K-4 and Diane kept glancing around with wide eyes. Small-town traditions like this were new to them. Their running commentaries amused Wendy, as well as others around them.

"Cool! This is so cool!"

"Oh, wow, look over there. That guy looks just like George C. Scott as Ebenezer Scrooge."

"Maybe it is George C. Scott."

"I thought he was dead."

"You have a really nice voice, JAM."

"Six years in the St. Vincent's Boys' Choir."

"No shit!" K-4 responded. "I was in a choir for a month one time, but I got kicked out for yelling 'Who farted?' in the middle of the Kyries. Which was really unfair because everyone knew that Billy Madison had gas like rotten eggs every Sunday morning."

"Girls never fart, you know," Geek remarked as if this was a subject appropriate for a Christmas caroling scenario. "That's what my older brother Sam told me one time. When I repeated that to my buddies in third grade they laughed me out of their club . . . the cool guys' club."

Aunt Mildred made a tsk-ing sound at the subject matter, but then she leaned closer to Wendy and said, "Remember how Grandma Patterson 'tooted' every time she bent over to tend the roses in the garden?"

Wendy had totally forgotten that, but she recalled now how embarrassed she'd been, especially when Laura had witnessed the "event" one time. She exchanged a glance with Diane, who winked at her, knowing that Wendy's initial nickname in WEALS had been Windy because she'd accidentally "perked" when doing duck squats. Thank goodness, the vulgar nickname was long gone in favor of Flipper.

Raul was talking then about holiday traditions in Spain, and Claudette described festivities in the Big Easy, many of them involving one-hundred-proof bourbon. The guys were now discussing among themselves a bar they'd heard about that featured a local drink called an OBX Bomb, "guaranteed to blow your head off." Diane had stopped to talk to Monique who stood in front of her boutique. All this was between carols and bell ringing as they walked.

Wendy tuned out their conversations and scanned the area. She assumed that Ethan and his grandmother were here, along with Cassie, but she couldn't see them through the crowd. She hadn't heard from Ethan today, but then she hadn't expected to. When he'd brought her home before dawn this morning, Wendy told him that she had a gift she wanted to give to Cassie. It was just a pretty blue sweater sprinkled with silver snowflakes that she'd seen in a store on the square, nothing expensive. He'd promised to bring Cassie to the open house tomorrow.

That was the only promise mentioned between them.

After they got home about nine, the seniors agreed to open the gifts from Wendy and her friends. They didn't want to do the mutual exchange among themselves since Gloria was asleep already. She could open the gifts from them in the morning.

Elmer was pleased with three red, white, and blue dog leashes, a new copper-coated pan, a pair of spiffy purple suspenders, a Navy SEALs sweatshirt, and a book titled *How to Cook Bear (And Other Wild Game)*.

Raul loved *The History of Spanish Music*, a set of taps that could be applied to any size shoe, an external flash drive for his laptop on which he was writing a book, a Navy SEALs sweatshirt, and a framed print of the saying, "Dance Is the Hidden Language of the Soul."

Claudette was surprised and gracious in accepting her gifts. Did she think they would leave her out just because she was so quiet? She got a pretty amber pendant on a silver chain, a book of piano music featuring Louisiana jazz favorites, Jessica

McClintock perfume, a colorful silk scarf, and a U.S. Navy WEALS sweatshirt.

Harry had been harder to buy for, but he laughed at a Donald Trump *The Art of the Deal* book and got misty-eyed over a picture in a silver frame of himself with his late wife, Julia, on a cruise ship, the year before she'd died. Harry also got a box of cigars, his guilty pleasure, a newly invented kind of cane that helped a wheelchair-bound person transfer to bed or a chair, and a Navy SEALs sweatshirt.

Wendy hoped that Aunt Mildred would understand the significance of the red coat she unwrapped. She was like a mother to her, and Wendy hadn't told her that enough over the years, nor shown her with her continuing absence. Her aunt gasped, then hugged Wendy tightly. Her other gifts were a set of Victoria's Secret hand creams, a pretty nightgown (not sexy sheer, but not grandmotherly either), a flamboyant Samba dress, and a U.S. Navy WEALS sweatshirt.

It was ten thirty by then and time to get dressed for church. By mutual agreement, Wendy and her friends wore dress blues for Midnight Mass at Our Lady by the Sea. It seemed appropriate as a sign of respect. Aunt Mildred, Raul, and Claudette went with them.

When they got to the church, an usher showed them to a pew near the front. The church soon became standing room only. Non-Catholics attended this service, in an ecumenical fashion, and just as many Catholics went to the St. Andrew's service on Christmas Day. The bell choirs and the choral groups were as much of an attraction as the rituals themselves.

JAM left their pew and went up onto the altar and then into the sacristy. Wendy exchanged questioning glances with the others. She'd known that he was asked to do some kind of deacon duties, but she wasn't sure what they would be.

Soon the church bells rang and Father Brad, in his white vestments bordered with bands of gold to mark the sacred holiday, led a procession down the center aisle of the church. He was followed by a half-dozen acolytes, boys and girls both, with JAM bringing up the rear with a plain white robe over his uniform, tied with a ropelike belt. The choir sang "O Come, All Ye Faithful," until the group walked up the steps to sit on the altar.

JAM stepped forward then, stood before the microphone, and into the silence said, "This is the day the Lord has made." He smiled then, stretched out his arms, and added, "Let us rejoice." He said it in such a way that it sounded like he was inviting everyone to feast.

At midnight, an altar boy and an altar girl carried a statue of Baby Jesus and placed him in the manger of the Nativity scene at the foot of the altar. They did it with such solemnity that everyone smiled.

The bell choir, accompanied by the singers, put on a spectacular performance. It was truly inspirational.

At the end of the Mass, Father Brad said in a jubilant voice, "May the peace of the Lord be with you now, and always."

The congregation replied, "And also with you!"

And, of course, there were more bells ringing.

There *was* a sense of peace as they left the church, more so than usual, it seemed. Like often happened when they were in uniform, Wendy and her friends were stopped repeatedly by people saying, "Thank you for your service." Which was also nice.

Aunt Mildred, Claudette, and Raul drove home, but the rest of them walked. Several inches of snow had fallen, and it was pleasant to breathe in the crisp air of the silent night.

K-4 took her hand and said, "Thank you for having us here, Wendy. It really was what I needed . . . a peaceful place to rejuvenate."

He was referring to how depressed they'd been after Flash's funeral.

"Just what I was thinking. Thank you, thank you, thank you." Diane took her other hand.

Walking behind them, JAM added, "Sort of a cleansing of the soul before we head back into the mire," and Geek laughed.

"I don't know how cleansed I am, but I might have found a new home. Do you suppose I could move in with your aunt Mildred for a while if I decide to go with the treasure-hunting venture?"

"Why not?" Wendy replied, although Geek was probably kidding. "The more the merrier."

Which turned out to be more accurate than Wendy had meant. When they got back to the house, they saw several suitcases sitting in the entryway. Aunt

Mildred was in the kitchen serving spiked ginger chai tea to the usual gang along with two new additions. Twin octogenarians, Mike and Ike Dorset, who had "escaped" from an assisted-living facility, which they referred to as "the nursing home from hell."

Oh, Lord!

Their thick white hair and trim bodies prompted Aunt Mildred to whisper to Wendy, "They look just like Bill Clinton, don't they?"

"More like Phil Donahue," Claudette interjected. Both women were clearly interested.

Oh, Lord!

"We got tired of being treated like children at Sunset Shores," Mike explained. "I mean, what grown man does coloring books?"

The only way they could tell the twins apart was Mike wore a red plaid shirt, and Ike wore a green plaid shirt. Both tucked into nicely pressed khakis.

"I like coloring books. Adult coloring books," Elmer joked.

Ike ignored Elmer's jest and said, "We want to dance."

Raul's eyes lit up at that remark.

"I do a mean Watusi," Ike added. "And Mike isn't too bad at the Monster Mash."

Oh, Lord!

"The ratio of women to men is about ten to one at Sunset Shores," Mike continued, as he sipped at his tea. "I got more marriage proposals than Elizabeth Taylor, bless her heart."

"She's dead now," Ike pointed out.

"Isn't everyone we know?" Mike countered. Then he sighed. "I still get a hard-on when I picture Liz in *Cat on a Hot Tin Roof.*"

Oh, Lord!

"Hah! You haven't had a hard-on since Nixon was president," Ike said.

JAM and Geek and K-4 and Diane were enjoying this conversation immensely, while Raul and Elmer and Harry were probably wondering where they would fit into the scheme of things if these two moved in.

Aunt Mildred cast a worried look of inquiry to Wendy.

Wendy just shrugged and said, "Merry Christmas!"

Chapter 20

And then the terrible trouble began . . .

Ethan saw Wendy enter the church for Midnight Mass in full military gear. Yeah, he'd known Wendy was in WEALS and that she did all kinds of warrior girl crap, which he didn't want to think about, but actually seeing her in uniform was a reality check he hadn't expected. He was shocked.

Any secret hope he might have been harboring was dashed as he saw her and her military friends walk proudly down the aisle to their seats. Especially when he noticed the many stripes and medals on the lot of them, including Wendy. Those kinds of things didn't come from sitting in an office on a military base. These were active-duty soldiers. Deadly soldiers.

The only thing that would have been more of a "Come to Jesus" moment for Ethan would be to see Wendy carrying a weapon, or worse yet, aiming it at some crazed terrorist. He could picture it now, though.

Wendy kills people for a living. Yeah, bad people, and,

yeah, someone has to do it. But she actually pulls a trigger and shoots human beings, when required.

And she puts herself in harm's way. Deliberately.

Wendy was one of those nutcase Navy SEAL types you see on TV, faces blackened, wearing camouflage, running in a low crouch with weapons ready as they rescued embassy kidnapees in some Middle Eastern place with a name like KissAss-Astan or Nigerian girls being held by Boko-Loco-Fucking-Haram. Wendy was not the same girl she'd been twelve years ago. Not even close. How could he not have seen that? He'd deluded himself into thinking she was the same Wendy, only twelve years older.

A Christmas tree farmer and Lady Rambo?

Yeah, right.

Ethan wasn't Catholic, but he often attended various events at Our Lady by the Sea. Tonight, he'd sought a little peace after a chaotic day with Cassie. Once she was in bed, asleep, exhausted after being on her feet way too long, he'd slipped out. His grandmother had been asleep, as well.

Even though he'd expected Wendy, who'd been raised Catholic—he wasn't sure if she still was—to be at Midnight Mass, he'd had no intention of approaching her tonight. Now, he definitely would not.

Time for Ethan to get on with the rest of his life. Without Wendy. She had her life, he had his.

He slipped out of church and went home.

The next morning, Cassie was up soon after dawn, waking Ethan and her nana to come open the many presents Santa had left under the tree. If she still believed in the jolly old fellow, this would probably be the last year that she did. So, Ethan and his grandmother put up with the "charade."

Cassie was one of those wonderful children who oohed and aahed over every gift, even the most mundane, like days-of-the-week underpants or a set of Sharpie pens. By ten o'clock, following a breakfast of French toast with maple syrup and sausages and orange juice, she had already set up her new iPad Mini, and was in the process of making a bead bracelet. But it became obvious that her flushed face was due to more than excitement. She had a low-grade fever and she could barely walk for the pain in her hip.

He and Nana soon had Cassie tucked into her new mermaid Snuggie blanket on the sofa, watching a Charlie Brown Christmas special on the television. They'd dosed her with over-the-counter pain pills and muscle relaxers.

"Do you think we should call the doctor?" his grandmother asked.

He shook his head. "Not yet. I think her overexertions of the past week have caught up with her."

"I agree."

"Cassie and I won't be attending church at St. Andrew's with you this morning," he told his grandmother.

"Cassie is going to be devastated not to play in the children's bell choir performance."

"I think she feels wonky enough to know she's not up to it."

"Too bad, after all those practices."

He shrugged. It wasn't the first time they'd had to cancel plans because of Cassie's condition. "And that open house afterward at the Pattersons' is out of the question, too. You go and give our regrets. I'll stay with her, and if she gets any worse, I'll contact that new doctor."

"Are you sure you don't want to go? I could come back after church and stay with Cassie?"

"No. It's better this way."

She narrowed her eyes at him, waiting for more.

He declined to explain himself.

A short time later, his grandmother came up to him where he was sitting beside the fire, reading the latest edition of *The Bell*, a cup of coffee on the side table beside him, Cassie fast asleep on the couch. She was wearing the new blue coat he'd bought for her.

"You look beautiful," he said, and she did. Her long salt-and-pepper hair was pulled off her face with a headband, hanging loose, showing off her mostly unlined skin, making her look way younger than her seventy-two years. The blue of her eyes seemed to be even bluer against the palette of the pale blue coat.

His grandmother did a little spin to show off the coat, then leaned down to hug him. "I love you, Ethan."

"I know that, Nana. I love you, too."

"I wish . . ." Her voice got choked up, before she cleared it. "I wish you could be as happy as your grandfather and I were."

"I know that, too, Nana," he replied. "But you have to realize that what you two had was rare. Not many people ever have that."

"Maybe. But there is a 'Wendy kind of love.'"

"Actually, Nana, there is not." And that was his final word on the subject.

The party's over . . .

*I*t was another wildly hectic day at the Patterson house.

The morning started out slow with practical efficiency. No big breakfast. Just muffins and coffee. Elmer stuffed his turkeys and set them aside to put in the oven after all the open house food prep was done. No one was going to church, though some of them would have under normal circumstances.

They opened some gifts, especially ones for Gloria who would be leaving that day. Gloria seemed to be cognizant for the most part. She thanked Aunt Mildred profusely for the book entitled *The Camel Bookmobile*, about an American librarian who moves to Africa where she finds a unique method for getting books to remote villagers. Then, while she recognized the framed picture that Elmer gave her of the Bell Cove Library, she didn't seem to associate it with herself in any work capacity. Until she suddenly wagged a forefinger at Wendy and said, "When are you going to marry that Rutledge boy and put him out of his misery?"

"What?" Wendy exclaimed.

"Well, I suppose you have to wait until after graduation, but, good heavens, girl, I'm tired of chasing you two out of the stacks on the second floor." She grinned as if she'd been aware all along of their shenanigans. When she saw her Navy SEALs sweatshirt, she frowned and glanced around, as if someone was crazy, and it wasn't her.

Gloria's daughter, Sue Ann, arrived earlier than they expected, and, thankfully, Gloria recognized her. Although she'd grown up in Bell Cove, Sue Ann was older than Wendy; so, introductions had to be made, all around. Gloria was a little puzzled about why she was going to her daughter's home, and no mention was made of her move to a nursing home tomorrow. Best not to confuse her with too many new things, everyone decided.

There was much hugging and promises to write amongst all the seniors while they loaded the car and it drove off. With tears in their eyes, Aunt Mildred and Claudette began setting up the dining room table with a lace tablecloth, silverware, and serving dishes for a buffet, even though it was supposed to be mainly finger foods. Wendy had suggested buying some quality paper products, but her aunt had looked at her with horror. Not for a Patterson Christmas Open House!

Claudette went off when Harry called for her to help him with something in the kitchen.

"What can I do?" Wendy asked.

"Get out the punch bowl and cups and set them on the kitchen island. You can pour one gallon of the punch that's in the garage fridge, but don't put in the ice cubes until just before the guests begin to arrive. Make sure you use the star-shaped ice cubes with the cranberries inside."

"Do you have a non-alcoholic version?"

"Yes. It's in the containers marked with a big red X. Put that on the dining room table to distinguish from the boozy one. Grandma Patterson's second-best punch bowl set is in the hutch."

"Okay. Maybe we should put placards next to each of them, just to make sure."

"Good idea, honey."

Raul came up and asked about setting up a music playlist for the afternoon.

"Make sure it's Christmas music," Aunt Mildred, the commander of this operation, ordered. "No dance music."

"Can't it be both?" Raul grumbled, but then he winked at Wendy and said in an overloud whisper, "Don't you love when your aunt gets all . . . what you say . . . bossy? Gets my Latin blood boiling."

"Oh, you!" Aunt Mildred said and blew a kiss at him as he walked away with a little dance step.

Wendy and Diane, who had just brought in trays of assorted crackers and gourmet cheeses, exchanged glances of amusement.

"Nice to know we have something to look forward to when we're old," Diane remarked.

"If we're lucky!" Wendy said.

"Are you saying I'm old?" Aunt Mildred protested.

The house phone rang and Aunt Mildred rushed off to answer it.

When Wendy began to set up the punch bowl on the kitchen island, she noticed that JAM was mixing a batch of his Santa's Wild-Ass Elf cocktails, which involved, among other things, peppermint schnapps, shaved dark chocolate, and vodka. A dozen stemmed glasses sat next to his pitcher, each with a mini candy cane hanging over the side. "Wanna taste?" he asked.

"At eleven thirty?" She glanced pointedly at her watch, then grinned. "Why not?"

He poured a small amount in two glasses and topped them with a sprig of mint for color. After tasting his, he added another dollop of vodka to the mix. She sipped hers and said, "Wow! You make a great Wild-Ass Elf."

"Aw, shucks, Flip, that's what all the girls say."

Claudette and Harry were sitting at the kitchen table making small sandwiches of party rye with paper-thin slices of ham, Swiss cheese, and stone-ground mustard, and crustless sourdough mini rounds with rare roast beef and horseradish sauce. Elmer had boiled up a pile of shrimp yesterday, not wanting to smell up the house today, and he was peeling them by the sink and placing them on a platter with a small bowl of his special homemade dipping sauce. K-4 was preparing some bacon-wrapped jalapeños from his late wife's family recipe, which he warned were not for the faint of heart, or tongue.

And Mike and Ike had surprised them all by going down to The Deli early this morning where the owner, Abe Bernstein, son of an old pal of theirs, opened the doors to them and allowed them to purchase, "at a bargain price," the remainder of the caviar he'd brought in as a new offering to lure in tourists. The caviar would be served over cracked ice with toast points and chopped red onions and lemon wedges for garnish.

And of course there would be an array of Aunt Mildred's Christmas cookies. And ginger chai tea for those who requested it.

A veritable finger feast!

The nice part was that everyone had a job, even Geek, who claimed his only talent regarding food was eating it. He was bringing in logs, having been relegated to "keeper of the fire." There was a feeling of family amongst them.

And the whole holiday festive spirit thing was helped by the snowflakes that could be seen coming down outside, sort of an omen of good cheer. A rare Outer Banks Christmas snow was always appreciated as one of the Lord's small blessings.

Raul's daughter, Bonita Arias, came early, but she was considered extended "family" and welcomed by everyone. *And I mean everyone*, Wendy thought, but not in a mean way, as she looked over Raul's thirty-something daughter who was an absolute stunner, with long, silky black hair, a svelte body in a figure-hugging red sheath dress that was demure at the neck and sleeves, but cut off midway to yee-haw in the back, with killer high heels, which were also red, and, *get this*, seamed black stockings.

"Who wears stockings today, let alone ones with seams? I wouldn't be surprised if she has a garter belt, too," Diane whispered at Wendy's side.

Wendy was pretty sure that Diane would be making some purchases on the Internet later today.

Anyhow, it was hard not to admire Bonita, and not just because of her appearance. She was intelligent, as evidenced by her talking to the guys about her experiences as an oceanographer, who sometimes consulted for ship-salvaging companies. And she had a warm personality, which she extended to all of them, not just to the guys, and not just to the younger people. She was especially kind to Aunt Mildred, her father's "girlfriend," which earned her many points in Wendy's book.

For a brief moment, Wendy wondered if Ethan had ever met Bonita. If he hadn't, would he be drawn in like all the others when he arrived today? She decided to go upstairs and change her clothes and put on some makeup. So did Diane.

It had nothing to do with Bonita.

Nothing.

Really.

The open house was a huge success and some of the folks stayed longer than four p.m., even though it was Christmas Day and they should be wanting to have their own holiday activities. They were having so much fun.

Midway through the afternoon, Eliza Rutledge arrived. Alone. It turned out that Cassie was having a bad day, and Ethan needed to stay with her.

"Oh, that's too bad. Is it serious?"

"We just think it's a reaction to being on her feet too much the last two days with the parade and everything. Her hip can only take so much stress before it screams for a rest. Plus, she might be coming down with a cold."

"Doctor Hale is here, if you need him to go check her over."

"Nice to know, but we'll wait and see."

"I have a couple little gifts for Cassie. Can you take them home for her?" Aside from the little blue sweater with silver snowflakes that Wendy had purchased earlier, she'd also put together a basket with a box of ginger chai tea, a bear squirt bottle of honey, and a tea set she'd found in an antiques shop on the square, composed of two delicate cups and saucers and a plate, all imprinted with hand-painted pink roses. And a dozen raspberry short-bread cookies, of course, thanks to Aunt Mil.

"Definitely."

By six o'clock everything was cleaned up, and they were all relaxing, mostly in the living room by the tree, where Bing Crosby was crooning something appropriate about a white Christmas in the background. Bonita was still here and was sitting in the dining room with Geek and K-4 and JAM looking over the treasure maps.

They would all be sitting down to Elmer's turkey feast at seven, but this was a brief respite before anyone had to get up. Despite all the food they'd prepared, and the masses of offerings that their guests had brought, most of it was gone, and ironically those residing here had eaten little if any of it, being too busy serving and circulating. They were all starved, salivating over the luscious smells in the air.

Aunt Mildred, sitting close to Wendy on the sofa, with their shoeless feet propped on the coffee table, said, "While we have a quiet moment, I wanted to say something to you, honey."

"Oh?"

"When you go back to California, if you would rather I not have all these people staying here in your house . . . well, I'm perfectly willing to evict them. Oh, not *evict* evict, but you know what I mean. It's your house, after all."

Wendy put an arm around her aunt's shoulder and hugged her closer. "Aunt Mil, how can you even ask that? What a joy all your friends are! You—all of you—have made this the best Christmas holiday for me and my friends, and, believe me, we needed this." She got a bit choked up and had to clear her throat. "Anyhow, as long as you want, or are capable of doing all the extra work, do whatever you want here."

"You're not going to sell the house, then?"

"Not right now."

"Do you think you'll ever come back here to live?"

"I can't imagine that I will. What would I do here? It's not like there's a call for special forces talents. But it's nothing I have to decide anytime soon. As I've mentioned before, I have another six months on my current contract before I have to decide whether to accept another extension." Wendy didn't add that she was surprisingly confused after this trip home, by her new association with Ethan. Where she'd been sure of her career plans a week ago, she was now thinking . . . well, enough of that for now.

The day had been so busy that she hadn't had time to think about Ethan, not too much anyway, but when she went to bed that night, he was on her mind. She hoped Cassie was all right, and she planned to call tomorrow to make sure, and if possible ask the little girl how she liked the gifts her great-grandmother had brought home for her. She wouldn't go over there, unless invited. She kind of hoped that she was.

But all that changed at 6:05 a.m. on the day after Christmas when Wendy's beeper went off, and she heard similar ones going off throughout the house. It was the signal from the Coronado command center for SEALs and WEALS to get on their secure cell phone lines ASAP.

Bottom line: Liberty was canceled. They were ordered to report back to the base immediately because of a new terrorist threat in Afghanistan, no other details provided but it must be urgent to recall them en masse. Further highlighting the urgency, command had made arrangements for a helicopter to be available at eleven-hundred, on one of the Outer Banks emergency medical airfields, which would take them to the nearest military base for air transport back to California. That meant that they had to be "good to go" five hours from now, when they would be boots off the ground, but it would take at least two hours to get to the pickup zone.

Allowing an hour to pack and inform Aunt Mildred of her departure, that gave Wendy only a two-hour window of opportunity for a necessary task.

She would not leave Ethan again without warning.

It was only seven thirty when Wendy arrived at Ethan's home. Thankfully, there were lights on in the kitchen. If her rental car didn't announce her arrival, Harvey did with his wild barking. The door was opened by Eliza Rutledge, wearing an open robe over a pair of flannel PJs, before Wendy even stepped on the porch, and the dog bounded out to give her doggie kisses.

"Harvey! You bad dog. Get in here," Mrs. Rutledge said. To Wendy, she gave a sudden look of concern. "Is something wrong? Has something happened to your aunt? All that dancing! I wouldn't be surprised if she fell and broke a hip."

Wendy had to smile at the old lady, who was as opinionated as she'd always been. "No, nothing like that. Sorry to barge in so early, but I just got notice that I have to return to base. Is Ethan here?"

"No. He went over to the tree farm—the one here in Bell Cove. They're grinding up the unsold trees for mulch, and they like to get an early start."

Wendy glanced at her watch. Seven forty-five.

"Come in and have some coffee, dear."

"No, I better not." If she hurried, she could go to

the tree lot, talk to Ethan, and get back to the house with time to spare.

Just then, Cassie came limping in. Her hair was a wild sleep mess, but, other than that, she seemed okay. "Wendy!" she exclaimed with pleasure, then hesitated, as if unsure about whether she could come over and give her a welcome hug.

Wendy took that choice out of her hands and not only hugged the girl but kissed her soundly on the cheek, which was thankfully cool. No sign of the fever Mrs. Rutledge had mentioned yesterday. "I came by to wish you a Merry Christmas, sweetheart, since I didn't get to see you yesterday."

"I was sick and Nana left without me," Cassie told Wendy, giving her great-grandmother a dirty look. Obviously, it was a sore point. "Thank you for my presents."

"Did you like them?"

"I love them. The sweater fits perfect, and it looks nice with my jeans. We can have some tea now." She glanced over to her grandmother. "Can't we, Nana?"

Mrs. Rutledge raised her brows at Wendy.

"No, I can't stay. I just came to say good-bye. I'm leaving for California this morning."

"Do you have to go?"

"I do. My boss needs me for some important work."

"I thought we might go to the pool again." There were tears in Cassie's eyes.

"Maybe next time I'm home, but you can practice with your dad in the meantime. And here, I've written my email address for you to write to me, if you want. Tell me what progress you're making." She handed her a slip of paper.

"My dad showed me a picture of you at the dance. You were wearing a pink gown, like a princess. Were you thinking about me when you wore that color because I told you that I like pink?"

The gown had actually been rose-colored, although Wendy supposed rose could be considered just another shade of pink. "Absolutely," she lied.

"I'll think about you when I wear the blue sweater, too," Cassie promised.

Now Wendy was teary-eyed. When she was back in her car, she wiped her eyes with a tissue and had to blow her nose. Twice.

The Christmas Shoppe was empty when she got there, but she could hear a grinding noise behind the building. A high-school-age boy came in carrying a small chain saw. With one synthetic diamond earring and tattoos on his arms, Wendy assumed it was the kid that Cassie had a crush on, according to Ethan.

"Can I help you?" he asked, giving her the once-over in her jeans and hoodie.

The arrogant snot! "I'm looking for Ethan Rutledge?"

"He's out back by the grinder. Do you want me to get him?" He gave her one of those half-lidded looks of conceit, as if wondering if she wouldn't prefer him.

Puh-leeze! "Please."

In the meantime, something was niggling at the

back of Wendy's mind, something that Matt Holter had said at the Christmas dance. He'd suggested that she go look at the tree. He couldn't have meant the tree that she and Ethan had planted together when they were only fifteen years old. It must have died the death of most Outer Banks Christmas trees by now.

Without thinking, she marched out the side door of the shop and to the far end of the lot. Amidst the straggly Rutledge Trees, there it stood. The Forever Christmas Tree. The one that had been destined to be the first Christmas tree that Ethan and Wendy had in their home after they were married.

Chills ran up and down Wendy's spine as she gazed upward. It was magnificent. A testament to something important, but she wasn't sure what. How had it managed to survive when all the others failed?

Through love, she realized. Faithful, long-lasting, forever love.

Ethan must have babied this thing, coddled it, protected it through harsh winds and storms. He must have been ridiculed, frustrated, angry at times. But he hadn't given up.

Why had she?

She hadn't realized that the loud grinding noise had stopped, only that Ethan was standing beside her. She couldn't look at him, not yet.

"You're leaving," he guessed.

She nodded. "Emergency callback."

"Dangerous?"

She shrugged.

"Thanks for coming to tell me that you're leaving." Unspoken was the word "again."

She refused to rise to that bait. He was the one who'd betrayed her all those years ago. All she'd done was leave. Yes, without giving him a chance to fix things, if he could have. But he hadn't the right to expect that of her. Had he?

Maybe in the final analysis, they had both been at fault.

She was still staring at the tree. "Why?" she asked. "Why did you go to the trouble of preserving the tree?"

"Ethan's Folly, that's what some folks called it. A fool thing to do. Maybe it's time I cut the damn thing down."

She turned now to look at him. "Don't you dare!" she said with such ferocity that he blinked with surprise. "If you cut down my tree, I will come back and haunt you."

He smiled then, a sad smile, probably because she'd referred to it as her tree. "You already haunt me, Wendy."

Just then, her phone rang. Checking the screen, she saw that it was a text message from JAM:

Hey, Flip! Where R U? Car packed. Ready to leave.

"I have to go," she said with a sigh. Then, on impulse, she grabbed his face with both hands, tugging him downward, and kissed him, hard. Over her shoulder as she walked away, then ran off, she said, "This isn't over."

"What does that mean?" he yelled after her.

"I have no idea. Just . . . just take care of my damn tree."

Chapter 21

The first step is the hardest . . .

The last time Wendy left, Ethan had gone around like a zombie. Now, he was more like a robot. For the past two months, ever since Christmas, so much had happened. Zap, zap, zap. There had been nothing he could do, except hang on and do what had to be done.

First, there had been the shock of Wendy's leaving.

"Dad, she had to go. She does important work, you know. It's not because she wanted to leave us so quickly."

Sad that he had to be reassured by his almost twelve-year-old daughter.

There had been a few chatty text messages from her, like he was her new BFF:

Arrived safely bk in CA. Miss OBX already.

Hmpfh! She missed the island, but no mention of me. Then, days later:

Op completed. All good.

She must have known that I'd be worried. Nice of her to let me know, but, face it: I would worry every time she went out on an "op" . . . if I knew where she was going or exactly what an "op" is.

Cold & rainy here. How's the island?

Great! Now we're reduced to talking about the weather!

How's my tree?

A bloody pain in the ass, that's how it is. I picked 117 mites off it yesterday.

Geek just gave notice. He'll be a Bell Cove-ite by
     June.

And what will you be by June, Flipper? Where will you be?

He may have had all these thoughts, but he never answered any of her text messages. Not because he was sulking or to prove any stupid point. He was just so confused. Honestly, he didn't know what to say. He knew how *he* felt, but was unsure about Wendy. To him, it felt as if the ball was in her court.

"You're a fool," Matt told him over lunch at the Cracked Crab one day when they'd met to discuss some issues that had come up with the land deal over on the mainland. He was referring to his "lack of action" regarding Wendy, not the surveyor's report. "There aren't many people who get a second chance, pal."

"What do I have to offer a woman accustomed to a life of adventure? Hell, I'm the same Ethan Rutledge I was twelve years ago, but Wendy is an entirely different person now."

"So the hell what?"

"This new Wendy does exciting things, meets exciting people, travels to exciting places."

"Yada, yada, yada."

"Case in point, I personally witnessed her taking off on a moment's notice when Uncle Sam called. And she was picked up by a military transport helicopter, for God's sake. How expensive is that? Which shows just how important she and her gang are to this country. Then she shoots off to some mountains in Afghanistan to rescue three Marines being held by the Taliban."

"Wendy told you that?"

"No, but from the CNN news footage of a special forces mission a few days after she left, I put the pieces together."

"I saw that report. Wow! Do you suppose Wendy was one of those yahoos parachuting out of a moving plane?"

"I don't want to know," Ethan said. "Face it, Wendy would be bored stiff in Bell Cove where the most exciting thing that happens is a grinch contest. And the most interesting person in town is Abe Bernstein and his Reuben sandwich."

"You have a point there."

Matt wasn't the only one calling him a fool. Laura called him a fool every time she saw him, for no particular reason, when she wasn't alternating it with moron, idiot, and mush brain.

Then lots of other things took precedence.

Firstly, the fire on the new land he'd purchased, which might possibly be arson. Apparently, Jeb Parkins, a prime suspect, was having second thoughts about the sale after a failed trip to the Bahamas with his girlfriend.

Second, after a routine checkup, Cassie ended up in the hospital for another surgery. Having inherited the Rutledge gene for height, his daughter had grown two inches since her last visit and, although the current temporary joint was made of an uncemented, flexible material, it was deemed necessary to replace it.

Most people grew to their full height by age fifteen or sixteen, but some continued up into college. He could only hope that Cassie would be in the former category, and that they could put in a permanent device, earlier rather than later, that would hopefully last more than twenty years.

Third, the biggest crisis in those two months after Christmas, as far as Cassie was concerned, was that she'd broken her iPhone and it took weeks to repair it, and even then her contacts and apps were lost.

Lastly, once the arson case was settled and Cassie was home following the operation, Ethan's grandmother went on some kind of half-assed crazy strike. She was no longer going to work in the Christmas Shoppe, which was open year-round, though the main business was landscaping in the off-season.

"No big deal! I've been urging you to take it easy for a long time," he told her.

"And no more cooking or cleaning, or laundry."

Huh? "Okay, I can accept having someone come in more often to clean and do laundry, but cooking? You love to cook."

"Not anymore."

"What are you going to do, then? Paint? That's a good idea."

"No, you fool, I'm not going to paint. I'm going to dance."

Another person calling me a fool! "What?"

"Also, I'm moving into Mildred Patterson's house on a temporary basis."

Now, that hurt. "Why? Are you that unhappy with me and Cassie?"

His grandmother threw her hands in the air, as if he was hopeless. "I love you two, you know that. But I've come to realize that I'm an enabler. That's what one of Mildred's new guests said last week. He's a retired psychiatrist."

"A dancing shrink?" he joked.

His grandmother didn't laugh. "Seriously, Ethan, you need to get off your butt and do something about Wendy. Either that, or forget about her, and find someone else. How about that Bonita woman, Raul's daughter?"

He ignored his grandmother's attempt at matchmaking. Besides, if she only knew! He'd already dated Bonita, in fact had a short affair, before he'd known it was her father who was living with Mildred Patterson. Bonita was very nice, but not really his type. If he had a type! "Can't you see how impossible it is? Wendy's life is in California, mine is here in North Carolina."

"If I'm not here, maybe you'll give it more serious thought," his grandmother went on, as if he hadn't even spoken.

"That is ridiculous. All I've done is think. The facts remain the same. No second chances at love here."

She shrugged.

"Really, Nana, tell me what this is all about."

"Sit down," she ordered.

He sank to a chair at the kitchen table, and she did the same.

"Do you love the girl?"

He felt his face heat. "Yes," he admitted, noticing that his grandmother didn't ask if Wendy loved him.

"You know the story of me and your grandfather, and how we got together."

Oh, crap! That again! "Yes. But that has nothing to do with—"

She put up a halting hand. "I couldn't . . . wouldn't move from the Outer Banks. He loved me enough to move here, even though his work was elsewhere."

"And made a fool of himself perfecting that Rutledge Tree."

"Is that what you think? That he made a fool of himself? You're the fool in this picture if you believe that."

I'm getting really tired of everyone calling me a fool. "Are you suggesting that I move to California?"

"I'm not suggesting anything."

"Like hell you aren't!"

"Don't swear," she said. Then she reached across the table and took one of his hands in both of hers. "Ethan, do *something.*"

Thus it was that two weeks later Ethan and Cassie were on a plane to San Diego. He had to wait that long for his daughter to be strong enough for the strain of travel.

Cassie, whose excitement was a palpable thing, thought that they should inform Wendy that they were coming. Ethan wasn't taking a chance that she would nix the visit.

After renting a car at the airport, they drove to Coronado where Ethan got them a room at the famous Hotel del Coronado, which Cassie loved because it resembled a big white castle, albeit with a red roof. Soon after, he found the cottage where Wendy lived with two roommates. He left Cassie in the car while he went to the door, just to make sure he'd gotten the right place.

Diane, the WEALS known as Grizz, answered his knock. Leaning against the frame, arms folded over her chest, she just grinned. "Well, well, well! You lost, buddy?"

That is some welcome! Not a good sign for how Wendy is feeling toward me. "Hello, Diane," he said, opting for politeness, instead of responding in kind. "Is Wendy here?"

"No, she's over at the command center. It's her turn this week to teach the newbie class."

He breathed a silent sigh of relief. At least she wasn't off on some dangerous mission that he would worry over. "Can we go over there?" he asked, indicating with a motion of his head toward the car that Cassie was with him.

Diane waved at Cassie, then told him, "I can give you a pass." Belatedly, she asked, "Do you want to come in for a drink?"

"No, I'll wait out here."

She went inside and returned with a card which she handed to him. Then, she gave him specific instructions on which entrance to the base to use and where the command center was located.

"Thanks, Diane," he said.

She studied him for a long moment and asked, "Has anyone ever told you that you're a fool?"

"A few people. Why?"

"What took you so long?"

If the mountain won't come
to Muhammad . . .

Wendy was on the O-Course of the grinder, the asphalt-covered PT area that sat like a prison yard in the middle of the command center buildings. Working out a group of WEALS trainees, she watched and occasionally yelled out orders to the scrungy women, hot and sweaty and dirty, just like her. After a three-mile run on the beach, wearing shorts, T-shirts, and heavy boondockers, they were rolling around in the sand for sugar cookies.

She set her stopwatch for twelve minutes and called out, "Ready, set, go!" The women immediately began a regimented series of exercises that involved the cargo net, the balance poles, the "hooyah logs," rope swinging, the "dirty name log jumps," the weaver, the tower climb, the monkey bar ladder, and the Slide for Life.

She'd performed and supervised this rotation so many times, she could do it with her eyes closed. For these few minutes, she had a chance to think. And any time she had a chance to think, her thoughts kept going back to that blasted Forever Christmas Tree. The blue spruce flourishing—heck, even the fact that it had survived—held significance. She wasn't sure what, but she intended to find out.

Because her Christmas liberty had been cut in half, she had another week coming. And a few more days on top of that because of the two live ops she'd engaged in since the Afghan mission. Maybe she would go home to Bell Cove for Easter and get some answers.

Like, why had Ethan failed to respond to any of her text messages? The ones she'd sent soon after her departure from Bell Cove, and then shut down when she hit a figurative wall.

Surely, Ethan understood, without the details, that the curtailment of her liberty, and that of her teammates, had been made for an important reason.

No sooner had they arrived back at Coronado than
they'd been given a briefing. Three Marines captured and being tortured in a remote mountainous
region of Afghanistan.

Being the professionals they were, a small team of
two WEALS and four SEALs (her, Diane, JAM, K-4,
Geek, and F.U.) were ready and HALOed within
days onto a flat portion of the mountain. Wearing
full-ruck, meaning about seventy-five pounds of
equipment, including assault weapons in a sling
over one shoulder, handguns in a thigh holster, and
Ka-Bar knives in their boots, they had made their
way leapfrog style out of the open area. Two operatives worked together, one running in a crouch
position while covered by a partner from behind
till the partner came forward and passed by to be
protected by the first person in the same manner,
over and over, till they reached cover.

They'd found the soldiers, one of them near
death from injuries and repeated beatings, in a
cave guarded by only two Taliban men, who were
quickly eradicated. The whole operation took only
two hours before they were back on the plane to
Kabul. Easy peasy, which was not always the case.
Like that 2005 incident in which sixteen SEALs and
spec op troops had been killed when they'd tried
to rescue four downed SEALs in those same mountains. Or the infamous Operation Gothic Serpent,
which was the subject of the movie *Black Hawk
Down*.

During SEALs and WEALS training, the instructors always drummed in the message that, in the

most successful ops, the goal was accomplished with no shots being fired. That had not been the case for Wendy's team that day two months ago. There had been three deaths. The two Taliban and the one Marine who died as he was being airlifted. Still, it was considered a successful mission.

Wendy was eight minutes into this PT rotation when Delphine, one of her roommates, came up to her and said, "Commander wants to see you. I'll take over."

She raised a brow. "What's up?"

"You have visitors."

"Me? Who?" Wendy couldn't recall the last time she'd had a visitor. Probably when her dad came out to see her more than five years ago, but, no, there had been that guy she'd met on a blind date last year, who practically stalked her when she'd declined any further dates. He'd been barred from the base, eventually.

Delphine just shrugged, but she had an odd look on her face.

Wendy passed Commander MacLean as he was exiting his office and motioning her inside. "I'll give you a half hour," he said and closed the door behind her, after she entered.

Wendy couldn't have been more surprised.

Standing by the windows that overlooked the grinder were Ethan and Cassie. Turning at her entrance, they both had smiles on their faces . . . Ethan's rather tentative, Cassie's wide open and enthusiastic.

Stunned, she just stared at them for a long moment. Ethan, whose eyes were shaded by a pair of dark sunglasses, wore a tapered, blue dress shirt, with the sleeves rolled up to the elbows, unbuttoned at the top, untucked, over jeans and sockless loafers. Cassie was in pink, of course. A pretty pink blouse over white shorts with white sneakers and pink socks.

"Ethan? Cassie? What are you doing here?"

"We're Muhammads," Cassie announced, limping over to hug Wendy around the waist.

Wendy hugged Cassie back and kissed the top of her blonde head.

"There was a fire, and my phone broke, and Nana told Dad to get his butt in gear because he was so grumpy, but then I had an operation, and Nana moved out, and Dad wouldn't let me call you, but Nana said . . ." All this Cassie said in a long rush of words, none of which made sense to Wendy, and still went on while Wendy turned to Ethan for an explanation.

Over Cassie's head, Wendy murmured, "Muhammads?" to Ethan, who still stood by the window, leaning against the wall, gazing at her with an enigmatic expression on his face.

But then he pushed away from the wall, removing his sunglasses as he walked, folding and tucking them into a shirt pocket. Blinking slowly, his wonderfully silky black lashes rose, fell, then settled at half mast, just the way he knew she liked, the way she at one time could not resist. Only then did he say, "We're coming to the mountain."

"I have no idea what that means."

"Turns out I have a bit of my grandfather Samuel in me. You know how he moved to Bell Cove because he loved my grandmother so much, even though his work was elsewhere?"

"Yeah." She still didn't understand.

"Well, here I am." He grinned at her.

"Are you trying to say that you would move here? For me?"

"If that's what it takes."

"But . . . but what kind of work would you do here?"

"Have no clue. Maybe I'll grow palm trees."

"You would uproot Cassie from the Outer Banks?"

"Kids adapt," Cassie interjected, even though Wendy hadn't been addressing her.

"Ethan," she whispered, unable to believe that he would make this kind of sacrifice for her. This was huge. The logistics were up in the air. But what did it matter? The fact that he would be willing was the most important thing. She took his face in her hands and said, "I don't know exactly what you mean, but I'm glad you're here."

"Thank God!"

"He was afraid you would tell us to go home," Cassie remarked from where she was now sitting on the edge of the commander's desk, her legs swinging. A definite no-no. "Dad's nervous."

Ethan gave his daughter a chastising look, and she pretended to zip her lips, a smug expression on her cute face.

This was all so confusing. "You traveled roughly three thousand miles, to see me, and you thought I'd kick you to the door?"

"That's just what I told him," Cassie contributed.

Wendy exchanged a "Men!" look with Cassie.

"My daughter has been giving me love advice for the past two weeks, ever since we first decided to come out here," Ethan told Wendy as he finally opened his arms to embrace her.

But, no, she couldn't allow that. "Don't get any closer. I stink," she told him.

"If you think I traveled 'roughly three thousand miles' to be put off by a little stink, you don't know me, sweetheart." Ignoring her order, he yanked her into his arms, stink and all, and kissed her. A hello kiss, but much more.

Through the buzz in her ears at the headiness of his kiss, she heard Cassie say, "Good touch, that 'sweetheart,' Dad."

"Hide your eyes, Cass," Ethan murmured against Wendy's lips and deepened his kiss.

"No way! I'm learning things. Wow! This is a great picture I'm taking with my iPhone, but maybe you should take your hands off her butt. Can I put it on Instagram?"

Ethan removed his hands from her butt and set her away from him, but he still held her by the shoulders. Turning to his daughter, he said, "Don't you dare!"

"I was just kidding. Jeesh! Who wants to see two old people kissing anyhow? It's not like you're Jamie Dornan and Dakota Johnson."

She and Ethan both looked at Cassie with surprise. How would she know about the *Fifty Shades of Grey* actors?

"Have I mentioned that my daughter is almost-twelve going on twenty?"

Cassie just grinned, pleased with having disconcerted them. But then, she said, "Can we get on with this, Dad? I'm hungry."

Ethan rolled his eyes, then dropped to one knee. Taking one of Wendy's hands in his, he asked, "Wendy, will you marry me?"

Wendy was shocked. It was the last thing she'd expected.

"Daaaad! You said it wrong," Cassie complained.

With a grimace, Ethan said, "Wendy, will you marry *us*?"

"Yeah, Wendy, will you marry us?" Cassie said.

Wendy was speechless for a moment, which Ethan interpreted as possible rejection; so, he launched into a pitch, which he must have practiced on the way here. "I love you, Wendy. I always have. Always will. Forever. If you won't marry me, I'm chopping down that damn tree and burning it on the beach by the lighthouse. And then . . . and then I'll probably move to friggin' Alaska, or something."

"I'm recording this, Dad. Maybe you shouldn't swear."

Without a clue as to how this relationship could possibly work, Wendy swiped at the tears that filled her eyes and said, "Yes." That's all, just yes. The love words would come later. The explanations for how this could possibly work out would come later. For now, love was the most important thing.

"You do know that I love you, too, don't you, Ethan?"

"I hoped." Ethan had tears in his eyes, too. After he slipped his great-grandmother Rutledge's tiny diamond ring on her finger, the one he'd promised her twelve years ago, he kissed her softly to seal the deal.

And the weight of twelve years fell off them both.

Epilogue

*And the wedding bells, they did
ring, and ring, and ring . . .*

Wendy Patterson and Ethan Rutledge were married on Saturday, July 6, in Bell Cove. It was considered the event of the year, next to the Grinch Christmas hoopla. The town used the wedding, which they considered theirs as much as the bride and groom's, as an excuse to have an extended Fourth of July celebration. The décor was "patriotic nuptials."

No invitations were needed; everyone came.

More than one resident was heard to say, "It's about time!"

Or, "I always knew they would get together eventually."

Or, "They were destined to be together. Everyone knows that."

One person in particular mentioned something about "a Wendy kind of love" always winning in the end, whatever that meant.

Another person in particular, who was known to have a long-standing dislike of Ethan, said, "The fool! I wouldn't take him if he were gold-plated and Hollywood handsome."

Ethan and Wendy were married that morning in Our Lady by the Sea Catholic Church, but the bells of both churches rang when the couple emerged afterward. Those SEALs and WEALS who attended in white dress uniforms formed an arch of swords for the recessional. Very impressive! The reception followed at Gabe Conti's mansion, which had been decorated in a red, white, and blue extravaganza.

Wendy wore her grandmother's wedding gown, discovered days before the wedding beneath a pile of vintage clothing in some crazy hoarders' attic in the Patterson house, which, incidentally, was still notoriously filled with dancing seniors. The veil was donated by Eliza Rutledge, who kept telling everyone that Ethan was just like her Samuel. Although they didn't quite match the outfit, Wendy wore strappy silver high heels, to which Ethan had some fond attachment.

Despite Ethan's protests that white tuxedoes were "tacky," he and his groomsmen wore just that, at the insistence of the townsfolk who claimed the color was more suited to a beach setting. (Did I mention that the town considered it *their* wedding?)

Laura was Wendy's maid of honor with Cassie, Diane, and Delphine as bridesmaids, all in pink, at Cassie's insistence. The girl still had a preference for that color, although she occasionally relented with a little blue. Matt Holter was Ethan's best man, with Gabe, Tony, and Geek as groomsmen. K-4 was off on some secret SEAL mission no one could talk about. JAM helped to officiate during the rituals. Claudette Deveraux played the wedding march on the church organ.

Mildred Patterson gave her niece away, although many in Bell Cove claimed that was only symbolic. Wendy was theirs to give in matrimony.

Ethan and Cassie would not be moving to California, after all. Wendy decided to opt out of the teams when her contract ended in June. What she would be doing in Bell Cove, she hadn't decided yet. "I just want to enjoy being a wife, and a mother to Cassie, for a while," she told Ethan, who had no objections, of course. Ethan predicted that she would probably become a treasure hunter . . . or the town's sheriff, if Bill Henderson ever resigned, as he often threatened to do after the parking ticket fiasco at Christmas. Ethan didn't care, as long as she was here with him.

And, yes, the Bell Forge Salvage Company, under Merrill "Geek" Good's primary ownership, was soon to be a go, occupying half of the old Bell Forge building. Bells would still be made there, but the two companies would share the renovated harbor and some of the facilities. The first project wouldn't start until the fall. Everyone in Bell Cove considered it *their* treasure-hunting company and were enthusiastic (a.k.a. annoying) in their suggestions/meddling.

The Conti mansion was the perfect setting for the wedding reception, especially on this warm summer day with the doors open onto the bluff overlooking the ocean. In the distance could be seen the lighthouse, which seemed to have a particular significance to the newlyweds.

Gabe was being generous in offering the mansion for this event. He'd refused many other requests, despite the urging of Laura Atler, his ex-girlfriend. Gabe had moved to Bell Cove and set up his architectural office in the wing of the mansion that once housed the taxidermist's hell (or heaven, depending on one's perspective). The Smithsonian had taken most of the stuffed animals, although he'd kept the gorilla as a reminder of good ol' Great-Great-Great Uncle Tomas. Too tall to be a coat rack, Gabe regarded "King Kong" as a combined conversation piece/burglar deterrent. The pipe collection had set eBay on fire for all of two days, to the disgruntlement of Mayor Doreen Ferguson, who'd wanted Gabe to not only donate the collection but build a museum in Bell Cove to house them. As if! He refused to go down in history as a connoisseur of tobacco-related products.

The band Nostalgia provided the music for the Rutledge wedding. The bridal dance was, of course, Whitney Houston's "I Will Always Love You," but midway through the song, the band broke into "Carolina Girls," to which the bride and groom did the best shag the crowd had ever seen. Everyone said so. Since this was a dancing crowd, including the seniors from the Patterson house, the band played all kinds of music, and the dancing went on to the wee hours, long after the bride and groom had left for a honeymoon to parts unknown. Some said the Bahamas, some said Hawaii. In fact, they were on a fishing boat off the coast of the Outer Banks. Why look for paradise when it's in your own backyard? Not that they planned to do much fishing.

That night after making sweet love, and then a rocking good love (the waves were choppy), Ethan told Wendy that his wedding gift to her was . . . a tree! A new tree they would plant together to mark their wedding and perhaps it would be a Christmas tree for their tenth anniversary year. They planned to use the current one this year, if Wendy could bear to let Ethan chop it down.

Ironically, Wendy's gift to Ethan was a little stick with two definitive lines. There would be another Carolina girl (or boy) born seven months hence.

Author's Note

Dear Readers:

I hope you enjoyed this first book in my Bell Sound series. Second chance at love stories are the best, in my opinion.

Those of you who have read my other books will recognize some characters, such as Wendy, JAM, Geek, K-4, Slick, and F.U., from my Viking Navy SEAL series that began with *Wet & Wild* and *Hot & Heavy* and continued through five other novels. That doesn't mean there won't be other Viking Navy SEAL books someday; they aren't all leaving "town."

For those of you who live or vacation on the Outer Banks, be gentle with me. Bell Cove is a fictional town, and some of what I portray might seem unrecognizable or even impossible to you. Artistic license, I say!

For those of you not familiar with the shag mentioned throughout this book, google "shag dance," then turn the volume up high. You will smile!

In these negative, often scary, times we live in, I

am constantly reminded of the power of books to help us through difficulties. That's especially true of stories with a dash of humor in them. Don't you agree?

I love hearing from fans and can be reached at sandrahill.net or my Facebook page at SandraHill Author, or just by emailing: shill733@aol.com.

As always s, wishing you smiles in your reading.

Sandra Hill

LYS10 1018